THE RIDERS CLUB

THE RIDERS CLUB

DENNIS NAGEL

*For Chris
with love*

There is a band of wild horses on the
  ridgetop.

They've been watching us for most of the day.

So, we'll just keep our distance

And let them go along their way.

PROLOGUE

Tony Levitt dispatched one of his top security specialists to San Jose to investigate an unacceptable business disruption. It affected one of his favorite suppliers–a gang led by a skilled thief named Jerry Williams. He was one of Tony's favorites because he sourced the ideal product, highly profitable and marketable prescription opioids. Between William's acquisition and Tony's distribution, they quickly made a hell of a lot of money, and Tony wanted to keep the cash flowing. His security specialist contacted Williams's group and found a potentially deteriorating situation. Two new players in the group had attempted a takeover and were demanding more money. The underlings, in full revolt, had brought the enterprise down to its knees. And then missed last week's shipment.

Tony was in his corner office on the twelfth floor of an old but still beautiful casino in downtown Reno. He called his security specialist, a man who used the pseudonym of Joe while on assignment. Joe answered quickly.

"Good morning, Mr. Levitt."

"Good morning. How is your trip progressing?"

"I have the situation defined. I'm glad you called. I'd appreciate your advice on a solution."

"Alright. Bring me up to date."

"Two of the newer gang members who joined six months ago are muscling their way into control. They roughed up Williams, but he is still here and part of the group. However, he is not happy, and he wants out. It is a typical money and control dispute that must be corrected quickly, or it will kill the business. The new guys are confident they can run the organization."

"Do you think they can?"

"If Williams stays, possibly. If he doesn't, it is unlikely."

"The new guys, how would you size them up?"

"Cocksure of themselves, ruthless and volatile; I wouldn't want them working with us."

"Do you think Williams could continue the operation without them?"

"Yes, but he needs to learn stronger management skills to survive."

"Is the rest of the gang intact?"

"Yes."

"Are they going to miss another shipment?"

"It's going to be a close call. I'm not sure."

"Okay, my recommendation would be a *Wine and Dine*. I think it will put us in a position to get up close and personal, and then resolve these problems, one way or another."

"I like that, Boss."

"Good, I'll send the jet up early tomorrow. I'll reserve three suites, set up an entertaining evening with some of our loveliest ambassadors, and comp three open accounts. We'll give them a special evening. Then, we will meet the following morning."

———

As he waited for his guests, Tony wasn't as hopeful about the outcome of their upcoming meeting. He sat in a private conference room in a secluded corner of the fourth floor. Joe was also seated at the table, and another employee was posted in the corner.

Tony was a middle-aged man, slim and trim, with dark hair, and a hawk-like, unreadable face. He dressed in all black: suit, pants, shirt, and tie. He was a cerebral individual who made tough decisions after a great deal of thought. Tony always balanced out the long-term with the short, which was a reasonable practice when you worked outside the law's confines. One of Tony's most exceptional qualities was his ability to think quickly and clearly. When he gave something a great deal of thought, a great deal could take five seconds.

He was proud of his distribution company; it ran with precision and had well-received false credibility. From laptops to diamonds to drugs, Tony sold his customers quality products at below market prices. His suppliers sourced stolen products, acquired through methods of burglary or robbery, activities that could get them arrested. And sometimes, the police did get involved, and sometimes internal issues would arise that could lead to an environment of severe risk. When that happened, Tony would have days like today, when he dealt with idiots who couldn't understand reason.

Tony had received upsetting reports that his *Wine and Dine* had gone astray. The two new California boys couldn't handle their liquor and had raised hell in the casino. The men had become abusive, first to their female companions, then to a blackjack dealer who had dealt them a king when they needed a six. Joe had to step in and quiet them down, which created a broader confrontation.

Tony had suggested the *Wine and Dine*. He planned to introduce the new men to the scope and benefit of working with his company. Often, after spending quality time at the casino, a new appreciation of Tony and his team would develop. When that happened, cooler heads would prevail, and positive discussions ensued. After the California boys acted out last night, Tony was less confident, and he felt disrespected.

Jerry Williams was the first to show up for the meeting. He sat on the far side of the table. Williams was an interesting man in his late thirties. He was tall, slim, and blonde with several tattoos and multiple piercings. He walked with a limp, had a nasty bruise under his left eye, and another on the left side of his long neck, all aftereffects of the attempted coup. Jerry was an intelligent and usually friendly fellow, but not this morning. He sat in his chair silently with crossed arms. He intensely examined the carpet weave.

Ron and Larry, the California boys, arrived next. Their bloodshot eyes and disheveled appearance did not impress Tony. Both men were a little shy of six feet, somewhat overweight, and looked to be in their early thirties. They had long, greasy hair and heavily tattooed arms. They both eagerly poured their coffee from the carafe on the table.

After brief introductions, the meeting began.

"Gentlemen, I hope you had a pleasant evening," Tony said.

"I turned in early," Jerry Williams said without lifting his eyes.

Ron and Larry both snorted in contempt.

"We had a hell of a good night with those ambassadors of yours. What babes," Larry offered.

"Well, I'm glad you had a good time, but let's get down to business," Tony said. "I have two main issues to discuss. First, I understand there has been a change in leadership in your organization, and second, you have missed a shipment."

Ron and Larry both snapped their heads up like a couple of deer on alert.

"Yeah, Ron and I are in charge now," Larry said. "There is also a change in our split. It used to be that Williams got the lion's share of the money, and we got the scraps. We've corrected that. I don't see where it is any of your damned business."

"Missing a shipment is my business," Tony calmly replied.

"Well, about that, if you want us to keep the drugs flowing, we need to correct our split with you too. At this point, you get half. That is too much."

"It isn't too much; you will never find a better deal. Don't forget a couple of things. We have the customers; you don't. Our product turnover is fast, and our payout is quick. With us, you'll make more money than is possible anywhere else."

"I don't think you get it," Larry said. "We are doing the dirty work, and you aren't. You don't deserve half. So, this is how it is going to go. Your share is changing from half to ten percent. If you want the shipments to continue, that's the deal." Larry puffed out his chest, and Ron snickered.

"Please take a moment to think about risk. There are two critical times in every transaction–the procurement of the goods, and their sale. At both times, you are subject to the possibility of criminal risk. When you work with us, you cut that risk in half."

"You and I both know that is bullshit, don't we, Tony? But since you are so good to us, putting us up last night and all, we are willing to continue with you. But your cut is going to be ten percent—final offer."

Tony let a smile tug on the corners of his mouth, then he allowed Larry to feel his icy stare. Larry looked back with a smirk.

Tony was silent for five seconds while he looked down at his finely manicured hands. He then asked, "Before continuing, I'm curious why Jerry Williams is still working with you. Obviously, he didn't agree to this change willingly?"

"He's still with us, just in a much lower capacity," Larry smiled.

"Can this organization run without him?"

"He's with us, so it doesn't matter," Larry replied. "And again, who works for us is none of your business."

"Jerry, can it?" Tony looked at Jerry Williams.

"Don't ask him! We don't understand why you even want him

here. If you want to make a deal, talk to us," Ron spoke up for the first time.

Tony ignored them and asked again, "Jerry, can the business operate without you?"

"It is doubtful," Jerry replied, allowing his eyes to finally meet Tony's.

"And can this enterprise still run without Ron and Larry?"

"Bullshit!" Larry snapped.

Tony rose to his feet, and he stroked his temples with both index fingers. He looked at Jerry. "Jerry, if you wouldn't mind waiting outside for a moment."

Jerry quickly stood and moved toward the door.

Ron, face red with anger, yelled, "What the hell is going on?"

Jerry opened the door and stepped out.

"You wanted the opportunity to make a deal—now is the time," Tony replied.

To the California boy's surprise, Tony turned and followed Jerry out of the room, securely shutting the door behind him.

Jerry raised his eyebrows when he saw Tony followed him into the hallway.

There was a startled scream, muted popping sounds, and what sounded like crashing furniture. Jerry's face illuminated with understanding, but a flash of horror crossed his eyes.

Tony walked very close to Jerry, invading his personal space. Once face-to-face, he spoke clearly and calmly, "Mr. Williams, as of now, you are back in charge of your enterprise. Please give us a call if there are any other problems. We expect the shipments to resume immediately."

That concluded the *Wine and Dine*.

CHAPTER ONE

Tom was in bed with his wife, enjoying a deep, restful sleep. All was well, except they were getting ripped off, big time.

The telephone rang at 4:16 Sunday morning. Tom was usually a hard man to wake. He was a deep sleeper and a dreamer. He woke confused and irritated, and after the second ring, he muttered, "What the hell is that?"

Tess, more alert, mumbled, "It's the phone."

"What time is it?" He searched for the clock on his nightstand, rolled over, and tried to sit up. He wanted to find the screaming phone and silence it. Half-asleep, he staggered from the bed, when, thankfully, Tess turned on the lights.

She looked concerned. She held the phone and said, "It's the alarm company."

That did it; he was awake now. He found his way to Tess, grabbed the phone, and answered, "This is Tom Coogan."

"Mr. Coogan, this is Andre with Northern Alarm. We received an alarm activation at your 1344 North Vista Avenue location. We have dispatched the police. Are you able to meet them at that location?"

"Yes, I can."

"Mr. Coogan, how long will it take for you to get there?"

"Well, I have to change, which shouldn't take too long, then I can head right out, so about twenty to twenty-five minutes."

"Mr. Coogan, what is the make and color of the vehicle that you will be driving?"

"It's a Ford F150 Pickup, brown."

The Boise traffic was light in the early morning darkness. Tess had offered to come, an effort of support typical of her; for 25 years, she was always there and always stable. Tom explained it was probably just another false alarm, so she should go back to bed. At least one of them should get some sleep. Still, four in the morning is a rough time to get an alarm call. He felt if there was a real problem, the police would be there, and it would be best to face the music alone.

Tom had just turned fifty and was relatively healthy for a business guy who spent too much time locked to his desk. His short blonde hair was partially gray, with even more of the color taking over his well-maintained beard. His best attributes were his constant smile and positive attitude. He tried to lead, set a positive example and work hard, possibly to a fault.

Tom drove up Capital Boulevard, and after climbing Depot Hill, he merged onto Vista Avenue. A half-mile later, he pulled into the newly renovated Vista Park Shopping Center, where two Boise Police cars stood parked in front of his store. It was immediately apparent this was not a false alarm. Even from a distance, Teton Outdoors's front entrance appeared to be compromised.

Tom had purchased the business from his dad when he was in his thirties and had since expanded it from one to three stores. He hoped his children would one day continue the tradition. Teton Outdoors was the best outdoor and travel store in the area, with loyal clientele who enjoyed a dynamic and active outdoor lifestyle uniquely available in Idaho. Still, retail was getting more difficult with time. With all the internet competition and the local media losing their advertising effectiveness, retail became very challenging. And then, of course, there were the burglaries.

Tom parked his pickup and carried his six-foot, 205-pound frame across the parking lot. It felt like a workout. Tom's once athletic build had started to fade, and he struggled to stay fit. He felt he was still doing okay, but today shook that belief. As he drew closer, he stopped, dropped his hands to his knees, let his head fall forward, and closed his eyes.

"Oh shit," He muttered. After three slow Yoga breaths, he erectly marched onward with his game face on. He needed to suck it up.

After the third burglary, they had upgraded the store's security features with reinforced doors, laminated glass, and roll-down steel mesh gates. With the improvements, the front entrances were supposed to be insurmountable. There was no way anyone could break into Teton Outdoors, or so everyone thought.

With each step, Tom checked out the mess. Fifteen yards from the store's entrance, a mass of twisted metal sat separate from the framework that previously held it together. So much for the security gate. A few steps closer, large pieces of laminated glass laid in batches on the asphalt. The glue binding the glass sheets held it together in cracked jagged chunks, some folded vertically, teeth-up, creating a dangerous landscape for the unaware. The glass belonged to the reinforced doors, which were now about six inconsistently sized chunks of scattered metal, with some small glass pieces still clinging to their frames. When he reached the front entrance, he saw why there were shreds of wood siding, and other construction materials lying in the parking lot; the structure around the front doors no longer existed.

It's not that the gate didn't hold, or the door's frame didn't bend, or the glass didn't break. Teton Outdoors's security measures were, once again, inadequate. With the entrance's framework torn free, it left the building with a gashed front opening with questionable integrity.

Tom walked up to one of the Boise Police officers and introduced himself. The officer was fit and carried himself with a military bearing. He introduced himself as Officer Andrew Taft. "Mr. Coogan, the alarm company received the alarm signal at 4:06 AM. They notified us at 4:10, and our first car arrived on the scene at 4:22. The perpetrators were no longer on-site when we arrived. The situation appears to be a very sophisticated smash-and-grab burglary."

"Did anyone see anything? I mean, with Vista Avenue being such a busy street, it's likely to have some traffic even in the middle of the night. I would hope someone saw something," Tom pled.

"I agree. Typically, when someone witnesses a crime, if they show up, they show up quickly. There could very well be a witness, someone driving by, but no one has come forward."

"Yeah, okay, but… crap."

"I understand, Mr. Coogan. We certainly will follow up. In situations like these, we may need to notify the media and see if the news departments can ask the public for help."

"Yeah, that's a good idea. Hopefully, someone might have seen something around here."

"Mr. Coogan, your alarm system did its job; its siren still howled when we drove up. It may have driven the group away."

"Group—you think there was a group?"

"Yes, sir, we think it was a large group. There was a significant amount of activity inside."

"Significant? Now you're scaring me. How bad is it?" Tom's voice cracked, and his composure weakened.

"Our other officers are making their final clearing of the building and adjacent areas. They will complete their process soon, and then you can go in. You're the only one who can best define how significant the damage is. What we know so far is there is a mess in there. A big mess," Officer Taft switched gears, "You have an excellent alarm system; do you have a camera system?"

"Yes, we do. We have eight cameras inside, and one out front with good coverage of the front door, and they are all backed up on a DVR system."

"Nine cameras. Excellent. When can we see the video?"

"Right away. My son, Nick, is our tech expert, and he's on his way. I expect he'll be here momentarily."

Officer Taft's stiff demeanor softened for just a second, and he let a consolatory smile show.

Nick showed up a few minutes later, and after getting briefed by his dad, they waited together for the police's all-clear. Nick stood strong at six-foot-five; he was clean-shaven with short brown hair, had intelligent green eyes, a square jaw, and a booming voice. As a business school graduate, he brought more than just his physical presence into the business. His technical skills added an element that was essential to the business's growth.

Finally, the police gave the all-clear, and Tom, Nick, and the store manager, Steve Smith, entered the building. When Officer Taft said there was a big mess, he wasn't kidding. The front entrance was a sea of broken glass with pieces large and small. There were several mounds several inches deep. Plus, there were large shards with jagged ends that looked like weapons. Even with good shoes, you could get cut.

As they entered the store, a line of free-standing glass showcases standard in retail stores stood on the right side. Behind them was a range of displays. They all once displayed high-end merchandise on glass shelves. The burglars must not have wasted time by sliding open the doors on either side of the showcases. Instead, they destroyed all the glass on both sides and then removed the merchandise from inside. A lot of damaged merchandise laid on the floor. Both the showcases and the towers appeared trashed. They looked like a pile of garbage you might find at the city landfill.

Tom, Nick, and Steve huddled together in disbelief. Tom demonstrated his calm composure by throwing an immature fit. His anger took over, and he completely lost control. Tom started by yelling a string of obscenities and then marched nowhere in tight circles. He stepped toward a free-standing display of Tilley Hats. Tom grabbed the display unit, hoisted it off the ground, military-pressed it, and tossed it across the room. Unimpressed with his effort, he charged the prone hat display as if it might put up a fight. Tom attacked the prop and its remaining hats with a series of sharp kicks and stomps while continuing his swearing litany. His first kick broke the hat display into two pieces, the second into thirds. Tom's final kick was a total whiff that threw him off balance and led him into flight. He landed awkwardly on a nice sizable chunk of broken glass that easily sliced through his pants and slit his leg. Who won the big fight between Tom Coogan and the Tilley Hat display? The Tilley Hat display by a TKO.

Good thing Teton Outdoors sells first aid kits. Tom rolled up his pant leg and checked the damage. His ankle was a bloody mess. There was a row of small punctures; it almost looked like a saw blade hit him. A deeper cut bled on his calf, a stab from the large chunk of glass that left a gash about an inch wide. He was pretty lucky; a jagged piece of glass like that could have impaled him, and if it hit a vein, his bleeding could have been severe.

Tom washed his leg and ankle with a wet paper towel and applied pressure with a couple more hoping to stem the blood flow, the blood flow that was ruining his pants and socks. He rubbed a coating of antiseptic gel on all of his wounds and used a butterfly bandage to close the deep cut, and then he wrapped gauze and tape all around his lower leg.

Nick stood above him with an incredulous look on his face. Tom looked up at his son, and as he stood, said, "I'm good to go."

"Are you sure you don't need stitches on that cut?" Nick asked.

"No, I don't think so. I've had worse."

"Really, how often do you attack Tilley Hat displays?"

Tom didn't say a word; he just stared at his son.

"You're always telling me to act professionally and keep my cool when an irrational customer is giving everyone crap," Nick added, sounding irritated.

Tom looked down, then turned back and said, "Okay, when you're right, you're right, and you are. So, let's get together with Officer Taft and check out how much these assholes stole, okay?"

"Okay, but Mom will be pissed about those pants."

"I'll bet she will cut me some slack on this one."

Officer Taft was shooting a series of photos to document the crime scene. Tom and Nick joined him and went to work. They stacked the empty boxes that matched up with the stolen merchandise. Then tried to guess what else was missing by memory. They were trying to build a ballpark estimate of the missing merchandise.

Taft asked, "Do you have an estimate of the loss?"

"Well, they knew what they were stealing," Tom replied. "They grabbed the high-end optics, like Nikon, Canon, Swarovski, and Zeiss. They cleaned out our Celestron scopes and a lot more. We are going to have to shut down and perform a physical inventory, and then we will know."

"Any general idea you can give me?"

"Yeah, easily six figures."

Officer Taft seemed stunned, then looked Tom in the eye and said, "Then this is serious. It is a major crime. I'm so sorry."

Tom shook his head and said, "Thanks."

"Are you insured?"

"Yes, but I doubt any insurance company will touch us after today."

———

Steve, Nick, Tom, and Officer Taft crammed into Steve's small office, staring at the surveillance system's LED screen. Nick was in control, with everyone's attention locked on the image.

"The master display shows all nine feeds at once. We can scan through them all together or individually, or if you want, we can do both. What first draws my attention is that camera nine is not sending a signal," Nick said.

"Which camera is number nine?" Tom inhaled.

"Outside, front door," Steve answered.

"Shit. How long has it been down?" Tom challenged.

"It hasn't been down. It was going yesterday."

"Are you sure?"

"Yes, sir," Steve answered confidently.

"Okay, let's start with camera nine and see what's up," Nick said. He brought the feed to full screen and scanned backward. Only a timestamp was displayed.

The timestamp counted down on the unchanging screen until 1:45 AM, when an image finally appeared. Nick stopped the playback and then played it forward until suddenly, the imaged vanished. Nick scanned back and played it again, this time in slow motion. Camera nine's angle captured the front door and thirty feet of the front parking lot. The storefront was reasonably lit, and nothing in the scene physically moved. Suddenly, the screen went dark, and then the image vanished. Nick scanned backed and played it, and once again, the screen went dark.

"Somebody disabled the camera," Officer Taft offered.

In one motion, everyone got up and marched out the front entrance.

Camera nine used to be mounted under an eave about eight feet out and thirty feet to the front door's left. It looked like someone had destroyed the camera with a bat. The camera spun unnaturally on its mount, and they tore its connecting wires free. It was mounted ten feet above the walkway, too high to be an accident. And it happened two hours before the burglary.

Tom thought whoever did this had pre-planned and covered their tracks at the same time. They probably disabled the camera and then observed the scene to see if the damage set off an alarm. Two hours later, they robbed the store, all the while knowing it would be hard to identify their vehicles since they eliminated the operational outdoor camera.

Everyone went back to Steve's office and watched the feeds from the other cameras. Some cameras showed nothing, like the ones in the offices and other areas away from the sales floor. Nick went through the feeds quickly, and everyone watched them all. Some of the floor cameras gave some valuable detail, and camera numbers three and four, which covered the front door and the showcase area, showed everything.

From the front door view, a couple of masked individuals in dark clothing quickly attached chains to both of the front doors and the steel mesh gate, and then attached cables. A large dark vehicle pulled up. Nick froze the playback, and everyone looked for details, hoping to see make, model, and, of course, a license plate. They couldn't see much. The uneven light made it impossible for the camera to get an accurate exposure of the vehicle. Still, they had enough light to see it was an oversized pickup truck. Unfortunately, most of the other detail was blurred, and only vague features appeared. Then, the big truck pulled away, the cable quickly drew taut, and the gate and one door broke free. The pickup reversed back toward the front door, and as quick as it returned, it sped off again. This time when the cable snapped, the other door broke free, along with the entire door frame, and just that quick, the front end of the store was gone. The timestamp showed 4:04 AM.

The truck pulled away, and a nondescript van backed in with its back doors wide open. The vehicle transfer was fast and smooth. A group of nine individuals met at the door, all in dark clothing and masks. They formed a quick huddle as if they were a football team, and when the group broke, they went into action.

Two masked men led the group–one wielding an extra-large iron pry bar, and the other carrying an aluminum baseball bat. They swept down each side of the showcases, swinging their weapons, destroying and wiping clean the glass on both sides. A step behind were four pickers, cleaning off the shelves from the right and left sides of the cleared showcases. A fifth was removing the merchandise from the display shelves mounted to the wall fixtures. Another rolled in a large trash container with wheels and an open lid. The pickers were taking merchandise and tossing it into the trash container. Some of their throws were up to six feet in distance, and some tosses went awry, which explained why some damaged products were lying on the floor. Speed appeared to be their primary focus.

"Look at that! They're not only stealing fragile equipment, but probably busting the crap out of it. That stuff will get scratched to hell at the very least," Tom exclaimed.

The burglars rotated trash containers as fast as they filled them and then slid them up and into the van. They hit the sections of the store with high-end merchandise on display. They executed the smash-and-grab with speed and teamwork. It would have been impressive to Tom if it didn't make him sick and angry. They rolled the last trash container into the van, closed the back doors behind it, and sped away. The timestamp was 4:13 AM.

Officer Taft and Nick worked together in Steve's office, finishing their security video analysis. "Okay, so you want the feeds off of camera three, four, six, and seven. And you want the time from 4:00 to 4:15 Would you like me to put them on a USB drive or a DVD?" Nick asked.

"Let's try the DVD."

"I'll make two copies for you and drop them off at the station when they're finished."

Officer Taft stood up and shook Nick's hand, said thanks, and then walked out into the storefront where Tom and Steve were huddling. Taft walked up to Tom, shook his hand, and said, "Mr. Coogan, I'm very sorry this happened. I hope you can get the store back together soon enough so that your business is not disturbed too much."

"That's the next project for today; clean up, recover, and reopen for business."

"I have the information I need to complete my report. I went over the surveillance video with Nick, and he's putting together copies for us. Do you have a business card I can add to the file in case we need to get a hold of you?"

"Sure," Tom handed him his card and said, "Call anytime. I want to get to the bottom of this one. I want to get these guys."

Officer Taft stiffened and said, "Here is my card, and on the back, I have written the case number we have assigned. Whenever you contact the department regarding this case, refer to this number. I will finish my report, and a detective will be assigned. In the meantime, my shift is transitioning, and I will be off for the next week. If you have any questions or discover any other relevant information, call the station."

CHAPTER TWO

T om waited until eight in the morning before he called his landlord at Vista Park. After being rousted out of bed at four, he felt sympathetic, at least a little. Still, it was time to get to work; door frames needed rebuilding, glass needed replacing, and a lot more needed to be done. Unfortunately, it was Sunday. Getting contractors out on short notice would be difficult, but it had to be done. You can't walk away from a building with a gaping hole where its front door used to be.

"Hello," answered a voice on the second ring.

"Max, Tom Coogan here. Sounds like I didn't wake you up."

"No, I've already had my second cup of coffee. What's up? Do you have a water leak or something?"

"Unfortunately, it's a lot worse than that. A gang burglarized us last night, and they tore the shit out of the store. Max, I think you need to get down here."

Max Night owned the Vista Park Shopping Center, along with his sister and business partner, Terrie. She ran the business end, and Max took charge of the physical plant. He had a positive relationship with the best contractors in Boise, and he had the know-how needed to personally take care of most of the shopping center's repairs. Vista Park saved a lot of money with his hands-on approach.

Max was one of the good guys. Most of the time, he had a ready smile on his face that matched his happy and mellow disposition. Max was a somewhat unaffected, mop-headed character and a big Boise State Football fan, still fragile from last year's bowl game loss. He loved to talk about sports. He liked his customers, and on carefree days, he just wandered around the shopping center and hung out in their stores. It was going to be hard to keep his smile going today.

Tom had just hung up when his cell phone rang.

Looking down at the caller ID, he saw the name "Mark Taggart."

"Hi, Mark," He answered.

"What's up, buddy? We about ready to hit the trail?"

"Sorry, Mark, I'm out. I've got huge problems here at the Vista store. We had a major burglary last night, and the crooks destroyed the place. I've got to hang in here and get the store secured."

There was a brief silence on the other end of the line, "That sounds terrible."

"Yeah, Mark, that's a good description of what's going on here."

"Is there anything we can do?"

Tom had known Mark for years. Their wives were great friends who threw the boys together, hoping they could develop a fun couple's friendship. That plan worked almost too well. Mark and Tom shared a common interest that ended up bonding them together, almost like brothers. They loved horses and horsemanship. At one of their first dinners, Mark mentioned he had just purchased his sixth horse. As he had many times before, Mark overlooked the fact that taking care of another horse was a massive amount of work, bordering on too much. He would get up early every morning, work on the basics of feeding, watering, cleanup, and then be unable to find the time to get it all in, especially with time left to ride. Riding, of course, was the reason he owned horses. Tom offered to help, and the rest is history.

When Tom was in junior high, he purchased a horse, a brown gelding named Dakota. Tom rode him throughout the Boise foothills with his friends and neighbors, both young and old. He loved Dakota, and Dakota loved to run. They flew through the foothills together. Mr. Smith, who lived down the street, owned a pasture where he allowed Tom to board Dakota for the token grazing cost of five dollars a month.

Twice a day, Tom would hike down to see Dakota. They loved to be together, and even if they were not out riding, Tom would feed, water, and hang out with him. Taking care of Dakota became Tom's most significant responsibility, and Dakota became very protective of him. Early on, his dad ordered a load of lumber, and over a weekend, Tom, his dad and big brother built a pretty nice corral and barn. The corral was Dakota's place; no other horse was allowed. There was a sense of pride and belonging there.

Once Tom entered high school, football, basketball, and friends became more important than horses. He rode Dakota less and less. When Tom went out of state to college, he sold Dakota to Mr. Smith.

Tom had always missed Dakota. He felt guilty selling him to Mr. Smith. At least Dakota never had to move and kept his home and social relationships with Mr. Smith's horses, but Dakota still lost Tom. Tom could visit Dakota when he came home from school, yet he felt guilty for letting his horse down. Looking back, Tom would have changed things, but he knew in his heart that his foolish actions were that of an immature teenager.

Time had passed, and Tom felt lucky; he had a great family and friends. But when Mark offered him the chance to get involved with horsemanship again, he couldn't pass it up.

Mark was five years older than Tom—a little shorter and in a bit better shape, being slim, trim, and fit. Mark's sandy hair was fading to gray; his intelligent green eyes hid behind a pair of orange-rimmed glasses. Mark was physically powerful for his size and age. With his muscular arms and a strong back, he could grab a bale of hay and sling it up and on top of a stack that was well above his head. Mark's hair ranged from short to long, due to inconsistent visits to his barber. Sometimes, with his shaggy hair and his orange rims, he looked a little unconventional.

Mark Taggart was unusual while also being brilliant and eccentric; traits that sometimes go together with the highly intelligent. Mark once said that he had a hard time controlling his mind. He was an idea-man, but sometimes his ideas came too fast. He could lose self-control and impulsively act out while leaving his common sense behind. Once, after a study session during med school, he and his friends stopped at a beer and pizza joint on the way home. He met a charming young lady mid-way through his first beer. Before he finished his second, he proposed. The young lady spent the next two hours trying to let him down easy.

Mark spent less time at work as he moved toward semi-retirement. When he was away from the hospital, he traded his white medical coat for jeans, a heavy shirt, and cowboy boots.

Mark appreciated all of Tom's support in maintaining his mini herd of horses, and they enjoyed riding together. Tom usually rode a large, spirited gelding named Buck. They were a good pair, reminiscent of Tom and Dakota. After a year, the two men solved Mark's problem of owning too many horses. Mark sold Buck to Tom, but continued to board him at Mark's pasture.

Tom appreciated Mark's call and his offer to help.

"Thanks," he said, "But there is nothing left to do except clean up, and we've got a good crew. We're rebuilding and putting the store back together again."

"I'll take care of Buck."

Tom's focus was on the burglary and all the stress that came with it. He wasn't thinking of Buck. "Yeah, thanks for taking care of Buck. I'm stuck here for a while, and that would help."

Tom felt compelled to bounce back from this burglary and do so quickly. He let every employee know that together; they were strong, and he was going to lead his team past this violation. The Vista store became a display of teamwork and effort. Store hours were usually ten until five on Sundays. The crew knew that opening at ten would be impossible, so they set the goal to get the store open that day. They refused to let the bad guys win. They would open, take care of their customers, and let everyone know they were okay.

Steve phoned the retail staff and let them know what happened and asked them to come in early. He asked everyone to be prepared to get dirty and bring a second change of clothes to wear when the store opened for business. They would deal with the broken glass and all the other debris. They would separate the empty boxes from the stolen merchandise, and set aside the damaged inventory. It could then be counted and classified correctly in their accounting of the loss. Then, after the cleanup, they would start pulling new stock from the back room and organize it to set up and restock displays as soon as they were repaired and functional.

Nick took charge of security. He called the alarm company and requested a technician to repair, replace, and test the security system, as it was no doubt damaged when the crooks ripped it out from the front of the store. He installed a new security camera to replace the damaged one that was outside. His biggest job was to have a team perform a physical inventory of the affected areas. He would then enter those numbers into the perpetual inventory system and run a variance report, all before the store opened. Then next week, Nick would combine all the data and file the insurance claim.

Tom was the foreman, organizing and directing the team. A huddle formed right outside the store with Max from the shopping center, Bill Howard from the alarm company, Jack Peterson from

Atwell Glass Company, Terry Long from Northwest Insurance, and Tom.

Max and Jack were working together, reframing the door jams. Then a trio from Atwell Glass started installing new, heavy-duty commercial glass doors. Another Atwell Glass crew went inside, straightened out the showcases' frames, and re-fitted them with custom-made glass. When they finished, the displays sparkled. As soon as the front doors were in place, Bill reinstalled the door sensors that would trip the alarm and require a security code entry within ten seconds. He also installed glass breakage sensors, which would set off an immediate signal. Terry, from the insurance company, had no role beyond moral support. He let everyone know that Northwest Insurance was on the scene, making sure they cover the loss.

Terry stood with Tom and said, "You know, if you can't get the store in shape to open, you have business interruption coverage."

"Thanks, but we're opening today."

———

At one-thirty in the afternoon, the store was ready to open. The retail sales force had cleaned up, changed their clothes, and put smiles on their faces. Most of the customers were aware of the burglary and the effort the staff had made to open. As the customers came in, sympathy and encouragement were expressed, along with a few hugs. Teton Outdoors was a family business, and that family included a connected customer base that showed concern.

Tom greeted customers and thanked them for their patience. He wandered to the front of the store where Max Knight admired some of his performed repair work.

"There's a big guy over there looking our way," expressed Max with a minor concern. "Do you know him?"

Tom looked over and smiled. "Yeah, I know him. That's Brett. Brett Wyatt."

"You mean Brett Wyatt, the …"

"Yep, the one and only," Tom quickly replied.

Tom walked over to Brett and reached out his hand, "Hey, buddy."

Brett grabbed Tom's hand, wrapped another arm around him, and gave him a man hug. "Hey, I'm so sorry. Mark filled me in while we were on the trail."

"How was the ride?"

"It was great; we just wished you were there."

"Yeah, me too. That would have been a hell of a lot better than this bullshit."

"How long have you been up?"

"Quite a while. The alarm call came around four-thirty."

"Have you had anything to eat?"

"No."

"Well, Tess is a little worried about you."

"Did she send you down?" Tom smiled.

"Of course, she did. I told her I'd take you out to a late lunch," Brett spoke in a serious tone with a piercing gaze. Tom could get lost in his work and forget to take care of himself. Brett was on a mission. Tess charged Brett with the task of taking care of Tom, and that started with lunch. He would not take no for an answer.

"Okay, let's go," Tom said, almost slightly intimidated, then he countered, "You don't need to be so damned bossy, you know."

"You know I've got your back."

Brett Wyatt was Tom's best friend and the third member of the Riders Club–a group of three guys who enjoy riding horses together: Tom Coogan, Mark Taggart, and Brett Wyatt. One day while on a ride, Mark referred to the trio as the Riders Club. Everyone got a kick out of it, and the name stuck. Mark was the senior member, then Tom, followed by Brett, the youngest, and their leader. They got together at least once a week to ride mostly in the Boise foothills, and sometimes they would trailer-up and get out into the backcountry of Idaho. They didn't ride to go hunting, fishing, or to play cowboys. The Riders Club just loved the outdoors, and they explored it on horseback.

Brett was a big, powerful man with a legacy of athletic prowess. In the nineties, he played middle linebacker for the University of Wyoming, Cowboys Football Team. He was an absolute terror on the field, earning national acclaim. In the Fiesta Bowl against Washington Tech, Brett made eighteen tackles, two of which held Tech out of the end zone during the game-winning goal-line stand. After graduation, college football led to a six-year NFL career, where he walked away after taking what he considered too many hits. After football, Brett enlisted in the Army as an officer. His service was specialized; he worked in the Military Criminal Investigation Division, which he never talked too much about. His friends assumed Brett was a specialized MP, probably working undercover on complex crime. After he left the Army, the FBI quickly recruited him; he worked as a special agent investigating white-collar crime. Brett loved the FBI, but his analytical skills drew him more and more into analysis via a keyboard, and as a result, Brett became stuck at a desk. The desk job tied him down too much, so he retired from the FBI and happily moved to Boise.

Now that Brett had entered his forties, his athletic fame, along with his athletic physicality, started to fade. Still, he was an impressive individual. Brett was a tall, dark, handsome guy, best described as multicultural. He stood close to six-and-a-half feet tall; his physique had thickened over the years, but he probably could still rip a door right out of a wall. His short-cropped hair was dark brown, his eyes green, and his smile natural. He was formidable and fearless, and nothing seemed to shake him. Naturally soft-spoken and calm, he could quickly slip away from any timid tendencies when he was with others. Brett believed in living an honorable existence and stood by that belief. He related to a code of conduct he liked to share with his friends. Brett felt he was a throwback to a simpler time when a handshake meant more than a contract.

Brett had never married; sure, he had some relationships, but nothing that lasted. Sometimes he'd like to blame his past lifestyle, but he wasn't the only man who had been a policeman or an athlete. He had known a lot of others who had lived dangerously, and they had families.

As they marched toward the new front entrance, Tom made a point to let his staff know he was out to lunch. They walked toward Brett's truck, which he parked at the south end of the building, near the store's back door.

"Hold up. Something's wrong back here," Brett said.

At the back of the store, an older lady struggled. She sat on the ground, at the edge of an asphalt and gravel area, and failed at her efforts to stand up. Next to her were two full bags of groceries, which she had carried from the Albertson's across the street. She also had one of those baggy purses hanging around her neck, and it by itself looked like a heavy load. Too heavy. Her breathing was rapid, she was rubbing her right leg, and she winced with each stroke. She looked up, saw Brett, and then purposely looked away.

Brett asked. "Are you alright?"

"I'm sorry. I'm having a problem with my leg. I'll leave here. I need a few minutes—please. I'm sorry."

"Nothing to be sorry about. You are just fine here," Brett replied. "You can stay as long as you like."

"I won't be long," she said in a weak voice.

Brett kneeled, but not too close, respecting her personal space. "We're not here to shoo you away or anything like that, but we sure would be happy to help if we can. My name is Brett, and my friend here is Tom. What's your name?"

"Lori."

"Well, Lori, I'm pleased to meet you. How about we pick up

those groceries for you and move you over to that bench?" he motioned to a six-foot wood bench on the side of the building.

Brett and Tom helped Lori stand up and walk away from the gravel strip and over to the bench. She looked more comfortable and less afraid.

Something in Brett's manner was infectious. When he talked to her, she relaxed. As she rested, she got stronger. They visited, and Brett found out Lori lived at a community housing facility. It was walking distance of at least a half-hour away from Vista Park. It was too far for her to walk, even without the groceries. She agreed to let them give her a ride, so they loaded her and her groceries into Brett's truck and drove her home.

At the door, Brett said with a smile, "Lori, next time you need groceries, please get a ride or call a cab."

"I have a friend who has a car, but she hasn't been around for a while. I'll try to find her next time, but cabs are hard for me."

"Lori, since we are friends, if you ever have a problem, please call me. Here is my card, so call or have someone get a hold of me. It's not easy for any of us in this world, so sometimes we have to help each other."

Lori took his card, stared at it for a moment, and then carefully slid it into her bag.

Then Brett reached in his wallet and pulled out some cash. "And just in case you can't find some help, here's some cab money."

Tom and Brett lunched at one of their favorite eateries, the Ridge Top Deli. As they walked in, Brett noticed Tom's uneven gate and asked, "Are you limping?"

"Yeah, I took a bit of a hit while cleaning up the store."

"And it looks like you've been bleeding?"

"Yeah, I had a cleanup accident," Tom looked at Brett and saw he was on the edge of laughter. "You've been talking to Nick, haven't you?"

Brett laughed, then Tom followed suit. By the time they sat down at their table, they had disrupted the entire restaurant.

As they ate their lunch, Tom told Brett the story of his day; the wake-up call, the burglary, and the cleanup. Brett listened with intense attention as Tom described the details. Every once in a while, Brett commented or questioned, and the dormant investigator's mind tried to connect the dots. The crooks had picked the optimum time of day. They had destroyed a surveillance camera hours before the crime, testing the waters while destroying potential evidence. Their attack was fast and organized, and they had a knowledge of what to steal and where to find it.

Tom looked at Brett and asked, "What do you think?"

"Well, first, it sounds like one hell of a mess, and second, a bunch of drug-crazed thugs did not commit this crime. Professionals did. What did the police say?"

"That's another issue. As of right now, it appears no one is on the case. The officer in charge is out, and a detective is going to be assigned sometime this week."

"He said sometime?"

"Exactly."

"Tom, I've got to believe he is downplaying the situation, maybe because the case is being passed to the detectives. I would bet they are already on the job."

"Oh, I hope you're right, but I've got to say I doubt it."

"Why is that?"

"Because this is our fourth burglary in the last eighteen months, and so far, the police have nothing."

"Keep your head up. You have done a great job. I'm impressed by your skills in dealing with the whole thing. It's a huge problem, and most businesses would be closed right now. Unfortunately, it appears you have too much experience with this kind of crap."

"Yeah, isn't that the truth? Still, the whole thing sucks; it's starting to get to me, and the reality is these burglaries create issues that extend beyond the crime itself. If this is the reality of being in a small business, I might have to quit."

"What kind of issues?"

"To start with, the insurability of the company. On our last renewal, we had a huge rate increase because of claims, and now—who would even insure us? We are bound to be considered a colossal risk. Our agent said we were close to cancellation, and now he suspects we could be uninsurable. Without insurance, a lot of business contracts, like leases, can be cancelled. They require proof of insurance every year. And of course, employees may prefer to work somewhere that isn't a popular crime scene, and who could blame them?"

"Tom, I believe you were born to be the owner of a business like this, so try not to get your head down. I recommend you call the police tomorrow morning and ask to speak to the detective in charge. Ask him where they are at with the case and ask what you can do to help."

"That's a good idea. I'll do it."

"On a positive note, Tess invited Mark, Cindy, and me over for dinner on Tuesday night. She hoped a couple of days would give you enough time to recover, and then get some moral support by getting together with friends."

"That would be great."

"And after dinner, I have a recommendation."

"What's that?"

"Let's get the Rider's Club together and talk this through. We may come up with some thoughts that may help with the investigation."

"Good idea. Right now, I have more confidence in the three of us than I do in some unnamed detective."

CHAPTER THREE

B rett arrived at the Coogan's house about an hour before dinner on Tuesday evening. He carried a brown cloth tote that contained two bottles, an excellent local red from the wine region west of Boise, and a fifth of Seven Devils' Whiskey. The two couples were taking charge of dinner. Tom barbecued marinated flank steak on the back patio, which Tess paired with one of her custom salads, homemade bread, and twice-baked potatoes. Mark helped by setting the table while Cindy set up the buffet. Brett felt envious of the dynamics of both couples.

Brett followed Tom into the kitchen in search of a corkscrew, where Tess directed the clueless men to the corkscrew's location, right next to the bottle opener in the corner drawer.

There was a lot to be admired in Tess Coogan. She was tall, trim, fit and shapely with soft brown hair that enhanced her hazel eyes. She had an engaging, magnetic personality. In almost any social situation, she would run into a friend. Often, it seemed, Tess knew everyone. She was the foundation of the family, both direct and extended. She knew when to indulge, when to help, and when to step in and take charge. Tess made Tom's life easy; he could sit back, follow her lead and relax, confident in the strength of his partner.

Back out on the patio, Brett opened the red wine, giving it time to breathe. Tom and Tess's house sat on a ridgetop with a backyard view of the Boise Front. Brett took a moment to scan the 180-degree view. The foothills rolled from east to west until they melted down into the valley below. The sun was low in the sky. Shafer Butte, the highest summit above the hills, caught the evening light. The light reflected off Shafer Butte's melting snowcap and glistened.

Soon they were toasting, sipping wine, and having a wonderful dinner. Evenings like this had become a common occurrence. The guys would ride together in the morning. The ladies were in constant communication with each other, and they all lived in the same section of the foothills, rising above the east end of Boise. When they had an opportunity to get together, they often did on the spur of the moment.

As dinner wound down, Brett commented, "Tess, there is nothing better than coming here for dinner. You are one of the world's great gourmet cooks."

"Not really. I just know how to read a recipe," she replied.

That comment brought a chorus of groans of disbelief.

The group cleared the table, cleaned up, and sauntered to the other side of the patio, where they relaxed and enjoyed the view. After a dramatic sunset, Tom lit up the fire pit, and Seven Devils joined the party. The guys cradled their drinks, gazed into the fire, and addressed the topic at hand.

"Mark, when Tom and I had lunch on Sunday, he told me burglars robbed Teton Outdoors four times in the last eighteen months. I knew the latest burglary wasn't the first, but four? I had no idea. Did you?" Brett asked.

"Four … four burglaries? Tom, we spend a lot of time together. How could I not know?" Mark replied.

"I guess I try to avoid talking about negative crap like that."

"Yeah, I get that. So, how does that work with your insurance?" Mark asked.

"Oh, we have a pretty high deductible, but after today, they will probably cancel our coverage when we go to renew—too high of a risk—uninsurable," Tom sadly stated.

"Well, I think we should talk about it," Brett said. "As I said the other day, if we put our minds together, we might find a thread to follow that may help put an end to it."

"Hey, I'm all good with that. I appreciate your help," Tom replied.

"So, how about you start at the beginning, burglary number one, eighteen months ago," Brett requested.

"Well, okay, here it is. As you guys know, the front of the Vista store is all glass. Our security system has glass break sensors and motion detectors along with your standard entry alarm, and we have high ceilings. The burglars found a weakness in the system. They learned the motion detectors were set too high and did not cover the first thirty inches above the floor, plus there was a small dead zone behind the showcases. The burglars crawled around below that level–they didn't trigger the alarm."

"But they still had to get in, right?" Mark questioned.

"Yes, that is where they beat the system again. The windows are made up of two horizontal glass pieces, a thirty-inch panel on the base, anchored to a metal frame, and an eight-foot top section. On the corner of the store, they removed a lower panel without setting off the sensors. Then one burglar entered and crawled through the store and pulled a bag that he filled with merchandise."

"How could he remove the glass without disturbing the sensor?" Mark asked.

"They removed the windows from the outside of the store because the glass contractor installed them backward. The inside man had patience because he filled the bag and returned seven more times before he quit. He was inside for hours."

"He must have been a small guy, or could it have been a woman?" Mark asked.

"No, it was a guy in dark clothing and wearing a ski mask, but a guy. He had help from outside the building, but it was always the same man crawling through the store. The light was low, but we still got the whole thing on video. They didn't beat up the store; it looked untouched, except they didn't put the windows back. The theft of our high-end inventory was significant. It was a major loss."

"The police, did they come up with anything?" Brett asked.

"No, they came up empty, the media never reported it, and we haven't heard a thing for a long time."

Everyone sat stunned and silent, so Tom continued, "Okay, burglary number two—at the Fairview store. Where the first burglary looked professional, the second was amateurish. As Brett would say, a couple of drug-crazed thugs burglarized the store. They hit us at two in the morning. A guy and his girlfriend broke out a back window in the office area. There were a few light-duty security bars on this window, but the guy managed to bend them out of the way. They crawled through the window, ran through the office, grabbed five telescopes off the floor, ran back through the office, and then tossed them out through the window and crawled out after them. The funny thing was, there was a door next to the window. The idiots could have walked out through that door, yet they still climbed out through the window when they left. There were jagged pieces of glass left in the window frame. They probably cut the crap out of themselves."

Brett shook his head, then asked, "Okay, same question, the police, did they come up with anything?"

"Yes. An hour and a half later, this darling couple needed some beer, so the pair visited an all-night convenience store. The guy held a knife to a clerk's neck, and they stole a couple of six-packs. While they were leaving, the police showed up, arrested them, visited their house a little later, and found our telescopes, but the telescopes were busted up and pretty much destroyed."

The story was so ridiculous. Everyone shook their heads. They would have laughed, but it wasn't funny.

Tom continued, "I went to one hearing, and I received a lot of communication from the courts. The burglary was the least of the couple's problems. The guy was a Russian, he'll be in prison for several years, and he will face deportation when he's released. The girlfriend got off with probation and counseling, but no long-term jail time."

"How do you feel about that?" Mark asked.

"Oh, I'd like to punch the guy, but beyond that, I just don't want either one of them to do it again."

"That doesn't seem likely," Mark said.

"When that guy gets deported back to Russia, he will be in worse shape. The Russians do not tolerate deported criminals," Brett offered.

"Yeah, that's what I heard too, and I guess the Russian guy does not want to go back, but shit happens, right?"

Tom stood. "I think I need a refill, and then I'll move onto burglary number three."

The guys all agreed, took a pit stop, refilled their whiskey on the rocks, and returned, eager to hear more.

Tom returned, sat down, and took a sip. "Okay, so burglary number three; about five months ago, and once again at our Fairview store. We had reinforced the windows and beefed-up security, but this time, the crooks came in with power tools."

Someone groaned.

"They found a quiet spot on the backside of the building, against a wall made of corrugated metal. The crooks set up shop with what must have been a pretty good power saw. They cut right through the metal siding, the framework, and the interior wall, and they climbed through. When they entered the building, they had to be surprised to find themselves inside our shop, which contains our repair area, a utility room, and a supply room. The shop is a confusing collection of workbenches, repair parts, and cleaning supplies, with a door connecting to the employee lunchroom. Can you imagine being in their situation? As soon as they broke through the wall, the motion sensor reacted, and the siren went off. They were probably in a panic, knowing the police would come, and when the crooks searched the place, they found themselves in an area of the store where there was nothing of value."

Mark questioned, "So, no real big loss on this one?"

"Correct, they just trashed the place, which we had to fix — it just pissed me off."

"Yeah, it would piss me off too. How does this keep happening? Boise is a low crime community, and this? This is ridiculous, and you keep getting hit repeatedly!" Mark complained.

"Sometimes, I think it's our fault. We've reevaluated our security after every burglary. We've added cameras and additional motion sensors, locked up merchandise, built stronger walls, added heavier bars to our windows, and we've trained our employees to be aware. Still, it's not enough; we're missing something."

"It's not your fault. These crimes are happening too consistently; something else is wrong," Brett said.

"Okay, we're listening. Why do you say that?" Mark replied.

"Excluding the crazy Russian guy and his girlfriend. The other three burglaries appear to be related, and they appear to be professional. To these guys, burglary is a business, and they are unlikely to quit until they get shut down."

"But each one was different," Mark countered.

"Yes, and after each burglary, they refined their methods, working toward improving their technique and reducing their risk. The first burglary was successful, but it took too long, and they were dangerously exposed. Plus, it was unlikely they would find the same weakness in another security system. The burglary took hours; it may have even moved toward early daylight. What if a car drove by and saw them, or a security guard? The crime took too much time, with too much risk. They were lucky they didn't end up in jail."

Tom said, "You're right; daylight was breaking when they finished."

Brett continued, "So, they needed to adapt if they wanted to stay in business. On the power tool burglary, they successfully avoided exposure, and they designed the burglary to be fast. Still, they left themselves blind and found themselves in an unknown situation. Even if they cased the store, it was unlikely they could know what is on the other side of a back-room wall. And as you can imagine, you don't have time to explore when you are burglarizing a business with a siren screaming. This burglary was sophisticated but unsuccessful, so it was once again time to adapt. Now, on Sunday's burglary, they improved their technique again. They reinvented themselves, and with this alternative method, they decreased their risk level. They evolved their technique with force and speed, a powerful combination. Their take was high, and their exposure low. I would bet we will see this again."

"So, are you saying they are going to hit us again?" Tom asked.

"Possibly, but it's more likely they will find another target, probably in another city. It is smart to keep moving. It lowers risk, and if they plan well, it helps ensure success. They probably have burglarized multiple other businesses already."

"So, how can they be stopped?" Mark asked.

"If a professional ring is committing these burglaries, the only actual solution is to bring the ring down."

"You are an ex-FBI guy, what do you think of the job the Boise Police are doing?" Tom asked.

"I'm concerned, but to be fair, I'm not sure what they are doing. Hopefully, they are working on it."

"I can tell you what they are doing. They are doing absolutely nothing. As of this morning, I still couldn't find out if a detective has the case," Tom sighed.

"Okay, Brett, let me rephrase the question. Our local law enforcement, what should they be doing with this case?" Mark asked.

"First of all, they needed an early response; most crimes are solved within a short time, right after they occur. A slow reaction makes solving the crime difficult."

"Well, we've got that going for us, don't we," Tom replied sarcastically.

Brett ignored him and continued, "Detective work is not rocket science. It is about asking a coherent set of questions and then following through, looking for answers. Basic steps need to be addressed one at a time, like looking for potential witnesses. If witnesses don't show up on their own, they should go public with sources like Crime Stoppers. Someone may have driven by and noticed some unusual activity. Plus, someone needs to interview the employees at the store and see if any customers were acting suspiciously. You should review the store's security videos to see if anyone looked like they were casing the joint, especially if they were coming in multiple times. If you find suspects, capture their image; there are sources out there that have face recognition capabilities. Maybe a suspect could pop up. Look for suspicious vehicles. Checking the pawnshops and internet sites for crooks who are trying to convert your merchandise into cash would be helpful, too. All of this is basic leg work that often can find a mistake. A mistake that may lead you to the criminal."

"I think I should spend the day tomorrow watching the security videos at the Vista store," Tom said.

"Probably a good idea," Mark echoed.

"So, assuming it is too late to catch the thieves quickly, what is the next step?" Tom followed up.

"I always like to start with patterns and predictability. If you can find a definite pattern, you can try to predict where the criminals may strike next, and then set up a stakeout and bust them. For example, have you ever seen movies about Bonnie and Clyde? The police were staking out banks and waiting for Bonnie and Clyde to show up. Now, with computers and the internet, we have a great advantage. There are large databases we can source, which can enhance our ability to predict an outcome or multiple possible outcomes."

"I know you can't talk about some specifics about your time at the FBI, but you did this type of work, right?" Mark asked.

Brett hesitated, then muttered, "Right."

Mark intensely looked Brett in the eye.

"So, Brett, can you still do it, and if so, could you do it now?"

"It has been a while," Brett said.

"Will you give it a try?" Mark asked again.

Brett looked back, waited a few seconds, smiled, and said, "Criminals burglarized Tom's business four times in the last year and a half. They victimized and violated him, and Sunday was the fourth violation—it needs to be the last. I will try."

—————————

CHAPTER FOUR

Tom, Mark, and Brett were neighbors. They lived within minutes of each other in the same section of the foothills, all on streets that branch off Willow Creek Road. Brett lived in a comfortable two-bedroom house; it was a nice bachelor pad built with a city view. Tom and Tess's family home was a short drive uphill from Brett's. It sat with a backyard exposure facing the mountains. A quarter of a mile further up Willow Creek Road, a lightly traveled street veers sharply off to the left and downhill into a tight rocky canyon. As the road enters the canyon, it quickly turns to dirt, and most of its traffic is runners and bikers. It is quiet. About a quarter-mile beyond the turnoff is a wide-open expanse with Willow Creek flowing through it. This very private spot is Mark and Cindy Taggart's home.

At the property's entrance, a pasture is surrounded by a common rail and pole fence. A private dirt road leads to their mid-century home, which fronts the core of their small, attractive, ranchette. They live in privacy, in a place that feels like the country, while still being in the city. Mark works at Les Bois Hospital, which is five minutes away.

Mark bought the property ten years ago. Initially, it was two smaller parcels, which were later combined. The previous owners were horse people, and for years, had stabled quite a few. The house and the road on the property were in good shape, but you couldn't say the same for the other buildings. In the middle of the main pasture, a barn wearily rested with hay and feed storage with a tool shed and four stalls. The barn's structure was adequate, but the roof, siding, and interior were pretty rough. Only two of the stalls were usable, and the hay was kept dry, but beyond that, it needed a significant rebuild. The corrals across from it were in about the same shape, usable but pretty well beat up. Another pair of dilapidated outbuildings, west of the barn, laid in ruin. One building was a small barn; the other looked like a stall with an attached tack room. In their day, these buildings were probably ideal for a one or two-horse operation. Unfortunately, by the time Mark bought the place, they were in such bad shape; they were almost unrecognizable. They needed to be rebuilt or leveled.

Mark recognized his property's sad state, and he wanted to improve it, but he couldn't get around to it. He generated multiple repair plans, but he'd drop one for another every time he came up with a fix, and then he'd repeat the process. He could see the outbuildings' sorry state, but he felt it didn't matter since they didn't use them. Then, there was the barn, and it was usable as long as you didn't need over two stalls at one time. The patched-up corrals were functional; everything kind-of worked. What would he do anyway, would he build or remodel, and what about a tack room? It would be great to get all of his gear out of the garage, and then maybe Cindy could park her car there again. He'd been renting pasture space to Brett, then sold Buck to Tom and started renting to him. Mark felt bad for both of them, knowing they might have to move their horses if there was a harsh winter. And of course, there was the money; he was in good shape financially, partly because he always parted with his money carefully. Mark had done nothing, partially because he couldn't settle on a single renovation plan, but what he didn't know was that Brett and Tom had.

When Brett and Tom first sat down with Mark and showed him their idea, he was shocked. Mark was so surprised, he couldn't believe any of it. It's not that he didn't like it, because he did, but the terms of the deal they had proposed seemed all too one-sided, and all the benefit was his. In the litigious world they lived in, it just didn't seem possible.

In their discussion, he asked, "So let's say I decide to sell the place, I benefit, and you are out. How can that possibly work?"

"You're going to sell the place? Great! What do you want for it —never mind, whatever you want, I'll pay," Brett said.

"No, that's not what I mean. It is not for sale."

"If you're selling it, I should get a first right of refusal. I've known you a lot longer than Brett has," Tom volunteered.

"It is not for sale!" Mark shouted.

"Now isn't that the point," Brett said in calm sincerity.

Tom chimed in, "You will never sell this place. You would be stupid to do that, and Mark, you are not stupid. But if you ever have a stupid moment, sell it to me, okay?"

"Can I quote you part of the code?" Brett added.

"Always," Mark grinned.

"Remember, some things are not for sale."

"I thought I was the idea-man in this bunch, but you guys have outdone me on this one. Where do we go from here?" Mark asked.

"Let's shake on it," Brett said.

They shook on it and made the deal. Mark was right about the benefit and the risk, and in both cases, he won. But as Brett said, this is not about winning or losing; it was a win-win proposition; no one could argue with that.

The Riders renovated the entire ranch. They removed the old outbuildings and replaced them with a new, tall building with a metal roof. It was a hay barn where they could lay in a full winter's worth of hay and keep it clean, dry, and safe.

They expanded the existing barn's purpose. With most of the hay storage moved, they had room to grow the stall area. Instead of having two good stalls, they had eight, plus a cleaning stall and other extras. Built out the west side of the barn was a significant addition; this one was for the guys. There were two entries; the entry from the stall area opened to a mudroom where they could clean up after riding or working with the horses. The next room was a well-designed tack room where all of their gear could be cared for and stored with room to spare. The most significant addition to the barn was the clubhouse. There was a small but complete kitchen, a well-stocked bar, a very comfortable open area with a fireplace and a big-screen TV. There was a music area, not a place to listen to music, more of a place to play it. The guys all played, not necessarily well, but they played. In the music room, they kept three guitars, a ukulele, and six harmonicas. Out the front door was a patio with a fire pit; it was a glorious spot to hang out and relax. They had one hell of a barn, giving a whole new meaning to "I have work to do in the barn."

The renovation was an extensive project for a few guys to pull off. They hired an architect, an interior designer, a consultant with expertise in horse facilities, and of course, Tess and Cindy helped a lot. Without them, the clubhouse would have been drab and utilitarian. Brett and Tom paid for it all. In the agreement, Mark kept ownership of everything, including all the improvements. If Mark decided he wanted them out, they would leave. If Brett or Tom wanted out, they exited with no ownership. What Tom and Brett got was unlimited lifetime access. It was worth every penny.

Rent became a thing of the past in this unique partnership. As for expenses and supplies like hay and oats, they split them up, one share for each horse. The new barn was hard to leave, and its connection was so magnetic that both Tom and Mark would randomly leave work early and head down to the barn to hang out. Sometimes, Brett just never left; he'd sleep there and then go riding at the crack of dawn.

———

Saturday morning, Tom drove up and parked in a spot next to the barn. Inside, he could hear the wail of Brett playing the harmonica. Tom winced a little, opened the door, and yelled, "The harmonica gods are mad this morning. Brett, you need to work on a new song."

"You're just jealous," Brett answered.

Mark, who was finishing his second cup of coffee, asked, "Do you want to trailer-up, or just head for the hills?"

"Let's do the Ridge. Pepper needs a good run," Brett offered.

"Sounds good to me," Mark said.

They all saddled up. Tom was riding Buck, and the big Quarter Horse was eager to go, throwing his head and fighting the bit just a little. These actions were typical of Buck; he was excited to leave, especially if other horses were heading out with him. He always leveled out as soon as they hit the trail. Mark was riding Trixie, a Golden Palomino mare with a long, luxurious, blonde mane and tail. Mark brushed and brushed her because she deserved it. She was beautiful. Trixie was a big, strong girl with a sweet personality and always ready to go. Brett was riding Pepper. Pepper was a tall gelding with a dark brown coat, nearly black; his hoofs were striped, and his mouth and nose mottled. A striking, white-speckled blanket covered his hind and flanks. Pepper was the perfect Appaloosa, a breed many consider the world's best all-around horse. The Appaloosa is a western breed originated by the Nez Perce Indians in Northern Idaho. Appaloosas are courageous and independent and have historically been the recommended breed to ride when heading into a difficult situation.

Brett and Pepper were an impressive pair. Brett was an expert rider, and Pepper was the smartest and best horse he had ever ridden. And Pepper was a hackamore horse; a bit had never touched his mouth.

No trailers were needed to ride up to the Ridge. They rode out a small gate on the north side of the main pasture and onto a trail which was the remnants of an old abandoned dirt road. They skirted the creek for a half a mile, then took a route that ran up a draw where they started to climb. They rode for a half-hour, continually gaining altitude until the canyon to the south ran out, then turned south and rode back to a higher section of Willow Creek.

As they worked their way through, they experienced the glory of early summer in the great outdoors. During May and June, Boise's foothills turn a luscious green with the growth of seasonal grasses. Wildflowers cover many areas. A couple of local favorites are the Blue and Purple Bachelor Buttons, a small flower that thickly covers vast expanses, creating entire color zones. The other is the Arrowleaf Balsam, which looks like a wild version of a yellow daisy. It grows in tight groups that cover hillsides and ridges. It is a flower that spends its day following the path of the sun.

They watered the horses at the creek, took a slight break, rode further south, and crossed a dirt road. They entered a short but dramatic valley that was inaccessible to motorized vehicles. The valley narrowed into a tight gorge and then terminated. After a climb up a steep trail, they found themselves on the Ridge.

If you ever looked on an official map, it probably wasn't called the Ridge. Even if they knew the proper name, they would still call it the Ridge. It was pretty high up in the foothills, and it was a pretty cool spot because the Ridge was long, wide, and flat. Trails that had been there for a half a century laced its surface. There were no dangerous ditches, holes in the ground, or garbage lying around that could impede, or worse, injure a horse. It was as if God had set up a natural race track specifically for horses.

When Buck stepped onto the Ridge, he knew where he was,

and was excited. Tom needed to hold him back and give him a brief rest from the climb. After he held him as long as he could, he gave Buck his head and let him go. A Quarter Horse would never win the Kentucky Derby, but they can run with the best in a quarter-mile. They are sprinters, not long-distance runners. Buck was strong, and flying low, and Tom was holding on for dear life. Tom couldn't imagine any horse keeping up until the Appaloosa ran by.

They rode back to the barn by early afternoon, a little hot, tired and hungry. The Riders let the horses cool down and then unsaddled and brushed them. When the horses were ready, they were watered and let out into the pasture where they lazily grazed.

The guys hit the fridge for beer and went out on the patio to relax. Mark lit the fire pit and broke out the hotdogs. All three roasted quarter-pounders over the fire. With a little mustard and a bunch of buns, they had the makings of lunch, quite the gourmet experience. But of course, nothing is better than cold beer accompanied by a hotdog cooked over a fire.

Before he came out to the patio, Brett spent time intently focused on his laptop. He was studying, scrolling, and reading. It was uncommon for Brett to carry a computer down to the barn. He had always embraced the opportunity to escape technology, especially at the clubhouse.

"What's up with the laptop?" Mark asked.

"Well, remember I said I would work on a database study relating to burglaries similar to the one at Teton Outdoors?"

"Yeah. How is that going?" Mark asked.

"Good, but it has been erratic. I've been getting pieces of information, and then I've needed to follow up with additional queries. I'm finally getting to a point where the picture is becoming somewhat clear."

"So, tell me, Brett, what kind of database do you access? The law enforcement systems aren't open to everyone on the internet, are they? Do you still have clearance to work within the FBI or some other hidden government system?" Mark asked.

Brett turned to Mark, and with a deadpan look on his face, he stared directly into Mark's eyes.

Mark's composure faltered, and after about thirty seconds of silence, he said, "Sorry Brett. Sorry about the stupid question; let's pretend this never happened, okay?"

"Jesus, Mark. How about the obvious question," Tom taunted? "Brett, what have you got?"

With the hotdogs consumed, the guys headed back into the clubhouse and sat around the coffee table with Brett and his laptop, eager to see what he had.

"Okay, guys," Brett said, "I'll try not to bore you with too much statistical crap, so here is the short version. I was looking to see if a specific region was experiencing burglaries at a rate significantly above the norm. Plus, I looked for an abnormal rate of similar techniques in these burglaries, meaning destructive force, smash-and-grab. I looked for coincidental occurrences on a recurring day of the week or time of day, meaning three to five in the morning. Another factor is a geographical pattern, such as a string of crimes from city to city leading our way. I also checked for the same type of merchants with overlapping stocks of merchandise, and, of course, I looked for a pattern. I checked for any arrests or any solid progress made toward arrests. Does that make sense to you guys?"

Tom and Mark, quite transfixed, nodded their heads in agreement.

"Several of these areas popped up with statistical aberrations that were significant," Brett continued.

"Such as?" Mark said.

"Regionally, burglaries are spiking all around us: Washington, Oregon, Nevada, Utah, Wyoming, Montana, and Idaho. It's a vast region, but one with a lot of commonalities. When you step into California, Colorado, and other bordering states; it drops off fast.

However, in this large of a region, you would expect a travel pattern. Such as a team working down the coast from Seattle to Eugene. But there is no pattern, and no arrests or any significant progress toward arrests.

"We also have some matches in the time of day, day of the week, and criminal technique. They are hitting businesses around four to five in the morning, ripping the doors right off the main entries, and cleaning out the stores in mass and with speed. It is very, very similar to what happened here."

"Sure as hell doesn't sound like a coincidence to me," Tom said with an edge in his voice.

"Agreed," Brett said, "And it only gets better."

Tom and Mark unconsciously leaned in.

"The merchandise was consistent. The thieves stole binoculars, riflescopes, spotting scopes, telescopes, cameras, and lenses. Almost every burglary is easily netting six figures of exotic optical products. Two types of retailers are getting hit. The first are shops like Teton Outdoors: outdoor product retailers who invest in sport-optics and are moving toward photography. The second type are camera stores. Whoever is behind this is knowledgeable about their targets and their merchandise."

"So, does any of this help us predict who they may hit next, and is there a chance Tom's place may get hit again?" Mark asked.

"I do think they are repeating, and the Vista burglary was at least the second time the same bunch hit Tom. I also think they may get complacent with their success, and that may make them predictable. The regional law enforcement agencies need to work together, and they may bust these thieves yet."

"So, what do you mean, 'they are getting complacent?'" Mark asked.

Brett brought up a page on his laptop. "This may help. I've put together a compilation of the statistically related burglaries in this intermountain area during the last quarter. When we've finished going through this, Tom could check the details and see if you agree with the match. You may know some of the other victims. We may want to talk to them and make sure we are on the right track. But first, take a look at this."

The three men slid together to view Brett's laptop.

Brett continued, "So, in the last quarter, we have similar burglaries in Portland, Pocatello, Spokane, Logan, Bozeman, Eugene, Jackson Hole, Seattle, and Boise. In some cases, up to two or three businesses in the same city were hit within two weeks."

"Holy shit," Tom muttered, "I'll tell you right now. These stores are related. I know all of these guys, and most of them are my friends. We talk to each other and try to help each other succeed. Oh, shit. Look at this. Blue Sky Camera and Outdoor just closed. Now I know why," Tom was shaking.

Brett moved on, "What isn't normal is the travel pattern. If you are working a region, you won't go from Portland, then to Logan and then Spokane, that's zig-zagging the west, with too many miles in between. It doesn't make sense, but the common factors are too strong. All the burglaries took place between four and four-thirty in the morning. Of the fourteen burglaries, ten took place on Sunday morning, and four on Tuesday morning. So, when they hit a town with multiple targets, they strike on Sunday, and then they repeat on Tuesday or the next Sunday. That pattern could be a big mistake. They may repeat it to a fault."

"Brett, you have done an awesome job. I can see how valuable this information could be in the right hands. My question is, what do we do with it now? There are a lot of regional law enforcement agencies. Which one gets it? Who will run with it?" Mark asked.

"Tom, did you get in touch with the detective assigned to your case?" Brett asked.

Tom nodded his head in agreement.

"So, he's our man. I'll give Tom a copy of my compilation, and he will get it to the detective tonight."

"Sure, I'll give it a shot," Tom hoped he could get a hold of the guy on a Saturday.

"I've got a better idea," Mark offered.

"Okay, what have you got?" Brett replied.

"I know this may sound crazy, but listen up. Tomorrow is Sunday, and that's when these guys could strike again. That's the pattern. Let's figure out who might be their next target and then let's do a stakeout and see what happens."

"So, you think that is a better idea?" Brett countered.

"Yeah, we could catch the gang and bust them."

"Are you listening to yourself? We are not law enforcement."

"Well, we could turn them in."

Brett shook his head and said, "A stakeout where?"

Tom interrupted, "I know of one place they might burglarize. I know their owner, and I was thinking about calling and warning him. They might hit Valley Camera on Orchard Street. That is one hell of a store, and they are heavy in all the targeted categories. It seems possible these crooks could hit them."

"Exactly, that sounds quite possible. Let's do a stakeout there," Mark excitedly said.

"Mark," Brett said, trying to stay composed, "You have come up with a lot of great ideas, but this sure as hell is not one of them. You have got to be kidding me. What are you going to do if you catch these criminals?"

Mark started to say, "Well …"

"Well, nothing!" Brett interrupted. "Have you received weapons' training? Can you disarm an assailant carrying a knife or a club? Are you prepared for the unexpected, or are you a trained police officer? No, Mark, this is not a good idea. It is a stupid one. What in the hell are you thinking?"

"Well, the local police haven't done much yet, so I just figured we could help, maybe."

"Help, maybe? Mark, this idea of yours could be dangerous!

You could get in trouble or get hurt! Hell, Mark, you could get killed! Is it worth it—well, is it?"

"Okay, okay, you're right. It's a bad idea. Tom can deliver the info to the Boise Police Department, and we'll let them take care of it."

"Thank you, and don't get me wrong, you've got your heart in the right place."

They had another beer or two and enjoyed the rest of the afternoon just sitting around the fire pit and then headed for home. On the way out, Mark and Tom made the eye contact that said, "Let's talk."

Brett noticed, and it scared him.

CHAPTER FIVE

Brett pulled his old Schwinn Varsity out of the garage and dropped it into the back of his pickup. He drove down to Municipal Park, jumped on his bike, and pedaled onto the green belt. Boise's green belt travels along thirty miles of the Boise River, and his ride today was an easy ten-mile round trip that ran through the north side of Boise State University and four of Boise's riverside parks. After passing the Fire Fighters Memorial, he veered off the main trail and merged on to a branch that crossed a converted one-hundred-year-old railroad bridge that spans the Boise River. The branch led him past an irrigation canal, some houses, apartments, and businesses, until the pathway terminated at Orchard Street, bordering Valley Camera's parking lot.

Brett worried the guys hadn't dismissed the idea of setting up a stakeout. They could be making a huge mistake. They did not understand the simple truth; if you set up a stakeout to observe criminals, physical contact is possible. No way was Mark and Tom equipped for that.

Too many times during his law enforcement days, he had seen seemingly quiet situations explode. Brett knew where to draw the line, but did Mark and Tom? He wasn't sure. Once you cross that line, it's hard or impossible to come back.

Brett steadfastly decided he would not take part in Tom and Mark's plan, but he felt he needed to be in the shadows to back them up if they tried playing detective. So, riding his bike on the green belt right up to the potential crime scene was a great way to see the lay of the land.

From the east side of the store, a wall of evergreens entirely obscured the bike path. They also gave Brett great cover. He could quietly blend in and easily observe. A short distance toward the river, a small apartment complex bordered the path. A cedar fence sealed the apartment's property from the green belt. It was built around the complex to provide privacy, but age had taken its toll, leaving the fence in poor shape, with gaping holes that offered a great escape route. For Brett's purpose, this was a pretty good layout; he was ready.

———

"Hello," Tom answered the phone shortly after ten.

"Hey, buddy, is this too late to call?" Mark asked.

"No problem. I'll be up for a while yet. What's up?"

"Well, I was curious how it went with the detective when you sent over Brett's report?"

"Not too great. I couldn't get a hold of him. I had to leave a message, and he hasn't called back."

"Shit! Did you try anyone else at the department?"

"Yeah. I called the main number and got nowhere."

"Shit, shit, shit! If we don't deal with this now, and I mean right now, it may be too late."

"Agreed, but what can we do?"

"Let's meet at the clubhouse and see what we can figure out."

"I'll be there in five minutes. Should we call Brett?"

"No, not right now."

Fifteen minutes later, the pair jumped into Mark's pickup and drove over to Orchard Street. They went back and forth in front of Valley Camera and the other businesses nearby, trying to find an inconspicuous spot to set up the stakeout. Orchard has no on-street parking, so they were forced to set up in a parking lot. Across the street, to the west, is a five-story State of Idaho office building. The parking lot servicing the building is on its west side, almost a block from Valley Camera. It was nearly too far away to hide and observe the store's front, but its advantage was concealment; there were quite a few government vehicles permanently parked there, so it was an excellent place to park and blend in. They agreed this was the best spot to set up the stakeout. Their plan was complete, so they drove back to the clubhouse to wait.

On the way back, they stopped at Tom's house, where Tom grabbed some supplies. Tom explained to Tess that they started a late-night project; he could be late, very late. Tess thought it was strange, but knew when the guys got together, they could lose track of time.

Tess wasn't worried. She had the comfort of knowing that when the three of them were together, they were safe.

At the barn, Tom changed into some dark clothes. He put together a stakeout kit with a high-power tactical LED flashlight, a Canon DSLR camera with a Tamron 100-400 mm zoom lens, a pair of Celestron twelve power binoculars, and his cell phone. Mark also was dressed in dark clothes, but forgot his phone at home, which was typical of him. When he wasn't on call at the hospital, he tended to leave his phone behind and escape. It didn't matter anyway; they only needed one cell phone.

Their plan was simple. First, park and blend in, and hope to have an acceptable view of Valley Camera's front door. About fifty yards closer to Orchard Street, in the office building's courtyard was a garden area with benches and raised planters. It was an attractive feature that dressed up the front of the building. If they couldn't see well enough from their truck in the parking lot and needed to improve their viewpoint, they planned to sneak over to the garden area, hide behind the planters, and keep a lookout. If the burglars showed, they would first call 911, notify the police before the burglary, observe through the binoculars, shoot video and stills with the DSLR, and wait for the cavalry. The burglars had previously shown themselves to be extremely fast and could complete the crime before the police arrived. If that was the case, at least Mark and Tom could build a stash of new evidence to help solve the crime spree.

Of course, the odds the burglars would show up at the stakeout were low. Predicting the next crime scene couldn't be this easy, or the local law enforcement would be there. The burglars probably wouldn't show, and Tom and Mark would probably waste their time and lose sleep. If that happened, they hoped to keep the entire episode to themselves.

At three in the morning, Mark drove down Emerald Street, crossed Orchard, and turned into the State office building's parking lot. They parked in a spot between a state-owned van and pickup. The parking spot was ideal; his pickup looked like it belonged. They sat, waiting and watching, knowing it would be a while before they could expect company.

Brett parked his pickup in a remote parking spot on a quiet street at three-thirty, a block south of the green belt extension. He was dressed in dark clothing, carried a black bag of gear, and wore a black ski hat. He carefully and almost invisibly worked his way through the apartment complex and on to the green belt. A short time later, he concealed himself in the evergreens bordering Valley Camera's parking lot. His vantage point was very close. Valley Camera had spotlights across its front entrance and a large sodium vapor light covered the parking lot. It didn't take long for Brett to spot Mark's pickup in the lot across the street. Brett shook his head; unfortunately, he wasn't alone. He wasn't surprised, only a little disappointed. Of course, Tom was angry. The burglaries wounded him in a profoundly personal way, and Brett couldn't blame him for that. Hell, he probably would feel the same way. Mark reflected his buddy's pain and was an enabler in this action, even if it was a stupid idea.

————

Shortly before four, Tom became antsy and agitated. He'd been watching Valley Camera's front door through his binoculars, and he felt like he had been watching for hours rather than minutes. Even though the burglary gang had not shown, Tom needed to do something, and he decided they were too far away.

"Let's move up to the planters so we can get a better view," He announced, then opened the door and started to get out.

"Hold it," Mark said. "Relax a minute—let's give it a little time."

"If we give it some goddamned time, we're going to screw up the whole thing and get nothing on those assholes," Tom grabbed his stuff, stepped out of the pickup, and slinked away.

A moment later, Mark, hesitant to leave the truck, reluctantly gave up and followed.

After an awkward low crab walk up to the planters, the guys set up a new position hiding behind a four-foot-tall planter bordered by several small bushes. Tom took charge of the photography duties with his DSLR-telephoto lens combination. A low-battery icon blinked on the camera's display. Mark was manning the binoculars. Tom fidgeted and swore at the camera. Mark tried to keep Tom cool and calm, but Tom told Mark to screw himself and acted like he was ready to fight.

At 4:06 AM, a large gray truck with dual rear wheels drove past Valley Camera heading north on Orchard. Two minutes later, it circled back, turned left into Valley Camera's employee lot on the north side of the store, then circled behind the east side of the building, drove into the front lot, and paused a short distance past the front door. The truck turned left to adjust its line, then reversed and backed up to the landing, right in front of the main entrance.

A man jumped out of the passenger side of the big truck. He was dressed in black and was wearing a ski mask that hid his face. He wrapped a chain around the handles of both of the front doors.

Mark watched through the binoculars, but was having a hard time holding them steady. Twelve power binoculars are hard to hold still, especially when your hands are shaking.

"Call nine-one-one!" Mark whispered.

"You call them! I'm going to get a little bit closer," Tom then disappeared, running low and weaving through the parking lot.

Mark whined to himself, "But I don't have my cell phone." Then he looked down and saw Tom's camera lying in the dirt.

Suddenly a loud bang came from the action as the truck lurched forward, and both of the store's doors pulled free from their frame. The large vehicle was still pulling them away when a gray van entered the parking lot and backed up to the landing. It looked like an ugly, but well-practiced move. A team, all dressed in black and wearing ski masks, jumped out of the van. They bunched together for a moment, then with bats and crowbars in hand, they charged into the store. At the same time, the store's alarm went off, and the sound was deafening.

Mark had lost track of Tom; he scanned every part of the scene and searched with the binoculars. Tom had run across Orchard to a position about 150 yards south of the store. There was a furniture business next to Valley Camera; he knelt in their parking lot and assessed the situation. He was winded and on the edge of hyperventilating. He was also full of anger and rage, and reason was leaving him.

He carefully moved through the furniture store's lot and crossed into Valley Camera's. He stood three car lengths behind the van when he pulled out his 1000-lumen technical flashlight and shined it into the front of the store. The burglars started to break the glass out of the showcases when the light beam hit them. They blindly looked into the light and then reactively scrambled away from the entrance and took cover by lining up against the store's interior walls.

Tom stepped right up to the back of the van and kept his flashlight aimed. The alarm screamed, and communication was almost impossible.

Tom yelled as loud as he could, "FREEZE, THIS IS THE POLICE! YOU ARE UNDER ARREST! EVERYONE ON THE FLOOR AND..."

He didn't finish the sentence.

Tom missed the fact that not everyone was inside the store. The man behind the wheel of the big truck grabbed his large aluminum bat and walked up behind Tom, and with a practiced swing, delivered a tremendous blow right to the middle of Tom's back. Tom's legs collapsed, and he landed face-first onto the asphalt. He tried to climb to his knees when the second blow smashed onto the backside of his thighs, and then his assailant proceeded to kick him in the stomach, kick him in the chest, and then as if he were kicking a field goal, he kicked him in the head.

Tom was in immense pain, but still conscious. The man pulled Tom halfway to his feet, dragged him to the back of the truck, and hoisted him into the truck's bed. Then, as Tom laid on the steel surface, the man lifted the bat and hammered Tom three more times.

Brett walked out of the cover provided by the evergreens. He smoothly moved down the front of the store, reached the side of the van, and lifted his shotgun. When he pulled the trigger, it sounded like a bomb went off.

Everything stopped.

The shotgun blast blew the front fender and hood halfway off the van's chassis. It shredded the right front tire, and the van's front end collapsed onto the exposed wheel. Brett instantly ejected the casing as he turned and loosely aimed the barrel of the shotgun further up the van's body. Brett's second shot destroyed the back tire and blew the bumper right off the van's rear end. He ejected the casing, stepped away from the van, and strode toward the motionless truck. The third shot hit the truck's back end and destroyed the dual set's outside rear tire.

The gang of burglars was in a widespread panic. They piled out of the store. Some ran out and across Orchard Street and then split up, some sprinted north and some south, and some sprinted around the store and through the rear parking lot. Another few ran up the green belt while another ran past the furniture store.

The man who had beaten Tom with the bat looked down the barrel of Brett's shotgun, frozen. Every one of Brett's shotgun shots had been aimed at an angle to avoid any blowback via a direct ricochet. The man in Brett's sights had scrambled away from the truck's back end when Brett fired. Brett did not shoot directly at him; he let geometry take charge. The buckshot's ricochet hit him hard. He was bleeding from his arm, shoulder, and face.

Brett motioned toward the back of the truck and said, "Get him out of there."

The man walked to the back of the truck, slid Tom out, and spilled him into the parking lot, and then he scrambled into the truck's driver-side door and drove away.

The environment had changed entirely. The van was dead in front of the store; it spewed steam and leaned hard to the right.

There was no sign of the burglars or their truck. The alarm still screamed.

Brett circled and checked the lot. He picked up the three empty casings, stuck them in his pocket, and stowed the shotgun. He walked over to Tom's motionless body, picked him up, threw him over his shoulder, and marched back up to the green belt.

CHAPTER SIX

Mark hid behind a bush, holding his binoculars, trembling. Their stakeout had turned south, and of course, it was his idea, another bad one. He watched as the lone black-clad gunman marched down the green belt, carrying Tom's limp body across his shoulder. Mark pulled his binoculars up to his eyes the last time before the two men disappeared, and then he illuminated.

"Oh my God! Is that Brett?" he whispered.

Mark snapped back to reality. He jumped up and turned toward his truck, and then he turned around. Not wanting to leave evidence behind, he remembered to grab Tom's camera. He double-checked, confirmed he had grabbed everything and sprinted back to his truck, slammed it in gear, turned down Emerald, and drove east. It seemed essential to get out of there fast. Once he was a few blocks away, he heard a police siren. The sound slowed him down a bit. He didn't need to be pulled over for speeding, and he'd feel even better if he didn't see any police.

Mark figured Brett would likely drive straight to the barn, and he hoped he would, since Mark kept a full mobile medical kit at home, just in case of an emergency. Mark drove across town, turned for home, drove right by his house, and parked next to the barn. Brett wasn't there yet. He hoped he was right and prayed that Brett was on the way. Mark opened up the clubhouse, turned on the lights, and walked back outside to wait. Five minutes later, he saw the headlights of Brett's truck.

When Brett drove up to the barn, Mark ran out to meet him. "Oh, thank God, you're here. Is he conscious?"

"I'm not sure," Brett replied.

"Let's get him inside."

Tom woke up while Brett carried him up the path that led to the clubhouse. He had been sliding in and out of consciousness while lying in the backseat of Brett's pickup. Brett tried to keep the ride as smooth as possible. Every time Tom opened his eyes, he moaned. He fought Brett's firm hold, and then he spewed out, "Stop it, goddamn it—put me down."

Brett stopped and looked at Mark.

Mark approached and calmly said, "Look, buddy, we're going to carry you in and set you on the couch, okay?"

Tom continued to struggle, which created a couple of problems for Brett. It was physically challenging to carry a struggling, full-grown man. He could handle the weight, except if he applied more muscle, he might accidentally hurt him.

"No! Put me down! Put me down now!" Tom demanded.

Brett slowly dropped Tom to his feet, kept a muscular arm around his upper body, and tried to stabilize him. It helped, but Tom lost his balance, and his legs went out from under him.

"Whoa, Tom, take it slow. We have plenty of time," Brett said. He pulled Tom back up onto his feet, and this time, with Brett's help, Tom's legs supported some of his weight. They walked together, past the fire pit and through the clubhouse door.

Mark was way ahead of them. He had cleared off the couch, spread out a blanket, and found a couple of pillows. Brett and Tom weaved their way over while Tom's walking ability improved step by step. Mark asked him to lie down. Tom sat down, swung his legs onto the couch, dropped his head onto the pillow, and let out a pain-induced grunt.

Mark borrowed Brett's cell phone, called home, and woke up Cindy. "Hi, honey, I'm so sorry to wake you so early, but I have a medical emergency down here at the barn. Could you grab some sheets, several towels, washcloths, and my med-kit? Also, please grab my cell phone and my big blue robe. And Cindy, please hurry."

"I'm on it. I'll be there in a few," Cindy didn't ask why or what happened. Being a doctor's wife for twenty-five years had taught her to act first and ask questions later.

Tom was bloody and dirty. Mark quickly completed an initial cleaning, and then he treated several bloody abrasions. Mark focused on stopping the bleeding and then dressed and bandaged the scrapes. He wrapped Tom's forearms, palms, thighs, and knees.

Tom's head had taken several significant blows and was swollen enough to be Mark's number one concern. There was a massive lump where he had taken a hard, direct hit. The two head wounds were rips rather than cuts, probably caused by grazing blows from the bat. They were both in his scalp, and they bled continuously, matting his hair into a bloody mess that was difficult to clean. Mark finally stopped the bleeding and cleaned the wounds, and had to give Tom a little haircut to provide the clearance needed to stitch him up.

His next concern was the potential of a concussion and, if there was one, its severity. He also needed to check for internal damage, muscle or bone bruises, broken bones, cracked ribs, and more. Medical imaging would be needed to determine the extent of the damage created by the heavy blows with the baseball bat.

Mark broke away for a minute to speak with Brett, who had been hovering throughout the entire process. Brett was concerned and wished he could help. Mark was in shock as much as Brett, but one would never have known it. Dr. Taggart took over, and Dr.

Taggart was one of the best. He told Brett that Tom was "one tough son of a bitch." Tom had taken a beating, but at first check, it could be much worse. He asked Brett to run out and purchase ten bags of ice.

———

Officer John Holt and Officer Paul Witt stood in the Valley Camera parking lot at five-thirty in the morning. They had never seen a crime scene that matched this one. The owner of the store had been inside with another police officer and completed a walk-through with the officer. They struggled to understand what in the world happened. The burglars had trashed the store. Broken glass laid in piles, with the front doors destroyed. It didn't look like a robbery had occurred. Boxed merchandise sat neatly stacked on the shelves. The safe and cash registers were untouched. Officer Holt asked what everyone else was thinking, "What in the world happened here, and why?"

A mangled cargo van stood in front of the store. The van's tires were flat; its bumpers hung limp. It looked like someone had sprayed it with a shotgun. It didn't belong to Valley Camera; the store's owner had never seen it before. The van's license plates were bogus, and there were no reports of a stolen van. Weird unknown after weird unknown defined the crime scene. Valley Camera was a pleasant business with happy customers, and most of the employees loved working there. The owner wasn't aware of any disgruntled customers or competitors. He was baffled.

A red Chevrolet sedan pulled into the lot and parked. A tall, sharp-looking young man stepped out and walked up to Officer Holt.

"I'm Nate Hale," he said. "I work the night shift at Fred Meyer's down the street. I got off at four, and on my way home, I witnessed the fight here."

Officer Holt looked surprised. He took a step back and asked for Hale's driver's license and copied down his personal information.

"What do you mean 'you witnessed the fight?'" Officer Holt asked.

"Well, it was a burglary, or it started that way."

"Okay, are you saying this was a fight, or are you saying it was a burglary?"

"I guess it was both."

CHAPTER SEVEN

Brett hauled ten bags of melting ice into the barn and helped Mark set up Tom's bath. They agreed Mark should call Tess and update her on the situation. They felt it would be best to keep the details to a minimum, and they thought it was Tom's responsibility to ultimately deal with his family. So, to start, they settled on a little white lie—Tom had a riding accident.

Mark called Tess, gave her the bad news, and let her know that Brett was coming over to pick up some clothes. Mark planned to go to the hospital as soon as he could schedule the tests. Tess wasn't happy and said she would come over right away, bring the clothes, and then stay with her husband. She wanted to know what was going on. Mark didn't want to give Tess a hard time; his white lie was terrible enough, but Dr. Taggert took over again. He informed her he was the doctor who was treating her husband, and he was in the middle of his treatment. He explained that he respected her, but he needed to be alone with his patient. He told her he was taking Tom to the hospital for tests and hoped Tom would not need to stay overnight. He planned to bring him home later in the day. He promised he would call and update her right before they went to the hospital, and that he needed to get off the phone and get back to work.

Tess was pissed.

Tom didn't like the ice bath. He bought the premise that it would reduce swelling, and he knew it was a popular method in the NFL where football players took ice baths right after getting banged up in a game. Still, he wasn't used to it, and wasn't as tough as an NFL player. Bottom line, he thought it was too damn cold.

Brett came back and tried to give Tom some moral support. He told Tom how he had taken plenty of ice baths when he played ball, and they helped. He tried to bolster Tom's spirits, but it was hard; his heart wasn't in it.

When he went to Tom's house to pick up the clothes, he had to deal with Tess. He told her Tom was in expert hands under Mark's care, and that Mark was devoted to the task. Still, Brett felt like an ass when he had to be positive while holding back and distancing the truth. He didn't lie, but he didn't tell the truth. The whole situation was beyond his underlying code of conduct. But what else could he say; the facts were more than believable.

Their activities were potentially criminal; especially his.

Brett promised one thing. He said when they came back from the hospital, they would clear the air.

Late that afternoon, Mark helped Tom limp into Tom's house. Brett showed up a few minutes later. Tess had waited long enough and immediately broke down into tears. Mark asked permission to take the stitched and bandaged Tom directly to their bedroom and make him as comfortable as possible.

Mark sat down with them in their bedroom.

"All in all, after what Tom has been through, I am surprised how well he is doing. He does not have any broken or cracked bones. He's severely bruised over a large portion of his body. He is very sore and will be for a while. Tom needs to rest, and with rest, he will heal. I'll check in a couple of times a day, change his bandages, and monitor his progress."

"I can change his bandages," Tess said.

"I'll be here often, Tess. Please, I need to do this."

It was quiet for a moment, and then Mark continued, "I have prescribed some anti-inflammatories, which should help with the swelling and some of the pain. However, if Tom is hurting, let me know, and I'll prescribe pain medicine."

"I don't want any pain pills," Tom said.

"At this point, heat will help. Tess, do you have a heating pad?" Mark asked.

"We do have one," she said.

"I'll bring over a couple of extras; he has bruised a lot of his muscles. Now, Tom, you are in concussion protocol."

"You think I have a concussion?"

"You may have a concussion. We will know for sure in a couple of days."

"So, I can't play until I'm clear?"

"Sort of. You can't go to work. You can't ride a horse, and you can't drive a car. Once again, it would be best if you rested. Stay inside, away from bright light. When I check in, we'll do some concussion testing similar to what we did today at the hospital, and we will go from there. Okay?"

Both Tess and Tom nodded in resignation.

"Alright, let me know if you have questions. How about I leave you two alone?"

Mark walked out of the bedroom, and toward the family room, where Brett sat cooling his heels.

"Hey, Mark," Tom shouted just as Mark cleared the bedroom door.

Mark turned back into the doorway, "Yeah?"

"Thank you," Tom said.

"Thank you," Tess echoed.

Mark hesitated for a moment.

"You're welcome," he said, with his eyes cast down.

Tom and Tess hugged and cried a bit. The time for hiding the truth was over. Even with his wife, he was embarrassed. He told her what happened, starting with the meeting at the barn where Brett presented his theories. Then, he went through the stakeout, the robbery, and the beating in detail. He explained the guys were all stuck in the "what in the hell are we going to do now" stage. After all, it wasn't the standard explanation many men give their wives when they have done something incredibly stupid, like drink too much or lose a paycheck at a poker game. This encounter with professional criminals marked a new level of stupidity.

Tess certainly could understand the frustration that drove Tom and the guys into their lunacy, but she could not understand their entry into danger. They were grown men, responsible for families and a lot more. Then, there was Tess and her ability to forget and forgive, and her ability to support. Tom was a lucky man.

Tess agreed this situation should not go public. Tom probably did nothing illegal; then again, in this day and age of correctness, why chance it? This story would never leave the house. They wouldn't even tell Nick, who sometimes felt his dad went overboard, and they wouldn't tell their daughter Sage, who looked at her dad as if he was someone too valuable to lose, or someone she needed to protect. The problem with Sage was that she was her father's daughter, and she could get distraught and go overboard, too.

Tess, ready to check on their company in the other room, kissed Tom again, smiled, and kiddingly said, "Next time you get in a fight, don't tangle with someone carrying a baseball bat."

With Tess and Tom focused on each other, they didn't notice their daughter standing in the doorway. Sage Coogan, tall, slender, and curious, asked, "What do you mean—next time? Dad, did you get in a fight?"

"Oh, boy," Tom said.

Sage Coogan was their youngest. After college, she had moved to San Francisco, where she was building a career. Sage missed Idaho, her family, and Boise, and she came home often. It was easy and convenient with many two-hour flights available, as long as her money held out. She was thankful that she had come home last Friday night.

Sage was five feet ten inches tall, had long flowing dark brown hair and perfect skin. Her bright green eyes showed emotion and intelligence. Her eyes telegraphed her feelings, whether she was going to laugh, cry, get madder than hell, or take charge. She was easy to read that way. Her good looks came from her mom and her temperament came from her dad.

Right now, she channeled her dad's attitude; she wanted answers.

Having to explain to his daughter why he had acted like an idiot was not something Tom enjoyed doing. So, unfortunately, during the next thirty minutes, Tom explained everything again. In the beginning, Sage was angry with her father. As she pressed for details, they eventually came out. The more the story grew, the more Sage became enthralled. She was amazed at what she learned.

The more she learned of her father's misadventure, the more she could relate to his erratic decisions. She understood how and why everything happened and was on her dad's team; the story stayed where it was. To Tom, it was almost empowering. Until Sage forcefully explained that he was getting too old for this kind of stuff.

———

Both Mark and Brett were biding their time, eager to leave Tom and his family alone. When Sage walked into the family room, they felt they could finally say goodbye and hit the road. Tess had offered them both a beer, which they declined. A beer was unappetizing, and it had been a long day.

Sage had turned on the television to check the nightly news. She waved the crime fighters back in, "Hey, guys, check this out."

The Channel Seven News's headline bordered the bottom of the screen, "Brawling Burglars Bungle Burglary of Valley Camera."

Tess, Sage, Mark, and Brett sat in amazement as the blonde-haired Nicole Swann presented the story. What an incredible, hard-to-believe twist, and the implications were staggering.

Finally, Brett said, "How about we rewind this and get Tom in here? He needs to see this, too."

They all watched it two more times, just trying to absorb the details. The story presented a scenario where around eight burglars tried to rob Valley Camera. Then, in the middle of the crime, they fought with each other. The fight started because of the misuse of a flashlight which led to anger. And then to pushing, punching, and kicking, which led to hitting each other with baseball bats, which led to a gunfight. An all-out brawl broke out, but it ended a short time before the police arrived. A vehicle was left behind with its tires destroyed. Evidently, in full panic, the burglars escaped on foot. It was a sensational report.

They interviewed a Boise Police Officer named John Holt, who explained the details and credited an eye witness who offered his observations. Officer Holt presented a confident story and seemed entirely credible and eloquent in his interview.

Next up was the star of the story, Nate Hale. Nate appeared to be a sharp and handsome young man who risked harm when he witnessed the crime. Nate looked poised and intelligent, and the camera loved him. He explained he was on his way home from work shortly after four in the morning, when he noticed a group massed at the front entrance of Valley Camera. Immediately, Nate knew there was a crime in progress. He pulled his car into a good vantage point and observed. Nate explained the beginning and the escalation of the fight, and finally, the eruption of gunfire. He mentioned how all the criminals dressed alike in dark clothes and ski masks. He explained that most of the criminals panicked and ran for their lives when the gunfire started.

Nicole asked Nate, "Were there any individuals outside of the group involved?" "Absolutely not," Nate said.

The atmosphere at the Coogan house went from somewhat morose to amazed and gleeful. "Can you believe that?" Tom gasped. "It looks like we're off the hook."

"Tess, can I change my mind and have that beer you offered?" Brett asked.

"Me, too," Tom said.

"NO!" everyone said in unison.

The entire group was ready to celebrate. Everyone hung out for dinner. Cindy stopped at the Incredible Pie pizza joint, which had the best pizza in town. She picked up a couple of large pizzas, salad, and breadsticks. It was a pleasant party. And then the telephone rang.

"Let's not answer right now. If it's important, they will leave a message," Tess said.

After the message ended, the machine played the message aloud, "Mr. Coogan, this is Detective Broom with the Boise Police Department. Please return my call. I want to meet with you regarding the burglary at your store last Sunday. We need to discuss some new information."

"I wonder what that is about?" Mark asked.

"I've been putting pressure on the guy," Tom said. "Maybe he is trying to follow up with me."

"I wouldn't think anyone could relate this to what happened this morning," Mark said.

"I sure as hell hope not," Tom replied.

"I looked the scene over before I left, and I didn't see any incriminating evidence left behind," Brett said.

"I checked the area where I was, too," Mark said, "It was clean."

"I think we're good then," Brett said, "I don't think it is about us. It's about last week's burglary. Still, I wouldn't return that call for a while. It would be best if you got back in shape. It would help if you didn't look like someone who took a beating. We need to stall."

"Well, let's all think about this. We better not be missing something here. We don't want Tom to be in the position where he could be lying to the police," Tess said.

Across the room, Tom laid on his oversized recliner. He had his hand on his head and a frown on his face. He looked like a man with a big problem.

Dr. Mark stood up and said, "Okay, that's it. This is too much for Tom right now. It's time for him to go back to bed and rest."

"No, that's not it," Tom unhappily said. "I hope we don't have a problem, but has anyone seen my cell phone?"

Tess got up and went to look in the bedroom. When she came back, she said, "I don't see it here. Did you guys leave it down at the barn?"

"I don't remember seeing it down there, but I'll go look," Brett said.

"Hold it for a second," Mark said. "Tom, where did you see it last?"

"Honestly, my last memory of it was somewhere around Valley Camera this morning."

"Let's not panic," Brett said. "I can check the barn in five minutes." Brett got up and started walking toward the door.

"I've got an idea. Dad, do you have the Where is my cell phone app on your tablet?" Sage asked.

Tess grabbed Tom's tablet. Sage intercepted it, set it on the table, and touched the app's icon. The display scanned, and a spinning ikon appeared on the small screen. A group formed around Sage and watched.

Then, after a few seconds, the tablet displayed the cell phone's location.

Brett said, "Zoom out a little." Then in amazement, he muttered, "How can that even be possible? How did it get there?"

CHAPTER EIGHT

Tom laid back in the recliner; he was uncomfortable, his body hurt all over, and he was tired. He looked across the room. Everyone was crowded around his tablet, trying to take control of the thing and asking questions to no one in particular.

"Where is my damn cell phone?" He yelled.

The group realized they had left Tom out of the conversation, turned, and Brett said, "Your cell phone, according to this, is about fifty miles out of town, in the woods above Idaho City."

"How did it get there?"

Finally, the scrum around the tablet ended, and Brett took control of the app and tried to make some sense out of the cell phone's location. He scanned in and out on the displayed image, but it was hard to tell if the cell phone was near any buildings. A perplexing lack of clarity existed. The area looked like a forest surrounded by trails or old logging roads. There were no markings or names displayed. If there were roads, they didn't deserve a designation. Some shaded spots looked possibly like buildings, but once again, it was hard to tell. Playing with the control panel, Brett found where the GPS coordinates were listed. He changed the view and couldn't find any meaningful detail. Then the screen went blank.

He couldn't bring up the location again, as much as he tried. It was as if the cell phone had just disappeared. Sage, bringing youthful tech know-how to the tablet, tried and failed, and then restarted the tablet and failed again.

She turned to Brett and said, "My guess—the phone's battery died."

"Yeah, power was probably cut somehow," Brett agreed, "I guess we were lucky to connect at all."

"Okay, everybody. The party's over. It's time we gave this family a little peace; Tom needs to rest," Mark ordered.

He was right, so the cell phone issue was over. One thing they knew for sure was that Detective Broom didn't have the cell phone, and that fact brought relief to the entire room.

Mark and Brett said their goodbyes to the group and took their leave. They walked out to their trucks and had a quiet discussion. It had been a long day, and they were ready to go home.

Just before getting in his truck, Mark asked, "You up for a ride tomorrow?"

"Sure, what time sounds good?"

"A little later than usual. I'm going to check on Tom in the morning, so I'll see you after that."

"Great, I'll see you then."

"Too bad we lost the signal on the phone. I would have liked to go up and try to find it."

"Well, maybe we still can. I wrote out the GPS coordinates."

"Well, gentlemen, let's get right to it," Roger Carlson surveyed the room, looking for eye contact. There was none to be found. It didn't surprise Roger. Even professional criminals take pride in their work, and the debacle at Valley Camera was an embarrassment.

Roger Carlson had been the mastermind and leader of the burglary ring for almost three years. He was an industry professional in retail distribution, a skill he had made much more profitable by stealing inventory rather than buying it. Jay Peters was his second-in-command. Roger planned the burglaries, and Jay managed the gang that executed them. Early on, they had a series of hits and misses, and Roger's money kept them afloat. Since then, they had improved their methods and had become very successful. After they cleaned out their victims, they transferred the goods to Roger's new wholesale partner, and the cash flowed.

Their new wholesale partner made it easy to turn their stolen merchandise into cash. They dealt with Tony Levitt, an organized crime boss and one of the country's largest stolen property wholesalers. Tony helped improve their cash flow, and in return, he had high expectations. The shipments from Roger's gang needed to grow. Tony Levitt required consistency and loyalty. Anything less was unacceptable. So far, their relationship was mutually beneficial.

Carlson's gang was well organized and set up more like a business than a confederation of criminals. Their headquarters were located less than an hour out of Boise in an old, isolated camp. The recently renovated camp was in a reasonably unnoticeable, but still functional, state. Here, they housed the leading players in three separate cabins. A massive main lodge with a central kitchen served as their headquarters. A large garage kept their untraceable vehicles out of sight. Another large building housed the distribution center where they sorted and prepped their stolen merchandise for shipment to Sparks, Nevada.

In Nevada, they blended the inventory into a diversified and extensive network of class two and used products. Their Nevada partner, trying to develop legitimacy, removed or replaced the stolen products' serial numbers and then distributed the products to retail and online outlets.

"What in the hell happened?" Roger looked toward Jay, who was avoiding eye contact. "If you believe the press, we're a bunch of fucking idiots. Come on, guys, give me something!" Roger repeated.

Jay remained quiet. He was an ex-con and a former athlete. He was a stocky, powerful man in his early forties, around six feet tall, sharp-looking, and an excellent communicator. Jay looked like someone you might see coaching a high school football team: short dark hair, clean-shaven, and intense. He was an excellent manager and was always looking for an opportunity to make more money.

Rick, who had a series of ugly sores dotting his neck and face, didn't like being questioned. He unfortunately, was the unhappy recipient of a face and neck full of buckshot. Rick was tall, around six-three, and powerfully built with shaggy dark hair and a sloppy appearance.

He was an expert mechanic who maintained and repaired their small fleet of vehicles. And at least for now, he was pretty miserable with his scab-ridden skin. He said, "What would you do if someone pointed a fucking shotgun in your face?"

"Just call him Buckshot!" Arnie laughed.

"You little shit!" Rick shouted as he stood up, ready to pounce on the smaller man.

"Okay, calm down, you guys, and shut up unless you have something intelligent to say," Jay interjected.

Arnie shuffled his feet and cast his eyes around the room. Arnie was a short (around five-six), mouthy man who could make or piss off friends, depending on how he felt at the moment. His facial expressions regularly changed from grinning to smirking to pouting. He was wiry and strong, but not as tough as he thought. He had sandy hair that jutted out the sides of his ever-present, backward-facing baseball cap. He typically sported a toothy grin and a three-day-old beard, and he had wild eyes that were continuously on the watch for something. Arnie was a lot smarter than he looked. He was an experienced car thief, burglar, and con-man who added his talents to the group's collective criminal skills.

Jay Peters had brought in Arnie and Rick to help him run the operation. They also employed six part-time thieves who filled out the team and then returned home to their friends and families in Boise until they received the next call. It was a very high paying part-time job for the crew.

"You see, Roger, it seemed like a setup," Jay grumbled. "We went through all of our prep, and it was a-go. But, when we hit the store, they were waiting. It seemed like the first guy came out of nowhere. We checked the parking lot next door on our last drive through, and it was clean. And then suddenly, this guy was there, holding a big fucking flashlight and screaming. Rick, with his bat, came up from behind and took him out. And then this other guy, a big guy, came out of the bushes and started shooting, hitting Rick in the face. So, we bailed, and it was the right call, goddamn it."

"Anybody have an idea who these guys were?" Roger questioned.

"The guy with the flashlight acted like he was a cop. He was yelling, 'Everyone is under arrest,' and shit like that, but he was full of bullshit. A cop; no way. Cops don't show up to burglaries in progress without backup. Hell, I've never seen a cop let someone sneak up behind him like that. He didn't even see Rick coming," Jay replied.

Rick spoke up, "The big guy, I don't know if he was a cop or not, but he was the real deal. He had this scary focus, like if I made the slightest mistake, I was dead. The only reason I'm alive is that he let me go."

"If he's so tough, how come he just shot you in the face and didn't blow your fucking head off?" Arnie grinned.

"Why don't you shut up, you little asshole?" Rick scowled.

"It's a fair question. Why did the big guy let you go when he had you dead-to-rights?" Roger asked.

"Because he didn't want to kill me; he just wanted the other guy back. I had thrown him on the truck, then knocked him out. The big guy told me to get him off. After I did, he let me go."

"I don't think these guys are cops. I think they are local and somehow figured out we were going to hit Valley Camera. My question is, how did they know?" Jay said.

"Good question," Roger said. "Could there be a leak in the organization?"

"I don't know," Jay wondered.

Roger sat down and tried to take in the information. Roger was the President of Carlson Distribution, a major player in the western region's wholesale distribution of outdoor travel, and electronic products. He had a team of sales reps that covered the territory. Roger was a great relationship man who traveled and built long-term friendships with his dealers. He was on a first-name basis with every single one of them.

Roger was a cocky rooster of a man who loved to hear his voice. When addressing even a few people, he would falsely lower his tone and raise his voice as if he was a bailiff singing out the next case in court. Roger was average height, moderately overweight, and was always wearing new clothes. He was in his sixties, and his hair had turned completely gray, which he corrected by wearing varying shades of the original color in his monthly dye job. His skin was smooth from multiple peels from cosmetic doctors. His eyes were close together, and his nose was small. He loved to pull the chains of people around him, but if anyone ever called him on it, he folded up like a card table.

He lived between his primary residence in Seattle and his vacation home in Idaho. His vacation home was his spot in the world where he could get away from the distributing business and relax. It also sets him up to expand his interest into something more exciting and fulfilling. He could get out of Seattle, hang out with a bunch of thieves, and become a major criminal. Although, in truth, the criminal part scared him.

Roger would visit his dealers, walk their stores, and pass on advice he learned from his travels, where he saw successful displays and promotions that had worked for others. He supported his sales reps who wrote orders while he, with his eidetic memory, cased the stores. When it came time to prep for the next burglary, Roger knew where every alarm sensor, camera, and security feature was, and how they deployed. He also knew the location of all the marketable inventory, which wasn't too hard since he sold a lot of those products to the dealers.

Before every burglary, Roger and his three key players would meet for a planning session. Roger would produce a map of every targeted business, both inside and out. They went over the plan step by step—the entry, the targeted sections of the stores, and of course, the targeted merchandise. He identified the security features that would have to be disabled. He defined the time-window that the alarm system would allow. It was burglary by the numbers, and it had been working well until last Sunday.

The meeting with Roger, Jay, Rick, and Arnie became contentious as it progressed. When a boss calls a meeting and asks questions, people get defensive and often try to transfer blame out of pure frustration; this meeting was no different. However, the more Roger learned, the more he realized he couldn't assign blame. The crew did their job as they should. Even when they bailed, they made the right move. When the big guy showed up with a shotgun and started shooting, it was time to quit.

"Alright, guys, I have to agree. There was nothing we did wrong here. You did the job by the numbers, and it should have gone smoothly. You did a good job, and I commend you for it. And Rick,

I am so sorry you got shot. Are you going to be okay?" Roger coddled.

"Yeah, I'm okay, Boss; it's just going to take a while to heal up."

"All I can guess is we may have been a little too predictable by planning back-to-back burglaries in the same city. Somebody might have spotted our tendency to do that, which was my mistake. So, we need to correct that right now. First, since this is likely a local problem for us, we'll back off the Boise market for a while. Plus, at least for the next year or so, we shouldn't plan back-to-back hits," Roger said.

"But won't that affect our take?" Jay asked.

"Yeah, it is easier and more profitable to do two or three hits in a row, so I'd like to go back to it at some point in time, but after Sunday's problem, I think we need to be cautious. So, we're down one blind vehicle, right, and another is damaged?" Roger asked. "And do we have backups we can use?"

"Unfortunately, no," Jay said. "We have a new van, but it's not blind so it could be traced. The truck took a hit, but all we need to do is a little minor bodywork and change out a tire. I'll order a new one and get it done."

"Well, the van is the problem then," Roger said. "I planned to set our next job for the coming weekend. Bend is up next, and I'd still like to pull it off."

Arnie spoke up, "Well, we can probably get it done, but it will be close. I like to go out of the market when we steal vehicles, and remember, we have to scrub their history, but I'm game; let's try."

"Yeah, time is money," Jay said. "Arnie, let's get together and figure it out."

Jay, Arnie, and Rick appreciated the positive words from Roger. It meant a lot, and they trusted Roger, at least a couple of them did.

"Alright guys, good meeting," Roger said, "Any questions?"

"Yeah, one," Jay said. "With all this going down, should we call Mr. Levitt?"

"No, we can handle this," Roger said quickly, sounding surprised.

An hour later, Jay walked into his cabin and called Mr. Levitt.

CHAPTER NINE

"Agent DeShawn Terry," DeShawn spoke with the firm, confident voice of a seasoned FBI agent.

"DeShawn, Brett Wyatt here."

"Brett, it's good to hear your voice again. How are you doing?"

"I'm doing well, DeShawn. The web access you set up for me worked great. I could pull the data I needed for my study, and it was beneficial. Thanks for your help."

"Hey, you're welcome, always. So, the master of analysis is back at it, just like the good old days. How did it feel?"

"It felt a little awkward at first. You know it's been a while, so I had to work through a bit of a re-learning curve, but once I got going, I pulled together enough that it painted a pretty clear picture."

Agent DeShawn Terry was one of the FBI's top investigators in the Pacific Northwest. Brett and DeShawn had a long, positive history together. They were recruited into the Bureau the same year and were considered two of the bright young minds within the organization. As Brett's career moved forward, he and DeShawn often worked as partners. They made a talented team, and their teamwork produced good results. While they worked together, they became close friends. DeShawn had originally strived to serve in one of the country's large metro areas until he worked in Boise.

DeShawn did not hesitate to help when Brett reached out. He knew Brett well, and he trusted him. When most people asked for access to FBI files, they would need to prove the validity and the legality of their request. With Brett Wyatt, a well-known name in the organization, that step was unnecessary and ignored. If Brett needed help, he would get it. If Brett's concerns were valid, his work could lead the FBI into a vital case. Agent Terry and the FBI also had a hidden agenda; they wanted Brett back. The FBI would be a stronger organization with Brett Wyatt, a part of it.

With their histories together, Agent Terry knew Brett well enough to know the potential importance of his investigation, and his cop instincts couldn't let it be.

"Do you have anything you want to share with me?" He asked.

"Actually, I do. The data I pulled forms a strong pattern. I believe there is an organized gang committing burglaries throughout a seven-state region, and they are committing the burglaries weekly."

"No shit, how tight is your information? Is it strong enough for us to step in?"

"Close, but not strong enough yet. I can't get my head around the pattern of their movement from one burglary to another, and I believe that is key. So, I'm still working on it. However, I have put together a pretty good summary, and I can give you a copy. Another set of eyes could help."

"Hey, I'd like to take a look. These guys, whoever they are, should have never ripped off a friend of yours. Can I help with anything else?"

"Actually, yes. Are you guys set up to print detailed topographical maps?"

"You bet. With up-to-date satellite imagery, even more detailed than when you worked here."

"Great. I have GPS coordinates for a spot north of here in some rough country. I want to go up and look, but I want to know what I'm getting into."

"Sure. Email me the coordinates, and we can print a good size map. I can get it printed today. What size do you want?"

"Can you print a sixteen by twenty?"

"No problem. We'll fire up the big printer and get it done. Why don't you come by this afternoon, you can show me your analysis, and I'll have the map ready?"

Brett ended the call and dropped his cell phone in his pocket. He was hanging out at the barn, biding his time until Mark showed up for their morning ride. He poured himself another cup of coffee, sat down, and relaxed.

Suddenly, he heard a loud sound outside, like something big hit the outside of the barn. When he walked out into the corral to check it out, Pepper was waiting.

"So that was you, huh, buddy? Are you a little impatient this morning?" He walked out of the corral and up to the Appaloosa. Pepper gave him a bit of a loving nudge which Brett returned with some welcomed stroking behind his ears. "I haven't forgotten you, and we are going out for a ride. Just as soon as Mark gets here, we will saddle up and go." Pepper gave Brett a nosing in response, flicked his tail, turned, and galloped off to play with his friends. Pepper was satisfied; he just needed to know the plan.

Brett went back into the clubhouse, grabbed a harmonica, sat back down, and started playing. Time passed as he became lost in his music, and before he knew it, Mark slipped in.

"What are you playing—Dylan?" Mark asked.

"Yup," Brett muttered in a one-second pause of the chorus.

"What key?"

"G."

Marked picked up his Tenor Ukulele and joined in. Thankfully, the odd impromptu jam session ended, and the guys set out on their ride.

This morning, they rode due north over a series of ridges until they came to the east end of Clear Creek Golf Course, a course that tortured the locals because it would steal their golf balls by forcing them to shoot through some reasonably rough canyons. They circled the north side of the course and watched the frustrated players, then cantered past the back nine. A friend of theirs owned Victory Stables, which was a mile north of the club. There, they took a break, socialized with some other riders, and watered their horses. It was always a great place to stop.

Back on the trail, they reversed course and leisurely rode toward home and talked. Earlier this morning, Mark had stopped by and checked on Tom. He let Brett know Tom was doing well, recovering from the beating, and was enjoying the attention of both his wife and daughter. Tom called the store and let Nick know he was taking two weeks off and would only come in to attend some scheduled meetings. Sage liked the idea and called her employer and requested the same time off. She wanted to help take care of her dad. Tom appreciated Sage's concern, but in truth, it scared him a little; he didn't enjoy being bossed around too much. He was, after all, the oldest member of the family.

Mark confessed how he accidentally slipped up and let Tom know that the two of them were going on a ride this morning without him, which pissed Tom off because he didn't like being left behind.

Their continued discussion was all about the disappearance and the relocation of Tom's cell phone. There were challenging scenarios behind this occurrence, and they questioned what they meant and what they could do about them, if anything. Tom's cell phone was lost and probably had a dead battery in the middle of nowhere. Sticking their noses into police business was a miss-step at the Valley Camera stakeout, and Tom got hurt because of it. And the fact that Tom got beat up changed everything.

The discussion was circular. Brett and Mark agreed the smart move was to get more information and then make an informed decision. They rode back to the barn, cleaned up, and took care of their horses.

———

After his meeting with Agent Terry, Brett drove up to the barn as Mark approached. They walked into the clubhouse together, and were shocked to see Tom sitting on the couch. A pair of walking sticks rested against the wall.

Mark looked at the walking sticks and then at Tom.

"How the hell did you get here?" He asked.

"Sage gave me a ride," Tom replied.

"You're not exactly following your doctor's instructions."

"You said I can't go to work, can't drive a car, and can't ride a horse."

"I said a hell of a lot more than that, and you know it."

"I couldn't stand it. I've been going stir crazy, and I want to know what in the hell is going on."

"Well, I'm glad you are here," Brett said. "I printed up a couple of topographical maps of the area around your phone's GPS coordinates. We need to look at these together."

Brett laid both maps out on the kitchen table. DeShawn had printed an exploded view of the area leading in from Highway 21. The second map showed more detail of the area around the coordinates of the phone's location.

"I like the way they printed these; it gives us a view from the highway, plus a tighter scope," Brett said.

"These are beautiful; who did you say printed these?" Mark questioned.

"I didn't say… but it's a fair question. These maps were produced for us by Agent Terry, an old friend of mine from the FBI. And, the images are printed from their satellite view, shot this morning."

"I'm impressed," Tom said.

Brett chuckled and pointed to an area on the map. "See, this is a dirt road in decent shape coming off the highway, and it seems to come to a dead-end right here, where it may end as a parking area for a trailhead. It looks like a few trails take off from there, and even what looks like a couple of old logging roads."

"If those are logging roads, they must be pretty old—they look so narrow," Mark observed.

"Yeah, but look at this one. A little less than a half-mile past its starting point, it widens, and it stays that way right up to the area adjacent to the cell phone's coordinates. The fact that the road starts small and then widens, probably when it goes out of sight from the trailhead, is pretty inconsistent, don't you think?"

"Yeah, I agree. It looks like someone could be trying to hide something. It could be something like a way station, although, it seems a strange place for one," Tom said.

"It's just another thing that is hard to make any sense out of," Brett grabbed the second map with a more focused view circling the GPS coordinates. "Yeah, here is the road that comes near the phone. This general area is mostly Boise National Forest land, but this northern plot is private. And look, there are a couple of groups of buildings. Interesting."

"Brett, look over here, right by the coordinates—that looks like it could be a truck. Could the phone be in the truck? Why would anyone leave the phone in their truck?" Tom commented.

"Yeah, this is quite compelling. I'd like to know what is going on up there, and I'd like to find out if it has anything to do with these robberies. It's kind of hard to figure from a map."

"Maybe we should just go up and check it out, and hopefully we can get some answers," Mark suggested.

"Oh, I agree, but it could be awkward to drive by this joint and get much information. We would need to get out of the truck and look around, and that could be tricky. If the crooks from the burglaries are up there, they must be doing something that requires privacy, and if we drive into an unknown situation like that, it could be dangerous."

"I've got an idea," Mark smiled.

"All right, Mark. I hope this is better than your last one. Go ahead, spill it," Brett said.

"Let's trailer-up the horses, drive up there, and park at the trailhead and take a scenic ride. We could take our time and check it out. Plus, we'll be able to get closer, and we'll see and learn a lot more by riding a horse than by doing a drive-by in any vehicle."

Tom looked down and shook his head, while rubbing his sore legs.

"What if we run into some resistance? How do we handle it?" Brett questioned.

"We will just tell them we're a couple of cowboys on a ride."

CHAPTER TEN

At six-thirty in the morning, the air was clean and crisp, and the boys were ready to hit the road. Brett had a well-designed two-slot horse trailer hitched to the back of his Ford pickup. He'd purchased the trailer a few years ago, used and in good shape. It had double wheels on each side, which helped it tow easily and ride smoothly. The horses deserved some comfort, too. Mark had a step-up, four-slot version, which was great when you had three or four horses to tow, but it was overkill for only two. Of course, Brett was riding Pepper; the Appaloosa was excellent both on and off-trail, and hard to spook. Mark loaded up Rondo, a gelding Roan that was handsome, strong, and rugged. Mark picked Rondo because he was a pure mountain horse who could navigate through the rough country with little or no direction from his rider. Rondo was an excellent pick for the day's adventure.

They were both carrying saddlebags with some extra gear for the ride. They had the new maps, which would likely stay in the truck. Brett had a brand new, state-of-the-art portable GPS unit he purchased at Tom's place, Teton Outdoors. With it, he could spot coordinates accurately and quickly from the saddle. They both carried a pair of compact, but still bright, ten power binoculars.

Mark had an easy-to-use bridge camera that was compact and had an impressive optical zoom lens. He also carried his field medical kit, just in case; he felt naked without it. Brett brought along his Wyoming Special six-shot revolver for the same reason.

Their objectives for the day were pretty basic. They planned first and foremost on an information-gathering expedition. They didn't care about saving Tom's cell phone; he could easily replace it. However, some questions needed answers. Why did the burglars take the phone, and why did they bring it into the backcountry? Could their burglary ring be headquartered there, or could they be hiding there, and if so, are they still there? The FBI was involved now; any relevant information could be useful. The objective was to avoid confrontations and gather information, hopefully, and then get out of there.

The drive took about an hour. The big V8 sailed with ease up and over some pretty steep inclines. They traveled past Lucky Peak Reservoir and through a long series of curves mirroring the path of a roaring creek. It was a scenic drive through canyons and forest; it was no wonder that folks from Boise enjoyed taking day trips here. Idaho City was an old mining town turned ghost town, recently turned into a small-scale tourism area. It had beautiful hot springs with private and public pools and a small hotel next door. It was a fun place to walk through, check out historical buildings, have a beer, listen to an ever-present band, and enjoy the area's beauty and history.

They left Idaho City behind, and the highway narrowed while continuously gaining altitude. Just when it seemed they had traveled too far, they finally found the turnoff. The dirt road was pretty basic and showed little signs of use. It was slow going and bumpy, so the guys took it easy; they didn't want to rock the horses too much. The road broadened slightly and then ended.

What looked like a parking area on the satellite map turned out to be a bumpy patch of dirt backed by a cluster of Ponderosa pines.

Off to their left, another dirt area fronted a couple of trailheads, with a small space where you could park a couple of compact cars, but there was no way their rig would fit. Brett spotted the old logging road that led up to their destination and considered driving up it in search of better parking. He dismissed the idea after studying the challenge of having to back out. Instead, he chose a carved-out place they had passed on the road just before it. They could park out of the way, leaving a partial lane open on their left.

They unloaded the horses and pulled out their gear. It didn't take long to saddle up and prep for the ride. They methodically went through their supplies and cross-checked them against the list Brett had put together. When Brett slid his revolver into his pack, Mark asked, "You brought a gun?"

"Yup," Brett replied.

They were just about ready to mount up when Mark noticed a sign, partially covered by a tree on the edge of the old logging road. They walked up to check it out. It read:

PRIVATE PROPERTY AHEAD

NO TRESPASSING

TURN AROUND NOW!

"I wish I had brought a gun," Mark mumbled.

CHAPTER ELEVEN

Brett and Mark dressed like dude ranch cowboys. For them, it wasn't too hard to do. They shined their boots, wore brand new wranglers, and of course, slipped on the biggest cowboy hats they owned. They wanted to look and act the part and hoped their impression would be that of a couple of clueless weekend cowboys, rather than a couple of men investigating a crime.

The logging road was narrow but surprisingly smooth; any four-wheel-drive vehicle could make it through quickly, as long as the driver didn't care about getting their paint job scratched. It was a walk in the park for a horse and rider, almost a little anticlimactic. Fifty yards down the trail stood another sign warning of upcoming private property. Since they could not yet see the property, the existence of the posters was irritating them, but being clueless weekend cowboys, they held back the urge to tear them down. It didn't take long until the road widened because of some recent work, and the private property warning signs became more visible, repeating about every two hundred yards.

They broke off the road and rode up an established hiking trail.

The trail ran parallel to the logging road and kept the Riders and their horses out of sight as they made progress. With the tree cover, they'd dismount periodically and glassed the area. They couldn't see much; the country was rough and thick with pines. The trail looped and connected back to the road at a point where they had to be getting close. Then they ran into the barbed wire fence.

It was a new, well-built, barbed wire fence. The poles were heavy duty, with four lines of barbed wire strung tight. It was not an insurmountable fence by any means, but for a barbed wire fence, it was secure. The extra strands would be difficult to crawl over or under, especially if you were in a hurry. If nothing else, it would be easy to tear up your clothes or your skin.

The signs they had grown tired of had finally changed. The latest one said:

PRIVATE PROPERTY

NO TRESPASSING

VIOLATORS WILL BE PROSECUTED

They had arrived. The property's southeast corner had one fence line running along the road heading west, and the other running north into open country.

Brett pulled out his GPS to determine the direction of the saved coordinates, "It looks like the saved spot is inside the fence line to the northwest. Let's ride the north side first and take a look."

"Sounds good," Mark agreed.

Since they were riding off-trail, they made slow progress working through trees, rocks, and ground cover. They rode up a hill which led to a steeper, more mountainous area that bordered the property's back corner. Their view improved with the extra elevation, so they dismounted and pulled out their binoculars.

This property, with all of its obnoxious private property signs, appeared to be a camp. Probably at least sixty years old. It looked like a former hunting camp rather than a camp for kids or families. There used to be several hunting camps located around this part of the state. They were popular until population growth squeezed out both the hunters and their game. Technology had boosted the speed of hunting, but not the enjoyment, and the need for hunting camps had mostly vanished. Back in the 1960s, hunters would venture out and hunt during the day, and then spend their evenings in a locale like this.

Checking out the camp's layout showed several small cabins and a large one, all within walking distance of each other. Once again, it was camp-like, with a main lodge supporting smaller cabins. A well-maintained gravel road twisted behind the lodge and wound uphill to a couple of recently built buildings. All the cabins looked old and worn, but under closer inspection, showed signs of repair and renovation, primarily new roofs, covered porches, and other structural repairs. The camp wasn't fancy, probably on purpose, but was in okay shape. It made the guys question whether the facility was in better condition than someone wanted it to appear.

As they continued riding along the north side, the fence continued to pull away from the camp and pushed them into steeper, densely wooded terrain. Brett pulled out his GPS and took another sighting; they had come full circle and were behind the spot. It was time to backtrack to the road and ride west. Suddenly, they heard a roaring engine; it sounded like a motorcycle. They quickened their pace.

It took a lot less time to ride down the hill and back to the road than it did to go the other way; at least, it seemed that way. Their riding returned to being smooth and comfortable as they rode along the logging road. Vehicle tracks covered the road, along with no trespassing signs. They came to an open area where a branch turned sharply to the right. About forty yards into the property, a closed gate signaled this was the main entrance. There was a sign on the gate which they guessed said "No Trespassing." They rode up to the gate to check it out. Their rationalization was that the gate was the property line, so their side of the gate was not on private property. At least, it was the excuse they planned to use if necessary. As it turned out, it would be necessary.

Brett and Mark pulled out their binoculars, but before they could raise them to their eyes, they heard the familiar sound of a loud engine. A rider on an ATV had spotted them and was racing down a gravel road, speeding toward them. With a sideways skid, he stopped on his side of the gate. He looked downright hostile.

The ATV was pretty big, with an engine that purred with power. It had a camo-style paint job, which would have helped it blend in if it wasn't so loud. Its rider was a pretty big man. He was tall, broad-shouldered, and wore a dirty, old Yankees baseball cap with messy, shaggy brown hair hanging out in clumps. And he looked terrible. He looked like he had recently taken a nasty blow to his face, leaving sores, pockmarks, and scabs. He was stiffly standing on the ATV's footholds, and his eyes were full of fire.

"CAN'T YOU FUCKING READ?" He screamed.

"Well, yeah," Mark muttered.

"You must be fucking idiots, then. We have private property signs all over the place."

Mark barely held back a chuckle when Brett looked toward him and gave him the keep-it-down gesture.

The pockmarked guy noticed their interaction, and it seemed to piss him off. "You think that's funny, do you dipshit? Well, are you going to think it's funny if I come over and kick your ass?"

Brett, in a calm voice, responded, "Hey, we're going to turn around and ride out of here. We don't want to be on your property."

"You are on our property right now, so get the hell out of here, you stupid cowboys. If I see you again, I won't be so nice. I'll shoot first and ask questions later! You got it?"

"Got it," Brett said, as they turned their horses and trotted away.

The pockmarked guy laughed as he watched the hurried retreat.

Brett said to no one in particular, "If I see you again, I probably won't be so nice, either."

CHAPTER TWELVE

Rick, still tender from getting blasted with buckshot, had had little to laugh about lately. He wasn't a person who laughed with his friends; he laughed *at them* or anyone else who inspired his bully instinct. Right now, he laughed at the Riders as they awkwardly bounced in their saddles while they rode away in panic.

He pulled out his cell phone and called Arnie.

"Yeah," was Arnie's abrupt greeting.

"Hey, I just rousted a couple of weekend yahoos that were riding around here on their horses. Keep an eye out for them."

"Okay, any problem?"

"No, I scared the hell out of them, and they took off running like a couple of chicken-shits. They are probably heading for home as fast as they can, but if you do see them, come on tough, and they'll run off and never look back."

———

Brett and Mark rode back out onto the dirt road that fronted the camp. Instead of turning back toward the highway, they continued west. The barbed wire fence was six feet off of the roadside to their right. No trespassing signs seemed to be everywhere. When they started riding west, multiple trails intersected the road; some were for hiking, and some were probably made by wild game. Now, they were thinning out. To their left was the Boise National Forest, and to their right was the camp. Brett kept checking the GPS, and the coordinates kept getting closer, but likely on the wrong side of the fence. Based on their view from the north side of the camp and the distance they had traveled on the south side, he was confident that the camp's cabins and buildings were just through the trees to their right. They had hoped to get a better view. One that would allow for some good shots with Mark's camera. Detailed photos were high on their wanted list today, but the thick trees and bushes on the camp's side of the fence obstructed their view.

They had traveled over a half a mile past the entrance. Brett pulled up again and checked the readout on his GPS. He dropped it back into his bag, extended his arm, and pointed to his right and across the fence.

"Straight across there, six hundred and thirty-six feet away is the spot that brought us here today. I want to jump this fence and inspect the place," Brett said.

"Before you go jumping fences, why don't we ride up the road a while and look? It is a beautiful day for a ride; maybe we can find a better vantage point. Maybe one that will keep the barbed wire from tearing the crap out of our clothes," Mark offered.

"Oh, you're right," Brett grinned. "Let's get the lay of the land before we get ourselves in trouble." He nudged Pepper, and they pushed forward.

They continued riding at a steady pace, with the camp to their right. The road bent north slowly. They were nearing the camp's eastern edge; the terrain became a bit rougher and rocky, and the trees thinned. The buildings became visible as they rode into an area where the density of the forest declined. They might get to Mark's better vantage point yet; all the buildings were coming into view. The large cabin was a central lodge, servicing a collection of small private cabins. They rode another fifty yards, then the trees disappeared, and they had a completely open view. Brett pulled out the GPS and located the coordinates one last time. He focused his binoculars and said, "There it is! There's the truck! I knew it."

Mark grabbed the Pentax digital bridge camera, pulled off the lens cap, and set up to shoot when they heard the unmistakable sound of an ATV coming their way. They both quickly stowed their gear, mounted their horses, and started riding up the road, the horses falling into a canter. Pepper and Rondo were ready to move after their continuous stop-and-go pace, and with just a little urging, accelerated into a full gallop. At the corner of the fence line, the narrow road split, with one branch following the camp's northern property line, and the other continuing straight into the forest.

Brett and Mark both let their horses gallop straight up the road. This branch was rougher and more rutted, but they were on horses, so no problem. Rondo and Pepper weren't bothered by the ruts and were thrilled to run. The whine of the ATV interrupted their fun.

This ATV raced down the northern branch of the road, made a hard right too fast onto the forest branch, and it nearly rolled out of control. Pockmarked Guy wasn't driving; instead, it was another angry man, and he was standing straight up on the footholds in an awkward posture. He was a short, wiry guy, wearing oversized sunglasses and a baseball cap with its bill pointing backward.

Brett was not a man who could be pushed or chased, even while playing a role as they were today, and Mark was inclined to follow his lead. They were already fed up with the jerk who gave them crap at the gate, and now, here came another. So, after they rode over a rise, they pulled up their horses, turned back, and waited for this new guy to bring whatever he might bring. Unfortunately, it would have helped if they'd given the ATV a little more room to stop.

The camo-colored ATV was almost identical to the earlier one, except this one's driver was lousy. As he went over the rise, he hit a deep erosion rut that caught one of his front wheels. The nose of the ATV dropped, the back end popped upward, and it nearly flipped. It bounced, and when it landed, it fell into an out-of-control 45-degree skid, straight into Rondo and Mark.

Rondo explosively jumped away from the ATV and almost threw Mark. Mark held onto the saddle horn while Rondo collided with Brett and Pepper and almost crushed Mark's leg. Rondo was big, robust, upset, and scared. He started bucking. Mark held tight on the first and second buck, and then on the third, lost a stirrup. On the fourth, he got bucked off. Mark was lucky to land in a pile of dirt, almost on his feet. Then he collapsed, rolled down a slight incline, and landed hard on his rear. He sat there and wondered what had just happened.

Rondo collided with Pepper as the ATV slid behind them. Brett pulled Pepper's head in the opposite direction and dug in his heels. Pepper reacted by leaping into Brett's lead, just past the skidding ATV, off the road and directly toward a thick, fallen Ponderosa Pine. This time Pepper responded. First, he jumped over the tree, landing six feet on the other side. Then he turned and ran past its length, down through a sparse patch and well past the ATV, then jumped back onto the road. Pepper looked back at the mess behind him, shook his head as only a horse can, and then whinnied. Brett leaned forward in the saddle, wrapped both hands around Pepper's neck, and hugged him.

After nearly hitting Rondo and Pepper, the ATV fish-tailed and followed the line directly toward the downed tree that Pepper had just leaped over. Instead of jumping over the Ponderosa Pine, the ATV crashed into it. The fallen tree didn't budge, and the ATV stopped dead. Unfortunately for the driver, his momentum carried him forward. He flew over the top until he caught his arm on the handlebar, and then he flipped. His landing was rough. The ATV's engine choked and then stopped. Everything went quiet.

In just a few seconds, everything changed. The men looked around and tried to take in the events that had just occurred. One moment everything was great, the next, not so much.

"You okay?" Brett looked at Mark.

"Yeah, the only thing that is hurt is my feelings. I can't believe I got bucked off."

"Four more seconds and you would have won a buckle."

"Don't make me laugh. It makes my butt hurt."

Brett looked down at Pepper again, patted his neck, and whispered, "Good boy."

The ATV driver moaned and said, "This is all your fault, assholes."

Mark got up, and gingerly walked over to the guy and asked, "You okay?"

The man was lying in a pile of dirt, holding his arm and grimacing in pain. "Shut up and leave me alone."

"No, really, you took a terrible hit. Do you need some help?"

"Not from you."

"Yes, from me," He walked a little closer and spoke clearly, "I am a doctor."

The man took a few seconds and reconsidered, "I think I might have broken my arm."

Mark kneeled right next to him and said, "Now I'm going to examine your arm. I want you to relax it completely; I may need to move it around. What's your name?"

"Arnie."

"You can call me Doc."

Mark grabbed his med-kit and washed his hands thoroughly before helping Arnie remove his shirt, and then he examined his arm, which hung loosely to his side. "Your arm looks fine. Is there pain up here in your shoulder?"

Arnie shook his head as an affirmative, while his eyes signaled pain and worry.

Mark looked closer at the shoulder, "Well, Arnie, it looks like you have dislocated your shoulder," and then he looked toward Brett and said, "Brett, come over here and help hold him steady. I'm going to try to set his shoulder back into place."

———

Jay had seen Arnie drive off when the cowboys rode by and hadn't seen or heard from him since. Knowing Arnie's innate ability to screw up, Jay jumped on the last ATV and searched. He followed Arnie's tracks around the curve and up the rise that preceded the scene of the accident, pulled up, and was—surprised? He didn't know what to do or what to think, so for a few seconds, he just stared. And the assembled group stared back.

"Who is that?" one cowboy asked.

"That's my boss," Arnie said.

Jay shut down the engine and stepped off. The sling attached to the front of his ATV held a rifle. Jay left the gun behind as he walked over to the group. He shook his head. Arnie's ATV was dead, jammed against a large fallen tree, and awkwardly stuck. Behind it, two horses munched on some tall grass.

Of the two cowboys, one of them was a big guy who looked familiar. Jay couldn't put a name to the face, but he recognized him; he felt he knew him from somewhere. It would likely come to him. He also had the feeling that this man was someone he should not take lightly.

The other cowboy turned toward Jay and said, "Give us a minute here." Then he manipulated Arnie's arm and shoulder and popped it into place. "How does that feel?"

Arnie rotated his shoulder, "Better." He grinned.

"I put your shoulder back into its socket; it should be okay, but you need to give it some time to rest and heal. Make a basic sling and keep your arm in it for a week," He reached into his med-kit and pulled out a couple of packets of pills. "Take two of these twice a day; they should help with swelling and pain. Put some ice on your shoulder and clean yourself up; you're scratched to hell and could get an infection." The cowboy then turned toward Jay and said, "What do you want?"

Arnie interrupted and said, "Boss, I wrecked the ATV and dislocated my shoulder. This guy's a doctor, and he fixed it."

"Yeah, I got that much," Jay paused, took his time, and then looked toward Brett and Mark. "But you're the guys we saw riding by our property, and you have been looking around with binoculars... Why?" Jay questioned.

"Because that's what we do; that's our hobby. We ride horses around the backcountry, look around, and have fun," Brett replied.

"Well, let me explain something to you. Our employer owns most of this area, and he is a very private person. He wants people to leave him alone, and he is dead serious about it. So, I'd highly recommend you get the hell out of here and don't come back."

CHAPTER THIRTEEN

The ride back down to Brett's pickup and horse trailer was comfortable and pleasant. They turned off onto a few intersecting trails and rode across some of the other old logging roads. They might as well learn the trail system while the sun was high, and they had plenty of time to do so. It was an exciting series of trails, and they had found a couple of options they could try when, or if, they came back. It was a beautiful area, but they hadn't taken this ride for scenery; they rode today to learn. And they had learned a lot, but unfortunately, not as much as Brett would have liked.

They had plenty of time to talk about the situation as they rode. Brett was confident that this camp's occupants were at the very least involved in the recent burglaries. The truck he sighted looked like the one he saw at Valley Camera, but he wasn't sure. Brett tried to put the scenario together, starting with the jerks and the cell phone. The cell phone's signal and the truck occupied the same coordinates. And the men occupying those coordinates acted like a bunch of thugs. They were over zealous in protecting their privacy. It felt like they were hiding something. Something criminal.

It would be nice if he could prove it. If Brett knew for sure the truck he sighted through the binoculars was involved at Valley Camera, then they could bust these guys, and the case might hold. But there were obvious problems, like the crooks hanging out in the middle of nowhere when they should be in some urban center on the trail of burglaries. There were at least eight burglars at the crime scenes, but only three at the camp, and they were guarding it as if it were a secret base. It seemed the most it could be was a way station to be used after a failed burglary, but that made little sense either.

He knew for sure that the men they had run into were a bunch of thugs. The boss carried a rifle on his ATV, and he didn't look like a hunter. Even if he did hunt, it wasn't hunting season. Why the rough time? Brett had never run into anything like it, at least with ordinary people, even ones who treasured their privacy. And the boss looked familiar.

The good news was that they had an exciting ride, and the horses got the exercise they needed. Mark was embarrassed about getting bucked off, but he didn't blame Rondo; when it happened, it was every man, and every horse, for himself. Mark might have done some bucking, too, if he were a horse. Brett let him off the hook easily and said, "You rode well. Anyone else would have lost it on the first buck. And consider the upside; in a few years, this will make a great story to tell all the grandchildren."

They rode back down the last section of the narrow logging road and entered the trailhead area. The area was deserted, except for Brett's truck and horse trailer. The trailhead was a quiet area with little traffic; it was likely their rigs were the only vehicles parked at the end of the road. It was time to go home; all they had left was to unsaddle, load up, and hit the road.

Mark found a spot behind the trailer to unsaddle and take care of Rondo, but when he looked at the back end of his rig, it looked off kilter. The horse trailer's right side had a funny tilt that could have been caused by the road's steep shoulder, but it wasn't the road.

"Hey, Brett, come over here and look at this," Mark yelled.

Brett walked over, knelt, and examined the tires. "Oh, shit."

Their horse trailer's tires had been slashed. The horse trailer had two wheels on each side, one behind the other. The dual-wheeled design improved the ride, but in this case, it backfired. Someone slashed them both. Brett opened the trailer's front compartment, and as he feared, it carried only one spare.

"Oh shit," Brett said again.

It wasn't the end of the world, just a huge inconvenience. If Tom were there, he probably would have been acting out. Brett was the opposite of Tom. He projected a demeanor of calmness and confidence. Brett did not sweat the small stuff, but was a strong man when it came to the big things in life. That didn't mean he didn't care, because he did; in his solitary thoughts, he seethed.

Mark's trailer used the same size wheels and tires as Brett's, so they decided the best plan was for one of them to go back to the barn, pick up Mark's spare, return, and change out the tires so then they all would drive back together. Brett volunteered to go; he'd pick up another spare and then return as quickly as possible. Mark would stay and take care of the horses. It would be about a two-and-a-half-hour round trip.

Brett was okay until they slashed his tires. He had to assume it was the guys at the camp; probably the pockmarked guy, but it could have been one of the others. It didn't matter. It just pissed him off.

A lot of things were pissing him off. It pissed him off that someone burglarized Tom's place, threatening the livelihood of Tom, his family, and his employees. It pissed him off it put Tom in the position where he now questioned the value of his life's work. It pissed him off that Tom got beat up with a baseball bat. It pissed him off these guys were such threatening jerks, and it pissed him off he didn't get into their camp.

Brett drove down the highway, and the longer he traveled, the more he focused on what he should do. He needed to answer some questions that were bothering him. They had made some progress, but at best, it was only a lateral step, not a forward one. He wanted to find out what was going on at the camp, and though it didn't matter, he wondered if the cell phone was up there. He didn't want to go behind his friend's backs and act alone. But, sometimes working alone is best.

Brett had a plan.

CHAPTER FOURTEEN

It was a quiet drive into town and down to the barn; neither Mark nor Brett felt like talking. Both men felt better but were still irritated. With Brett driving back and forth to fetch a spare tire before he could change them and then load up the horses, they lost half a day. Half a day they wouldn't get back; half a day stolen by some real punks.

On a positive note, there was a surprising amount of activity at the barn while they were gone. Sage had never seen the newly remodeled and improved barn area. Earlier, Cindy had come over to the Coogan's house to visit Sage and Tess, and when the subject came up, she had invited the girls down to see what the guys had created.

Cindy's blue eyes sparkled with pride when she gave the full tour. Her short curly brown hair complimented her upbeat attitude as she pointed out each feature. She beamed when she saved the best for last. She brought Sage through the barn's recent addition. They entered from the stall area and walked through the mudroom and into the tack room. The modern kitchen, bar, and the music room stood out in the clubhouse. Sage couldn't believe the guys were keeping guitars, harmonicas, and ukuleles down there. When she saw the furnished area with a big-screen TV, Sage just stood and smiled. They had everything a rider or a horse would ever need, plus a great place to hang out and relax. She loved the entire setup and was a bit jealous.

Out at the new corrals on the opposite side of the barn, a Pinto named Tonto started fussing over Sage. He was a good-looking horse with a white face, and a brown body and mane. A full white band ran from his shoulders down his front legs, and a similar band ran over his rump and back legs. He was a postcard Pinto.

Cindy showed how they had built the new corral system that linked up to the barn. It was a modular system that added flexibility to the corral's setup from being open to the pasture to a cluster of one, two, or three corrals open to the barn. The key to the system was a newly designed gate control that provided the functionality to customize the layout. Sage was looking at one gate when she noticed Tonto examining the same detail as if he were part of the conversation. With Tonto's nose about six inches away from her face, he was hard not to see. At first, a little surprised, she stepped away. Tonto responded by looking at her with a quizzical gaze. He seemed curious, amazed, and wanted to be involved.

Cindy led them around to the next gate. While she demonstrated the mechanism, Tonto once again found space between them, nosed in, and continued his participation.

"Is he always like that?" Sage asked.

"Yes," Cindy laughed. "He is the most curious horse I've ever seen. He wants to know what is going on all the time."

"He's so cute," Sage said.

When they finished the tour, Cindy pointed to Tonto and asked, "Sage, would you like to take him out for a ride?"

Sage wanted to try, but had not been on a horse since she was a teenager when she took riding lessons at Victory Stables.

"It has been a very long time," she replied.

"Then, Tonto is perfect for you. He is gentle and easy to ride," Cindy encouraged.

"Oh, I don't know," Sage said nervously.

"Hey, we have five horses. That is too many, and the only reason we have five is so friends like you can ride. Go for it, and believe me, Tonto will love it."

While the ladies took the tour, Tom practiced a Jimmy Buffett song on his guitar in the music room. He'd been struggling with a chord progression and lost patience. Finally, he gave up and played "Home on the Range."

When the guys pulled in with their horses in tow, they saw Sage gliding across the pasture on the back of Tonto. Mark jumped out of the passenger seat and walked over to Cindy and Tess. Tom joined them. They watched Sage ride while they leaned against the pasture's fence.

Mark kissed Cindy and commented, "They look good together, don't they?"

"Yeah, Tonto charmed the young lady. She had no choice. She had to take him out for a ride."

"She's riding well. How often does she ride?" Mark questioned.

"She hasn't ridden since she was in high school," Tom replied.

"That's remarkable; look how smooth she is and check out her posture."

"Hey, Brett, check out Sage's riding. It's pretty impressive," Mark yelled.

Brett walked over, "No kidding; she looks good. She must do some riding down in California."

"She hasn't ridden since she was a teenager," Tess repeated.

"Well, then—she must be a natural."

Brett and Mark unloaded the horses, fed and watered them, then let them out into the pasture. Brett took the slashed tires out of his trailer and threw them into the back of his truck. He was still edgy and quiet from his day, but the girls helped him ease up a bit.

Sage came in from her ride. Cindy and her mom helped her unsaddle and brush Tonto. Then, they got him settled and sent him out in the pasture with Pepper and Rondo. All three horses had a pleasant ride, and all three seem quite happy about it.

Tom followed Mark into the barn and pulled him aside.

"How did the ride go?" he asked.

"We learned quite a bit, but it got a little rough. Brett was quiet on the ride home. He's a little edgy right now. Let's find a little time later when we can talk privately, and I'll bring you up to speed."

Mark watched as Tom walked through the clubhouse and back out to the patio.

"Hey, Tom," he yelled.

"Yes," Tom said after turning around.

"Where are your walking sticks?"

"Back at the house."

"I don't see even a trace of a limp."

"I feel good. You know, I've got one hell of a doctor."

Mark went into the kitchen and brought out a cooler of beer and non-alcoholic drinks. He was quite a beer guy, and he was recommending a new beer he had just purchased. This one was a creamy golden ale produced by a local downtown brewery, and it was perfect for a warm afternoon.

Brett sipped an iced tea.

"I've got a thought; it's getting late. How about we get together for dinner? It would be fun," Tess said.

"What have you got in mind, Mom?"

"How about a simple cookout right here at the barn? It would be easy to put together."

"That sounds good to me," Mark said.

"Sorry, I've got plans," Brett said. He stood up, said goodbye, stepped into his pickup, and drove away.

CHAPTER FIFTEEN

Brett wasn't worried about hurting any feelings after his abrupt departure. He was among friends. They all knew he had a pretty black-and-white personality, and would let people know when and if he had a problem. He did, after all, have plans.

The drive to his house was mostly downhill, and it took just a few minutes. He pulled into his garage, walked inside, and started his process. It was still a little early for dinner, so he fell into his favorite piece of furniture–an oversized leather recliner. He grabbed the entertainment system's remote control off the side table, dialed up one of his favorite music compilations, laid back, and listened to the music. Step one, relax.

Back in his football days, Brett had developed an almost superstitious routine on game day. He wouldn't hang out with any of his buddies, teammates, or even a girlfriend. He wouldn't touch alcohol for forty-eight hours before game time. Beyond that, he hardly touched the stuff at all during those years. Brett would stay home, reject company, and relax alone. If he didn't eat with the team, he would make a simple, healthy meal, usually with high energy protein, some carbs, and vegetables. Brett avoided burgers,

French fries, pizza, and all fast food. Once, when he was in high school, a buddy of his, a really big offensive tackle on the team, talked him into a pregame meal of the famous "Monster Burger Combo" at the local drive-in back home. It turned into a digestive disaster and a valuable lesson.

Brett looked at his watch; it was time to cook. He wasn't a gourmet cook, or even a good cook, but between his rice cooker, barbecue grill, and television cooking classes, he could get by. He dropped a lean steak on the barbecue grill, cooked some brown rice in the cooker, and threw together a spinach salad. Overlooking the city, he sat on his patio, sipped ice water, and enjoyed his dinner. He had plenty of time before he went out tonight — Step two, pregame meal.

After dinner, Brett cleaned up and changed his clothes. Instead of his riding outfit, he wore an athletic outfit of running socks, black running shoes, black lightweight sweatpants, and a matching lightweight sweatshirt with a hood. He filled up a 16-ounce water bottle and built a small collection on his bed. He had visited his favorite store, Teton Outdoors, and purchased a group of outdoor gadgets, and the coolest one was a pair of state-of-the-art night vision binoculars. Brett set the night vision binoculars on his bed and started adding items to the supplies, including his thick leather work gloves, a black ski mask, and a few other specialized items. He dropped them all into a small, lightweight travel backpack.

In the back corner of his home office, behind a closet door, he opened his gun safe. He selected his favorite compact pistol with its matching laser sights. He added a lightweight fabric holster and a pouch of ammo. It all fit nicely into his backpack. He picked it up and checked the weight.

He went back out to his overhanging deck, drank a cup of iced coffee, and watched the sun work its way toward the horizon. He had a magnificent view from his patio. The city was slowing down, going home, and ending its day. The sounds of the city never stopped, and it had a pleasing effect that echoed from the valley below. Brett drifted into self-imposed isolation and thought about the night to come—Step three, think about the game.

Thirty minutes before sunset, he moved back into his garage and pulled the tarp off of his ten-year-old Honda road bike. It was a beautiful machine that rode smoothly and quietly, but was versatile enough to handle off-road conditions. The more he rode horses, the less he rode his motorcycle; somehow, the two worlds didn't fit together. Brett was a horseman now; riding his Honda had become a contradiction. His attitude had changed to where he believed the two should not mix, and while riding Pepper, if he crossed roads with motorcycle riders, he found the motorcycles to be an intrusion. There is a time and a place for both worlds, and tonight was the time for the Honda. He put on his backpack, biking coat, and helmet, and then he pulled out and drove down the hill on Willow Creek Road.

For the third time today, he drove up the highway toward Idaho City. The Honda was a lot more fun to drive than his pickup. He flew over the hills and glided through the canyons. Idaho City was full of nightlife as Brett cruised by; it looked like a fun place to hang out. He drove past, and as he rode up into the high country, the only light came from his headlight and the night sky. The small opening of the dirt road appeared on his left; he made the turn, turned off his headlight, and rode the rest of the way in darkness.

The night sky was mostly clear, with a scattering of clouds and a waxing moon. A full moon would have been ideal, but the crescent moon cast just enough light to help Brett navigate. The lack of light pollution brought a star-filled sky, although some stars were hidden behind wispy clouds. A brighter sky would have been ideal, yet Brett's eyes had already adjusted, probably to his advantage. The conditions were perfect. Brett's confidence was high. He knew the strong would prevail.

He rode down the bumpy dirt road slowly, quietly, and carefully.

As Brett came to the end of the entry-road, his choice was to continue down the old logging road to his right or enter a trailhead. He entered the trail they had explored that morning. It swung out to the left while winding through the trees. It was narrow and bumpy, and in the darkness, he had a hard time seeing the upcoming curves. Brett took it slowly and tried to close the distance to the camp quietly. He found an excellent spot to stop and hide his bike under cover. If Brett rode any closer, the sound of the Honda's engine might have been noticed. He pushed the bike behind a couple of thick bushes and shut it down.

He removed his helmet and riding coat and changed into his running outfit. The lightweight hoodie and sweat pants were comfortable, and when he pulled the hood over his head, he was black from head to toe and nearly invisible in the night. He slipped the backpack on and started running. He was a couple of miles out, but the chilly night felt good, and the moonlight provided enough illumination to lead the way. Soon, he broke into a light sweat, and his second wind kicked in. He increased his pace and felt alive.

He exited onto the logging road around an eighth of a mile ahead of where he planned to cross the barbed wire fence. Once there, he slipped on his ski mask and his heavy gloves. He grabbed the top barbed wire strand, and with a spring off of the second rung, he was over and clear. Brett stood inside the camp's perimeter, southwest of the buildings, just as he had planned.

He hiked into the camp and worked toward the buildings on the west side. He walked carefully and observed. Three of the cabins glowed from interior lighting. He had suspected, and this confirmed that people were living there. With their window drapes closed, their occupants were hopefully down for the night. The main lodge was partially lit, probably by a single light fixture; it was hard to tell if there was any activity. The entire camp looked quiet; little if anything was taking place around any of the buildings. It was comforting to see them closed down, but in a way, some activity would help define the situation.

Brett spotted the truck. Someone had moved it to a pad next to one of the large outbuildings. Viewing through the binoculars, he could tell some repair work had occurred. They'd replaced the flattened tires and had straightened out the body, mainly by bending the fenders and bumper enough to clear any moving parts. The truck wasn't pretty, but it looked roadworthy.

Brett was very curious about the function of the large outbuildings. He speculated one was a garage of sorts, designed for the storage and maintenance of their vehicles. The other building was a mystery.

He slowly approached the two outbuildings; both were windowless and dark and probably closed for the night. The first building had a main entrance, and next to it, a large, oversized garage-style door big enough to allow in a good-sized vehicle. He checked both doors, and they were locked. Slowly and carefully, he studied the perimeter and found no other access.

Behind the building and in front of the road, stood a large wooden container. It looked like a custom-made garbage bin. The homemade bin made sense; there wasn't any garbage service out here in the middle of the forest. Brett pulled a small red beamed flashlight made for astronomy from his backpack. The red light was less harsh on the eye and harder to spot in the dark. He opened the garbage bin and aimed the flashlight before turning it on. He needed to be quick and unnoticed. Inside the container were stacks of cardboard boxes, paper goods, and Styrofoam packing materials. He was curious about the type of rubbish in the bin. The top layer was mostly Styrofoam, which made squeaky sounds if mishandled. He needed to be careful. The cardboard boxes were broken down and organized. He heard a door slam somewhere ahead, probably from the next outbuilding. It wasn't worth searching the container right now. It was time to move on.

Next was the other outbuilding. It was probably the location of the slamming door he had heard. Brett had used his night vision glasses from three different angles before approaching. He wanted to check out this area, and he didn't want to deal with anyone. Not until he was satisfied and had completed his search. It all looked clear, so he approached carefully. This building was like the last, with an entrance next to an oversized garage door, but it was more likely a garage designed for vehicles. Once again, the building was windowless and locked. However, a large cement pad was laid on one side, and the truck was parked there.

Searching around the building, he found another garbage bin, but this one looked to be full of garbage. It was filled with greasy towels, empty cans, rags, food wrappers, and boxes. Nothing of importance. A quick look at the truck confirmed his belief that this was the truck at the Valley Camera burglary. It was also locked. It was hard to understand. When you're out in the middle of nowhere, why lock everything up? It would have been nice to get inside something.

Right behind its cab, there was a large metal box with a flip-top attached to the truck's bed that was also locked. Brett pulled out the red light once again, and holding it low, examined the truck's bed. He saw something wedged into a gap between the box and the bed. He reached down and pulled on whatever it was and failed to move it. A little better flashlight would sure help. He tried again, and it popped out. It was a cell phone.

He dropped the phone into his backpack and crawled back out of the truck bed. He thought he heard something. It was a shuffling sound, and it was close. He took a quick look and then hustled over to a stand of trees, twenty feet away. He leaned into one tree and tried to blend in as much as possible. He was glad that all the lights were off outside of the garage.

The shuffling sound turned to footsteps, and then Brett saw the reflections of a flashlight. The light was moving in from odd angles, almost as if someone was swinging it back and forth in a search pattern.

"Arnie, is that you?" A man's voice yelled. And then, thirty seconds later, "Arnie?"

The footsteps were close, very close. Someone was checking the truck and walking this way. Then that someone stood between Brett and the truck.

Brett stood motionless. He realized his gun was in his backpack–it was useless, but he was calm and prepared to strike. Had he been spotted? He didn't know. Even if he had, it was so dark, unless someone pointed a flashlight his way, no one could see if he was there or not. Brett planned to give the man one more step, only one. He couldn't allow him to move in any closer. Brett didn't know if he was armed and knew little except that he'd have to take him out. He calmed his breathing, became focused, silent, and alert.

And then the footsteps moved away. After a minute, Brett risked a look. He could see the beam of a flashlight move downhill. He let a small sigh escape his lungs.

After a few more minutes and a little more time searching the area, Brett completed his task. He passed on the cabins; they were likely living quarters and not worth the risk. His aim was the outbuildings. He just wished he could have gotten inside.

With everything stowed, he started jogging, and as he moved back into the thickness of the trees, he began running. It didn't take long until he found his fence crossing point. He slipped on his heavy gloves again, repeated his vault over the fence, and then ran downhill on the logging road.

When Brett found the trail's intersection, he stopped and looked back. There was a new, red glow coming from the property, and it wasn't electric lights. It was a fire, and it looked like a hot one.

The truck was burning.

Brett chortled, "It's probably a fuel leak."

CHAPTER SIXTEEN

Roger Carlson drove his old Jeep Wrangler up the logging road. He kept the Jeep at his vacation residence in Idaho for times like this when he left the major roads and did some real driving. He also drove it because he didn't want to scratch his Mercedes.

He closed the gate behind him and paused to take in the view; it was clear and crisp, and the morning sun highlighted the resident forest. The camp was built in the middle of a growth of Ponderosa pines, Lodge Pole Pines, and Douglass Fir. Wildflowers were sprouting, and Huckleberry bushes were coming on strong. Someday, it would be nice to convert this from a business property to a real family escape. It had been created back in the day as a camp for deer and elk hunters, and now it was used for his personally designed crime ring. Unfortunately, the use of this property was trending down, not up.

Roger felt the same way about his life; it was trending down, not up. He spent more time in his Idaho vacation home, a half-hour from here, and less time with his distanced wife and disjointed family in Seattle. Similarly, Roger spent less time with his legitimate business, Carlson Distribution, and more time with his burglary scheme. And more importantly, he felt like he should have never teamed up with Levitt in Reno. What looked like a good infusion of cash and an improved distribution source had turned from positive to negative to frightening.

He had only himself to blame. If you get yourself involved with organized crime, expect to come out of it both morally and financially broke. When he first got involved with Levitt and PGB, he hoped he had found an alternative source of product distribution that would solve his financial problems. It turned out to be too good to be true, and now he had a new partner. A partner from hell.

Back in the Wrangler, he followed the improved gravel road up the hill and behind the processing building and to the garage. At the garage, he stopped and stared at the burned chassis of their truck. His burglary ring didn't need another problem. He hit the gas and drove the rest of the way.

When Roger walked into the lodge, Jay, Rick, and Arnie were already sitting at the table, expecting him. Jay and Rick were both cradling coffee mugs and projected a look of seriousness. A grinning Arnie sat and stared at Roger.

"So, I see we have a problem with our truck. That seems like a good place to start," Roger said. He had prepared to address a different topic, and he was irritated that another problem had to be addressed. Under his right arm, Roger carried the full set of documents for this weekend's planned burglary at Bend, Oregon. He had maps, security weakness zones, layout sketches, and a lot more. He could feel the project slipping away.

"Yeah, the truck caught fire last night and burned hard and fast. It took all our effort to keep the fire from spreading," Jay said.

"What happened?"

"I had been working on it. I changed out the tires and pounded out the fenders and rear bumper. It wasn't pretty, but everything mechanical was okay. I was in my cabin when I saw the flames," Rick said.

"That's not what I mean. How in the hell did it catch on fire?" Roger muttered.

"That is what we have been trying to figure out," Jay said. "It doesn't make any sense—it just happened."

Roger looked at Arnie, "What do you think, Arnie. You're just sitting there grinning."

"I don't work on them, Boss. I steal them. I'm no mechanic."

"Did you steal us another cargo van?"

"Yeah, but there is still some work we have to finish before it is blind. Until then, we can't use it on a job. It's in the garage right now, and Rick is working on it."

"So, do we have any theory on how the truck caught on fire?" Roger asked again.

"There are just a few ways a vehicle fire starts, like a fuel leak or an electrical short or both. Other than…" Jay looked away. He slowly looked up and said, "Other than somebody torching it."

"Great—fucking great," Roger moaned.

"The only thought we had was if some hidden electrical damage finally showed up as a short," Rick said. "Beyond that, I just don't know."

"So, last weekend on the Valley Camera job, we ran into a couple of people who shot us down, right? We don't know who or why, but we know it wasn't the cops. Now, last night, someone may have torched our truck. Could these events be connected?" Roger asked.

"I don't know, but it seems possible. But we didn't see or hear anyone around here last night," Jay replied.

"Well, whoever showed up at the Valley Camera job last weekend sure as hell made themselves known," Roger observed. "Has there been anyone suspicious around here lately?"

"Just those cowboys who were riding their horses yesterday morning, but we scared them away pretty good," Rick offered.

"Two guys were joyriding on their horses, and we caught up

with them and ran them off, and as Rick said, we sent them a pretty clear message to leave and never come back. They didn't seem the type of guys who were looking for trouble," Jay explained.

"One of them was a doctor," Arnie grinned.

"A doctor, how do you know that?" Roger asked.

"Arnie here wrecked his ATV when he chased them down," Jay said.

"Yeah, and the doc fixed me up. I had a dislocated shoulder, and the doc had his buddy hold me still, and he pulled it back into the joint and fixed it. Then, he gave me some great medicine, and I slept like a baby."

Roger leaned forward, rested his head on his arms, and he couldn't help himself. He chuckled. It was too much, just unbelievable. He looked up, and everyone was staring. It was like Murphy's Law; what can go wrong, will go wrong. And now a cowboy doctor? They all restrained themselves, but couldn't help but have a good laugh; it all was ridiculous. They could agree on that.

Jay brought them back, "I thought I recognized the other guy, and this afternoon, it hit me, and I remembered. Back when I played football for Boise State…"

"Jay the Pain—Jay the Pain," Arnie chanted.

Jay was an outstanding linebacker for the Broncos, and he drew a lot of national notoriety to the point when he was on the field and made a play. The fans would chant, "Jay the Pain, Jay the Pain." He was a fast, hard-hitting defensive football player who brought the pain, hence the nickname. It was a surprise and a disappointment when he didn't make it into the NFL.

Jay smiled, "Okay enough, Arnie, that was a long time ago. So, there was a guy two years ahead of me who played for Wyoming. We were both linebackers, and while he played, I was pretty much in his shadow. After he graduated, everyone was always comparing us like it was a big honor. The thing is, I didn't care for that bullshit.

I just wanted to be judged on the field, but the press guys couldn't leave it alone. It still pisses me off. He ended up playing in the NFL for years. He was a big star. Yesterday, he was wearing a cowboy hat instead of a football helmet, but I'm pretty sure it was him. His name is Brett Wyatt."

"I'm not a big sports fan, but the name sounds familiar," Roger said.

"There is no way that a rich NFL guy and a rich doctor are trying to move in on our turf," Arnie belched. "If they wanted that, the doc wouldn't have helped me out."

"Arnie, I think you're right. Why would a couple of wealthy individuals like a doctor and a professional athlete be interested in torching our truck in the middle of the night? It doesn't make sense," Roger agreed.

He paused a moment and scanned the men, then said, "But guys, we have a lot at stake here, and it sure as hell looks like we have a problem. Everything needs to go on hold. I'm calling off the burglary at Bend this weekend. I sure as hell don't need *these*," he said as he shuffled his plans to the side. "I want everything by the numbers. Our truck is down, and we don't have time to replace it. And something stinks; we are getting trashed, I don't like it, so we need to fix it."

Jay stood up. He was red-eyed with emotion. "No way in hell. We're not calling off Bend—that will screw up our take!" he said.

"We are short a truck."

"So, the van can do double-duty."

"It's not just busting out the front doors, Jay. We need all the vehicles to perform our pre-hit sweeps. The van can't be in both places at one time."

"So what? It will happen at three o'clock in the fucking morning. How conservative do we need to be?"

"That's enough! Arnie, Rick, give us the room. Jay and I need to talk," Roger ordered.

Roger and Jay had been working together since the crime ring's beginning. Roger had rescued Jay from prosecution during an employee theft incident in Nevada. Jay avoided a life-altering legal problem but lost his job, and Roger hired him as the foreman of his new venture into crime. They started with an employer-employee relationship, and later, as time passed, they became a team. Roger had worked with Jay and educated him in business and life's lessons. With Roger being Jay's senior by twenty years, they developed a father-son connection. And like a real father-son relationship, the son would sometimes rebel. Today was that day.

Jay was steaming, so Roger used his skills to remind him of all they had accomplished together and calmed him down. Then, they reviewed the big picture and the long-term value of their plans. They were in a high-risk venture where even a minor mistake might ruin them. As they worked through how and why they followed strict methods, it became clear to Jay that safety was vital. Still, he felt Roger's techniques were sometimes over the top. When they finished their talk, Jay apologized, and they both promised to work together.

With Rick and Arnie back in attendance, they all agreed to skip a week of burglaries and instead work toward solving their problems. Jay was going to notify the road crew of the delay and have them hang tight. Rick and Arnie were in charge of the vehicles. They needed to finish up the cargo van, replace the truck, and repair the ATV. They all needed to check supplies and weapons, clean their guns, and clean up their act in general.

Security was the number one issue. There were big questions that needed answers. They needed to investigate and communicate any possibilities or coincidences that could help identify any possible adversaries. They would update and improve security at the camp. Carlson had learned a lot about security methods through his relations with retailers. He would design a system; isolation was not enough. In the meantime, they would double up on general surveillance, and they would arm themselves at all times. If they ran into any threats, they all agreed to shoot first and ask questions later.

Roger gathered up his plans for the Bend job, said his goodbyes, and walked back to the Wrangler.

"Hey, wait up," Jay yelled. He ran down the lodge's steps and caught up to Roger at the Jeep. "Roger, I just wanted to apologize again. You've done so much for me, and I should have never challenged you. I'm sorry."

"Don't worry about it. We've had big problems here lately, and problems can cause stress. We are all feeling it. So, we're good," Roger reached out, and they shook hands.

Jay walked away and then turned and asked. "Roger, should we call Mr. Levitt?"

Roger closed his eyes and winced at the prospect, "I'll deal with Levitt."

CHAPTER SEVENTEEN

Early the next morning, Brett and Mark saddled up for one of their favorite foothill rides. It was good to be home. A brief rain shower had cleaned up the trails and knocked down the dust. The wispy overnight clouds wasted away, and summer brought back blue skies, cumulus clouds, and warm morning light. After being bucked off Rondo, Mark gave the big horse a break and instead rode his faithful Palomino, Trixie. This morning they were hitting the Shadow Creek Trail, a meandering trek that covered a stretch of the foothills unnoticed and unknown by most. Starting in a draw hidden behind a ridge, it was one of the most stunning and quiet rides in the Boise foothills. They deserved a peaceful ride, one that would hopefully mellow them out; they had a lot on their minds.

Often, on a morning like this, the guys would be silent, enjoying the ride while sorting their thoughts. Today was typical. Yesterday's events were top of mind, but the two men had different perspectives. Mark was still frustrated. Brett, not so much. They needed to talk.

"Those guys we ran into yesterday, do you think they are

crooks, or do you think they are just jerks?" Mark asked in frustration, breaking the silence.

"I think they are both," Brett replied.

"I'm glad to hear that; I was hoping it wasn't just me. You know, for those crooks to give us all that shit and try to run us down and then after we helped them out — they slash our damned tires— Unbelievable! I'm an adult, so I know better, but I feel like we should go up there right now and kick their asses. Does that make me immature?"

"Yep."

"Well, you're right, of course, but still, deep down, wouldn't you like to do that?"

"Nope."

"Really—okay, then. Help me out here, Mister Mature; why not?"

"Because I already did last night, and I feel a hell of a lot better."

Mark and Trixie pulled up. Mark's temperament moved from anxious to curious. "What did you say?"

"I said, I already did last night, and I feel a hell of a lot better," Brett grinned.

"What in the hell did you do?"

Brett pulled Pepper around, so they were eye to eye. "I rode my Honda up there, parked it in some cover, jogged up to the camp, jumped the fence, searched the truck, found the cell phone, and then I lit the truck on fire and came home," Brett smiled.

"No shit?"

"No shit."

"Is the truck destroyed?"

"Yep."

"Okay, Brett, I need details."

While they rode, Brett explained it all in detail. The full version took a while longer to cover. It also had less shock appeal, but still brought satisfaction. Brett explained how frustrated he was after yesterday's journey. He was upset, just like Mark, but while he drove home and back with the spare tire, he became increasingly irritated. He had fumed while Mark waited. If they had stayed away from his rig and hadn't slashed his tires, maybe. Brett could have left it alone. Instead, they sent him a message, and since Brett never could tolerate a bully, he sent a message back. The tale enthralled Mark, and Brett's hero status moved up a peg.

Now they had a big question. Where should they go from here? They had positively determined the men at the camp were crooks. They were burglars and thieves. Tom's cell phone proved that. It went missing at the burglary of Valley Camera and then traveled to the camp—undeniable proof. Why would they hide a burglary ring in the woods? There had to be more involved. The situation was an enigma, but they knew one fact; the purpose of the camp was criminal.

The two men discussed alternatives and generated a few more. Instead of settling on a plan, they searched for better ideas, but couldn't find one. They were stuck. They enjoyed the ride and let it go until they got back to the barn. Tom had planned to meet them there, and knowing Tom, he was probably already in the clubhouse. They needed his input; he had a substantial stake in this decision. They could move toward a moral conflict, and that was a questionable line to cross.

The Riders arrived at the turnaround point on the trail. It ended on a dramatic bluff where they could see some incredible rock formations right below the tree line. After taking it all in, they circled back and rode toward home.

They wound their way back down into the draw and climbed up to the top of the ridge. This ridge was long and skinny, and as they rode west, it narrowed. They let Trixie and Pepper run until they neared the next connecting trail. The new trail ran down the steep southern exposure. They rode through a couple of tight switchbacks and then crossed the face of the ridge. The ride had a completely different feel on the downgrade. The entire valley opened up in front of them. Downtown Boise loomed like a gleaming abstract, and the Treasure Valley seemed to go on forever.

Once they bottomed out, the landscape widened out into a valley that was crisscrossed by a few intersecting trails. A horse and rider jutted out from behind a small bunch of scrub trees, and a feminine voice called out, "Hey, wait for me."

They turned to see Sage and Tonto trotting onto the trail, surging to catch them. Sage had brought Tonto up to a full gallop. Together, they rode smoothly around a couple of curves until they pulled even.

"Hi, guys," Sage beamed.

She sat tall in the saddle. She was wearing a pale violet long-sleeved shirt, slick sided Nikes, a black and gold University of Idaho Baseball Cap, and her long, dark brown hair was cascading down her back. Sage was a pretty impressive sight, but not your typical cowgirl.

"Hi, Sage," Brett and Mark bellowed in unison.

"You and Tonto are becoming quite the pair. You looked like a PRCA barrel racer the way you took those curves," Brett grinned.

"I'm not sure what that means, but thanks."

"It means you are riding Tonto like a pro," Mark said. "Except to pull it off, you need to improve your wardrobe."

"How's that?"

"If you're going to ride in a rodeo, you'll need the appropriate boots and hat."

"Okay, I'll put them on my Christmas list, and Mark, thanks so much for letting me ride Tonto," Sage smiled. "I just love him."

"You can ride anytime you want. Tonto needs the attention. And what's up with your dad? Is he coming down soon?" Mark asked.

"He's down at the barn right now. We couldn't hold him back; he's been going stir crazy. Mom dropped him off and left me in charge of getting him home. You'll see. Dad is so happy to be down there with Buck, and it looked like Buck missed him too. When we left on our ride, Dad was thoroughly grooming that horse."

"We are riding there right now, try to keep up if you can," Mark jabbed.

"You've got to be kidding," Sage challenged. "Eat our dust."

And with that, Sage and Tonto flew away.

Brett and Mark rode back to the barn, took care of their horses, and then let them loose in the pasture. Sage had rebelliously disappeared up another trail, and they hadn't seen her since. Tom was waiting inside the clubhouse. His feet were on the coffee table, and he was wearing a sly grin. Tom had a coffee cup in his hand and a fresh pot brewing. Judging by his caffeine jitters, he'd probably consumed the first pot all on his own. Brett and Mark poured coffee for themselves and joined him.

"Tom, you missed a bunch yesterday. A lot happened, and we need to talk," Brett said.

Tom was shocked at what he missed as Brett explained it all, giving Tom a thorough understanding of their encounters and where they stood. They almost had enough evidence to turn over to Agent Terry, but the critical evidence, Tom's cell phone, painted a problematic connection, namely the burglary at Valley Camera and their potentially illegal involvement. They generated a second alternative; it was Mark's idea, of course. The three of them would take another trip to the camp and dig for enough evidence to nail the crooks. They decided they needed more, and there was only one place they could find it. They all agreed. It was time to head up to the mountain camp, one more time.

First, they needed to deal with a couple of issues. Tom was confident that he felt fit enough to be part of the team. Mark demanded proof, meaning another medical exam and a complete fitness test before he would allow his friend to get on a horse and ride into a potentially dangerous situation. That pissed off Tom, who believed he was as physically fit as they were. Second, Mark mentioned that *this time*, he was bringing a gun. Brett questioned that, which surprised and pissed off Mark. Coming back together, they agreed that that afternoon after Tom's medical exam, they would go down to Boise High's Track, and they all would take Mark's fitness test. If it went well, then tomorrow they would drive out to the Rabbit Cliff Shooting Range to test their shooting. So, in fairness, everyone would have to prove themselves.

Sage had finished her ride, cooled down Tonto, and was putting her saddle back into the tack room while listening to her Dad, Brett, and Mark talk. She walked into the clubhouse area and sat down with the boys.

"Hi, guys. So, Mark, when are you going to give Dad this medical exam you have planned?"

Mark, who wasn't sure where the question came from, said, "Right away?"

"Okay, that will work out perfectly. Dad, I'm going to run home and pull out our guns and make sure they are clean. If not, tonight, we'll have to take the time to get them cleaned up and ready to shoot tomorrow. It's been a long time. I'll be back in about an hour and a half to pick you up, and then we can go home, have lunch, with enough time left to change into our workout clothes before we go down to Boise High. Okay?"

Sage stood tall with her feet spread shoulder length apart and scanned the three men, daring a challenge.

None came.

CHAPTER EIGHTEEN

Brett didn't stick around long after Sage left, which left Tom at the clubhouse along with Mark, who subjected him to another medical exam. Tom had grown weary of the continuous checkups. He swore if he were ever injured again, he'd keep it from Dr. Mark because the cure was bordering on being worse than the injury. Tom believed he was physically fit, but Mark still felt guilty about the Valley Camera incident, and he just wouldn't let it go. After the checkup, even Mark had to admit that Tom's recovery was extraordinary, but Mark still had concerns.

When Sage drove back down to the barn, her dad was riding Buck around the pasture while Mark was leaning on the fence, critically watching.

After greeting Mark, she asked, "How is he doing?"

"Remarkably well; he is one tough guy."

"Is he recovering from the concussion?"

"I never said he had a concussion. I said he *may* have one. After he took those head blows, concussion testing became medically necessary. As it played out, your dad has one hell of a hard head. He needed stitches. Beyond that, he is clear.

"I'm sure he is experiencing pain in his back, thighs and legs.

My only concern is whether he is hiding his pain and stress. That's why I asked him to ride. I'm watching his body language. Bouncing around on a horse can create discomfort, especially if you have a muscle injury."

"You mean he could be faking being well?"

"Exactly. He keeps telling me he is fine, and he is getting a bit crabby about the exams."

"Sounds like Dad. But he looks good out there on Buck. As a matter of fact, I think he is enjoying himself."

Mark turned to Sage and smiled, "I agree."

After lunch, Sage made her dad look at their guns. The last time they used them, which seemed like a long time ago, they had been cleaned and stored correctly. They were in pristine condition, ready to fire. It had been a long time since Tom taught the kids about guns, how to clean them, how to handle them, how and where to store them, and how to respect them. Tom and his kids had spent a lot of quality time together enjoying the sport of shooting. It was a great memory.

Next on the list was Mark's fitness test, initially aimed to assess Tom's condition. Now everyone would be involved, which could be interesting. Tom and Sage both changed into lightweight workout clothes and then jumped into Tom's pickup to drive down to Boise High. On their way to the truck, Tess said goodbye, kissed Tom, and with a twinkle in her eye wished him luck.

Tom grinned and gave her an extra hug. He didn't think he needed luck. He was ready.

Once in the truck, Tom said to Sage, "You know, honey, you don't need to come with us. We could run laps all afternoon."

"It sounds like fun," Sage replied.

"But when we go shooting tomorrow, you don't need to get involved. You should stay home, okay?"

"I'm going, Dad. I don't come home often, and I want to spend some time with you," Sage said firmly.

There was no way Tom could argue with that.

Even though it was Mark's deal, Brett naturally took charge. They started with stretches and a few calisthenics, and then they huddled up. It was a cloudless day with blue skies and intense sunlight. Beads of sweat already appeared, and the endurance tests hadn't started.

"Everybody, listen up. I think we should keep this simple. So, let's do a fitness run, and I mean *run*, not jog. Six laps; each lap is a quarter-mile, so a mile and a half. As I said, this is not a jog, but it's not a sprint either. It's an endurance test, so we need to run at a steady pace. That's it; is that okay with you, Mark?" Brett boomed.

"Yeah, sounds good," Mark said, looking worried.

The first couple of laps, they ran a steady pace, comfortably and together. At the beginning of the third lap, Brett was a little edgy and, with his long legs, extended his stride and pulled away. Early into the fourth lap, Sage, full of confidence, accelerated and surprised the group. Being the trimmest of the bunch, Mark became engulfed by a competitive urge and sprinted until he caught up to Sage, and then matched her new pace. Tom, who was a pretty good athlete when he was a kid, knew they had made a mistake. At a hundred yards past the mile mark, Sage and Mark were gassed. Tom carefully quickened his pace to finish strong. He sailed past Sage and Mark, who were struggling together, and on the bell lap, expanded his lead to fifty yards.

Brett finished first, and then Tom was next, followed by Sage and Mark. Mark and Sage both stood, stooped and spent, with their hands on their knees.

"You know what happens when you keep your head down, don't you? You kiss your ass goodbye," Brett scolded.

Tom smiled. He made his point.

The fun part came the next morning. Target practice at the Rabbit Cliff Shooting Range. Rabbit Cliff was in the desert about five miles off of the interstate south of Boise. It was a private club, and Brett was a member. The club owned a piece of private property that was next to a cliff that formed a natural backstop. It was a well-designed range that was safe, responsibly run, and not overwhelmed by numbers.

It seemed everyone was excited to go to the shooting range, even though the trip's justification was not to have fun; instead, it was another test. Tom and Sage both showed up with their rifles, and Sage brought her old twenty-gauge shotgun, hoping they would shoot some clay pigeons. Mark and Brett both showed up with their strapped-on pistols in their matching holsters. Brett, like Sage, also brought his twelve-gauge shotgun, hoping to shoot some flying pieces of clay.

There were several ranges set up, all separated by the type of gun fired. They all stayed together and watched each other until it was their turn. They would shoot from three postures: standing, kneeling, and prone. A professional shooting instructor named Glenn, employed by the range, ran the entire group through a firearm safety session and then led them through their paces and coached.

Brett led off at the pistol range. He wore a hearing protection headset. He started at the standing position, fired and emptied his pistol, reloaded and dropped to a knee, fired, then reloaded again and finished in the prone stance. Everyone applauded.

Glenn checked the target with his spotting scope, "Excellent marks."

Mark was up next, and he said, "I don't think I'll be as quick."

"Don't worry too much about speed; we're concerned about form and accuracy," Glenn offered.

Mark went through the same stages as Brett. He wasn't as fast, despite that, he moved from one position to another smoothly. When he finished, he felt pretty good about his effort. Once again, there was applause.

Glenn scoped the target again, checking Mark's score, and then compared it to Brett's.

"Very nice shooting Mark, and you were plenty fast enough. In reviewing the targets, your score is a little better than Brett's—congratulations," Glenn said.

"Good shooting," Brett said as he walked over and patted Mark on the back.

Tom and Sage led the way over to the rifle range, where Sage asked her dad to go first. Sage was shooting the Marlin Bolt Action 22. She had acquired it when she was a teenager. Tom was shooting a similar rifle in a larger caliber.

Tom followed the same posture progressions: standing, kneeling, and prone. It was a little different with rifles; they were more awkward to handle due to their size. Tom was successful in his efforts to shoot smoothly, and he felt his accuracy was alright.

"Checking your target, you shot an outstanding score. Nice shooting, Tom," Glenn complimented.

"Okay, let's do this," Sage smiled as she put on the headset.

She wasn't as smooth as her dad, but she was faster. She snapped from one posture to another and fired quickly. It was kind of impressive, and once again, applause erupted.

Glenn glassed the card and said, "Hey Brett, look at this."

Brett walked over to Glenn's tripod-scope setup and viewed through the scope. "Wow, incredible accuracy. This looks like a target you would see at the Olympic Games."

Brett expressed his confidence in the group, then led them over to the sporting clays range. Only he and Sage had brought shotguns, so Glenn loaned out two of Rabbit Cliff's twelve-gauge shotguns.

Brett went first and said, "Check this out. We're going to have some fun now."

Clay pigeons sailed one after another, randomly and in different directions and angles. Sometimes they flew up, sometimes straight out, sometimes left or right, but totally unpredictable. It was a great way to end the day, everyone had fun, and no one kept score.

Tom and Sage packed up their guns and said thanks to the good folks at Rabbit Cliff. They walked back to Tom's pickup. Tom sat behind the wheel and smiled. It was a good day for him—he officially was off concussion protocol.

"Dad, I have a question for you," Sage said.

"Sure, honey."

"I heard you talking to the guys about taking a ride up to that camp above Idaho City."

"Okay?"

"I want to go with you."

"Absolutely not! It's too dangerous."

CHAPTER NINETEEN

Tom delayed Detective Broom's meeting request long enough to avoid looking like a man who lost a fight. For the meeting, he wore a long-sleeve button-up shirt, slacks, and a blue blazer. Tom was covered up and looking business-like. It was as good a day as any, so Tom agreed to meet that morning at his Fairview store office. After he took a couple of weeks off giving no notification to his staff, he left behind some pending issues that could become problems. That, plus the meeting with Detective Broom, made working a half-day a good idea.

Tom and Nick huddled first to clear up a few lingering problems. Then Tom planned to meet with a couple of his manufacturer's representatives, and then Detective Broom. Once he finished with the meetings, Tom aimed to leave and stay away for the duration.

Nick and Tom cleaned up their to-do list and then met with Larry Reynolds, who sold TVA Backpacks. Nick, who was the Vice President of the company, made most of their purchasing decisions. He was an avid outdoorsman. He enjoyed purchasing the outdoor products, and he field-tested a variety of them. He liked the TVA

Backpacks but had concerns; they were a little overpriced. So, he ordered a few to see if they would sell. He believed in the old retail method: try everything, and re-order what sells. Tom, who was clinging to his limited involvement in purchasing, agreed.

Next up was Roger Carlson, from Carlson Distributing. He wasn't there to show products today; he had sales reps who worked with Nick. He just wanted a few minutes to explain a unique program. Tom and Nick were happy to see him. They were old friends.

Roger walked into the office in a bigger-than-life manner. There were handshakes and family questions; all the typical personal banter that occurs when old business friends first get together. Finally, the conversation turned to business.

"Tom, Nick, first of all, I wanted to tell you how bad I feel about the burglary," Roger offered.

"Thanks, Roger. What can I say about that kind of crap? It was awful," Tom replied.

"I heard they busted up the place, but it looks great in here now. You must have put in a lot of work to get it back in order."

"Yeah, it was a royal pain, but our crew worked hard, and we are back on our feet."

Roger shifted nervously on his feet, but Nick and Tom didn't act like they noticed his discomfort. "Do the police have any theories who committed this crime? Do they have any leads at all?"

Tom was a little slow to answer, and then Nick spoke up. "Nope, not a thing."

"Nothing?" Roger repeated.

"We are meeting with the detective on the case today, and we'll see what he has to say," Nick replied.

"Oh, I hope he has some good news for you."

"We do, too," Tom said.

"I have some good news to offer; that is why I'm here today. We know how hard it is to get back on your feet after a crime like this.

You can't sell inventory you no longer have, and you can't restock without the cash flow from that inventory. On top of that insurance claims can take months to settle and leave you in a bind. I'm here with a special offer. During the next three months, you will get special payment terms on every product you buy from Carlson Distributing and all the manufacturers we represent. Instead of the standard 30-day payment, we will give you 90-days. You can restock with confidence, knowing you won't have to pay for any of the inventory you purchase from us until you get your insurance money."

Tom and Nick both appreciated Roger's offer. It really would help to get some extended payment terms. They had a hundred-thousand-dollar hole blown into their cash flow.

It was time to meet with Detective Broom. Nick stayed with his dad so they could both meet with the detective. Roger Carlson hung around after the meeting. The store manager was an old friend who proudly gave Carlson a quick tour of their upgraded security improvements. Breaking away, he browsed as he walked down aisle after aisle and checked out how well his sourced merchandise was displayed. It was a routine review he made every time he visited one of his customers. Roger appeared to be thoroughly supportive of his dealers.

———

Brett walked into Teton Outdoors, hoping Tom hadn't finished up and gone home. He didn't come in only to see Tom; he went into the store to make a purchase. He wanted a quality portable two-way radio system to take up to the mountain camp on their next trip, hopefully, within a couple of days. They had planned on using their cell phones, but reception could be spotty up in the high country, and an improved communication system might be necessary. A sales associate let him know Tom was still in meetings, so Brett started shopping on his own. He found a compact set of waterproof multichannel radios that came in a set of four at a pretty reasonable price. Usually, he would go ahead and buy them, but in this case, he wanted Tom or Nick's recommendation since it was their store, and they were the experts.

————

The meeting with Detective Broom went pretty well. Detective Broom was a soft-spoken, cerebral individual. He was a plainclothes detective, average-sized, with bright green eyes that likely didn't miss much. He was the type of investigator that could make suspects comfortable enough to open up and talk. He was there for a couple of purposes. First, he needed to let Tom and Nick know that there were no real leads on the case. And second, keep the lines of communication open. Broom relayed that similar burglaries had occurred in both Spokane and Portland, and he believed the crimes might be related. He asked if Tom was familiar with the other victims, and if so, he might call them and compare notes. Hopefully, some useful information could arise.

Tom was supportive and business-like and agreed to follow up. He sincerely thanked the detective for his efforts. Tom didn't even consider disclosing anything about their crime-busting activities; at least, not yet.

Tom walked with Detective Broom to the front of the store, where they shook hands before the detective left. When Tom turned around, he saw Brett playing with the merchandise in the radio section.

"Hey, stop playing with the merchandise," Tom barked.

Brett threw his arms up into the air, feinting surrender with a big grin on his face. "I'm sorry, sir. Please don't call the cops."

"Okay, I'll let you off the hook this time," Tom laughed. "By the way, speaking of cops, the gentleman I just walked to the front door was Detective Broom."

"Oh, so that was Detective Broom. How did the meeting go?"

"It went well. The detective was a real nice, sincere guy who is concerned about the case. He said as of now, they don't have any leads, but he thinks it could be related to a couple of other burglaries in the region."

"Wow," Brett winked, took a breath and changed the subject.

"Tom, I was looking at getting some of these two-way radios, and I liked this set. Is this one you would recommend?"

"Yeah, we've sold a lot of those, and our customers have loved them. They are rugged and waterproof; it is an excellent choice," Tom answered.

"I don't see a distance spec listed, but I'd guess it would cover ten miles, right?" Brett asked.

"More like twenty," Tom replied.

"They are good for twenty-five miles of coverage, and they are underrated, at that," a voice behind them said.

They both turned around and saw Roger Carlson standing there.

Tom smiled and said, "This is Roger Carlson. We buy these radios and a lot of other products from him. So, when he says the radios cover twenty-five miles, they cover twenty-five miles. His company is a valuable supplier of ours, and he is a longtime friend." Tom addressed Roger, "This is Brett Wyatt. We are good friends and riding buddies."

They shook hands, and Roger looked appraisingly at Brett. "Brett Wyatt, now that is a familiar name. Hold it a second. Are you Brett Wyatt, the famous football player?"

"I don't know about famous, but I used to play a lot of football —a long time ago."

"Don't let his modesty fool you. He was All American and All-Pro. He was, and is, awesome."

"You look like you could put on the uniform and play today," Roger said.

An employee of Teton Outdoors interrupted. "Excuse me, Tom; you have a call on line two."

Tom looked back while he was on the phone. Brett and Roger were visiting; both men were smiling and appeared to be getting along well.

CHAPTER TWENTY

The sun rose above the foothills, and the sky cleared after a brief shower, leaving the sagebrush smelling sweet. The horses trotted in line with Brett riding Pepper, Tom riding Buck, and bringing up the rear was Mark, who was riding Rondo for the first time since the powerful gelding bucked him off. It was good the horse and rider were back together again.

The Riders were out for a quick trip that left time for other plans. They were riding an old favorite, the Loop Trail. The Loop Trail circled the edge of a prominent plateau that, if not protected from development, could someday become a very popular subdivision. It rolled along as a narrow track with smooth terrain and moderate elevation gains. It was a fun trail where riders of any experience could ride at the speed of their choosing. The trailhead was nearby with easy access, allowing the opportunity to ride out and back while saving time for other life matters. When they wanted to ride but had limited time, The Riders Club usually rode the loop.

After cooling down and taking care of the horses, they were surprised to find Sage in the clubhouse. She had brewed a fresh pot of coffee and was sitting on the couch, watching television. She picked up the remote, switched off the TV, smiled, and said, "Good morning, guys."

Tom looked at his daughter and closed his eyes in frustration. They had talked little since he told her she couldn't come with them on the ride to the camp. They didn't say a word to each other on the drive home from Rabbit Cliff, and now, it looked like he had a problem.

The previous night, Sage had reacted as if it didn't concern her, but Tom could tell she was thinking about it. In the evening, he hoped to talk, clear the air, and make sure his daughter was okay. Time went by as if nothing happened.

Sage spoke up quickly. "Dad, I came down here because I know it is important for us to talk about—you know what."

"Honey, I said no because I care. I can't put you in danger, and I'm sure Mark and Brett feel the same way," Tom said.

Mark and Brett had an inkling, but they weren't sure what the Coogans were talking about, and they didn't want to be involved in any family drama. They turned back toward the tack room and walked away.

"You don't need to leave. I just have a thought; I'd like you guys to hear," Sage said.

Tom waved them back. "Sit down, guys; it's okay."

Sage smiled, and that seemed to make everyone feel a little better.

"Sure, go ahead," her dad said.

"Okay, your last trip up to this camp got dicey, if not dangerous, and if I understand it right, the next trip could be worse."

The guys nodded their heads slightly, wondering what was coming next.

"Second, Brett, you guys had a problem last time, didn't you?"

"Yes," Brett said.

"They slashed your tires and left you high and dry, right?"

"Yes," Brett again answered.

"Consider this. I propose I come with you guys, and as you are riding up to this camp, I'll stay behind and guard the truck and trailer. I can ensure the rig's safety, and I can have the truck ready to roll and the trailer ready to load up the horses. So, no slashed tires, and we can leave quickly if necessary. Plus, if you guys have a problem up there, I may be in a better position to call for help. Being downhill and closer to the highway, I may have better cell service, and if necessary, I can drive the truck back to Idaho City and grab the county sheriff."

There was a moment of stunned silence, and then all eyes again fell on Tom.

"That may help," Tom said. "What do you think, Brett?"

"Sage, your idea is—pretty good. If it's okay with Mark and your dad, I think you should join us."

Everyone agreed.

———

Brett scanned every person's eyes, one at a time. "My old friend, who is a local FBI agent, has been supportive and helpful in our efforts up to this point. However, we have two problems. First, he is concerned that we may get in over our heads; imagine that," He chuckled.

Everyone smiled.

"If he knew everything that has happened, I would bet he'd ask us to back off. Plus, other than Tom's cell phone, which we can't even talk about, we don't have enough clear evidence to wrap up the case. Our goal tomorrow morning is to change that. We need to find that evidence.

"Of course, our overall goal is to nail these bastards in a way that will destroy their crime ring. Only then will we clear the air and prevent these crimes from ever happening to Tom's business and others. Only then will problems like insurance issues disappear.

Only then will these violations that destroy good people's lives go away."

Brett paused, acknowledging their support. "We need to go on this trip with a coherent plan. To start, we are going to use the joyriding cowboys cover again. I know it is almost too much, but it is believable. If we find ourselves in an adversarial position, we should be treated more like a nuisance than a problem. And with our horses, we can move quickly and quietly, especially on some trails. We need to move efficiently and communicate effectively. We need to bring a small camera that can shoot still and video images. And we may need to record audio. Sometimes, thieves and criminals can have loose lips if you allow them the opportunity to talk."

Tom interrupted, "At the store, we sell a compact Ricoh weatherproof digital camera that shoots still images and video. It also has a built-in audio recorder. I'll get us set up with them."

"Great, and Tom, I'd like you to review supplies and other needs. For example, what will Sage need at the truck?"

"I think my shotgun should do the job," Sage threw out.

"Yeah, in a life and death situation, but beyond that, I'd rather see you start with a little mace or bear spray," Tom replied.

"Bear spray is potent and debilitating, especially if you hit someone head-on; it packs one hell of a punch," Mark pointed out.

"We have four two-way radios that we will all need to monitor continuously. Sage will stay with the truck and trailer. The rest of us are going to split up. Mark and Tom will ride to the south side of the camp. Once you're there, split again, and we can triangulate the camp. One of you needs to cover the south side, while the other covers the northwest. I'll cover the northeast. We need images of the camp from all three areas to both illustrate and map it. Try to stay on the trail system that starts south of the old logging road and stay out of sight. And remember, take your pictures from as much cover as possible."

"Mark, give Tom as much detail as you can on the trails. Sit down together and study the satellite photos. If you need to, try to sketch out some trails and coach him. I don't want him to ride into any surprises."

"We'll get to that right away," Mark replied.

"I'm going to enter north of the camp, picket Pepper in cover, and then hike down and cross into the camp. Once inside, my goal is to search the outbuildings. If we are going to find hard evidence, I bet that is where we will find it. If the camp is vacant, it should be smooth sailing. I'll call you in, and all of us will search the camp in mass. If I run into problems and can't search the buildings, I will call for a diversion. Then, Mark and Tom, you'll need to pull the thieves away and draw them toward you."

"What do you have in mind for a diversion?" Mark asked.

"How about gunfire? I've got a gun that shoots blanks. It's louder than hell," Tom answered.

"If we do that, we may need to play the part of drunken cowboys if we get confronted," Mark suggested.

Brett paused, and everyone looked at Mark with raised brows for just a second. Then Brett shook it off and continued.

"I don't know about acting out as drunken cowboys, but gunfire should work. It should certainly get their attention. If we have to create a diversion, we need to be careful; their reaction could be unpredictable and possibly dangerous. If the diversion brings on a conflict, radio me immediately. I'll drop everything and come to you. Tom, after you fire the gun, keep moving and avoid confrontation. There are a lot of trails you can take to stay hidden. If the diversion works, I'll finish my search, and radio Sage when I'm ready to come back."

"Sage, I want you to be in charge of communication. You'll need to know everyone's status, and you'll need to monitor us at all times. If you think it is needed, have us check in with you. It would be efficient if you could find a basic code system for us to use. When it comes to using radios, especially communicating emergencies, locations, and issues. Brief, clear, concise communication is always best," Brett said.

"I can handle that," Sage replied.

"Let's break up and work on our assignments and then meet after dinner tonight and finalize our plan. Questions?"

Everyone sat quietly and nodded at each other.

"We will move out at dawn."

CHAPTER TWENTY-ONE

om spun the cylinder on his compact pistol and inserted a bullet into each opening, one at a time. It was a simple task, but he was struggling, and it looked like his hands were shaking when one round bounced off the floor.

"Hey man, be careful. Shouldn't you wait until we've stopped?" Brett asked.

"Too late," Tom said as he finally slid in the sixth-round. "I'm pretty stupid to try to load a gun while we're driving down a dirt road."

"Don't drop the pistol. You wouldn't want to scratch it up; it's a thing of beauty. It looks like something you'd expect to see at a wild west show. Is that a real ivory stock?" Brett asked.

"I think it is ivory-like plastic, but the other parts are nickel-plated. It is good looking, but when you hear it fired, you'll be shocked. It is so loud; I don't think we could find anything better for a diversion."

The sun still hid behind the mountains to the east, but the local birds were awake and singing, letting the world know that their day had started.

Mark was driving his burgundy F-250 V8 pickup and was

pulling his four-horse trailer. Once they arrived at the turnaround point on the dirt road, he turned the truck and trailer around, so they were aimed east back toward the highway. He then backed up into a position where they could easily load the horses and then drive straight out quickly.

The group unloaded the truck and trailer, saddled up the horses, and gathered up their gear. Mark was riding Rondo again, knowing the horse would remember the trails as well or better than he. Brett was riding Pepper, and Tom was riding Buck.

All three of the Riders carried binoculars, plus an outdoor camera that shot in multiple modes, and the firearm of their choice. Tom packed his rifle, and both Brett and Mark were carrying their pistols. Tom also brought his DSLR camera mounted with a Tamron 18-400 mm zoom lens. With a lens like that, he could shoot wide-angle and then zoom in and capture images from a great distance. The camera-lens pairing was small enough to carry it in a compact case, and it would not impair his movement while he slipped in and out of cover. This high-res setup would perform well in producing detailed images that could help them illustrate a map. And just in case, if they needed a diversion, Tom holstered his overly loud replica pistol that shot nothing but blanks.

Sage stayed with the truck and trailer. She carried two cans of bear spray that could accurately shoot a stream of the toxic mixture at least fifteen yards away. She also brought the twenty-gauge shotgun that she had fired at the Rabbit Cliff Range. They had selected a channel on their two-way radios that would hopefully keep their conversations private. Sage had put together a set of codes that would help keep their chatter down while still letting them check in at consistent intervals of time. She had the trailer tires blocked and the gate open and ready, so they could load the horses quickly and get out of there if the Riders came back on the run.

A freshly-made barricade of downed trees blocked the entrance of the old logging road. The barricade would do little to stop a horse but could slow down any wheeled vehicle. It didn't matter to the Riders because they were staying off the roads and riding some trails to allow a stealthier approach. Still, it was the first sign that the group who lived up at the camp had beefed-up security.

Brett rode Pepper north of the logging road and skirted the east side of the camp. They found a narrow wildlife trail that blended into the forest. He pulled up and dismounted to crawl into a clearing and stayed low while photographically documenting the camp's perimeter. He was making consistent progress while being as quiet as possible. The mountainous terrain was still diffusing the sun, but the eastern horizon shimmered with golden light.

Tom and Mark rode on a trail south of the old logging road. Once they arrived at the eastern edge of the camp, they split up. Like Brett, Mark rode through cover on the camp's southern border, sometimes dismounting to shoot photos, then moving back into cover, repeating the pattern as he rode west. Tom continued riding a hidden trail until he neared the camp's southwestern corner, then he followed the same pattern. Tom could get the best shots of the cabins and their inhabitants. The Riders were positioned in a triangulated design around the camp, and they were shooting a complete panoramic set of images.

Once Brett had completed his sweep of the northern edge, he backtracked to a section of barbed wire fence, well suited to cross and enter the camp. First, he rode Pepper a couple hundred yards north of the fence line through a rocky incline and into a small clearing rimmed with pine trees. He set up a picket line between two trees and picketed Pepper in an area where the horse happily munched on some tall grass. Brett then quietly worked his way back to the fence, found a spot with a robust uphill incline, and with his hand positioned on a fence pole for leverage, leaped over the barbed wire and into the camp.

The camp was pretty quiet, with the inhabitants still waking up. The interior lights were lit in a couple of the cabins and the main lodge. Brett could hear the sounds of doors opening and closing along with some quiet conversation, but that was about all.

The first outbuilding he approached was the large garage. There were not any lights on or any signs of activity. He went to the side door and found it locked, as it had been the last time. This time he was prepared; he pulled out a pair of lock picking tools. He slid the blade of a snap gun into the upper section of the keyhole and a thin tension wrench into the bottom. On the third pull of the snap gun's trigger, the lock's driver pins leveled, and with the tension wrench, he turned the tumblers and unlocked the door.

"I still got it," he whispered.

The garage was larger inside than what Brett had expected. It was big enough to both store and service vehicles. Brett saw it had three separate areas. The repair area contained a supply of tools, jacks, and parts. Next to it was a paint shop with a portable enclosure. The other side of the garage was a parking area. Six vehicles were parked; three were licensed and appeared legal. Brett shot photos of the license plates, and in a quick search of their glove boxes, he found and copied their registration and proof of insurance. There was a large white cargo van, built on a tall suspension; it was the only vehicle registered to a company instead of an individual. It was well suited to haul a heavy load.

The other three vehicles did not have license plates, and their glove boxes were empty. They appeared to be recently painted a nondescript gray. There was a passenger van with three rows of seating, and an extra-long cargo van with an empty cargo bay, plus a sizable beefy pickup truck that looked powerful enough to tear the front doors right off of a building.

The snap gun worked flawlessly on the locked door of the second outbuilding. Even though Brett was moving efficiently, time was passing, and the morning sun was bathing the camp in full daylight.

If anyone planned to work in this well-designed building, they could show up at any time. There were what looked like several work stations inside. Behind a large motorized roll-up overhead door, there was a loading and unloading area. It bordered several oversized shelving units built directly into the wall. The shelving units were empty, as was most of the building. Several large permanent tables sat in the middle of the wide-open floor space. Another set of shelves were stacked with folded boxes, ready to be filled. Packing materials were stored nearby in cardboard vats. Along the back wall was a computer with an attached small laser printer filled with a stack of shipping labels. Also on the back wall countertop were box cutters, tape dispensers, and Sharpie markers. This building was a well-designed warehouse with everything needed, except something to store and process. The building was nearly empty.

Along the far wall was an oversized garbage container filled with emptied boxes of all shapes, sizes, and colors. These were not shipping packages like the others. These were product display boxes with colorful photos and printing emblazoned upon them. And sitting on one of the shipping tables were two medium-sized boxes that appeared to be ready to ship.

Voices suddenly and loudly came through the walls. So much for acoustics. Brett heard a key in the lock, and he dove behind one of the big tables before a man opened the door and walked in. The man walked over to the garage door and pushed the button next to it. As the motorized door rolled up, the white cargo van from the garage backed up to the opening. The man that opened up the warehouse walked through the open garage door and spoke to the driver through his rolled-down window. Both men took their time; they seemed calm, indifferent, and oblivious to what could come their way.

Brett made a quick decision. He needed more time in this building. Brett wanted to finish his job and wanted to know what was in those boxes. If he got aggressive and overreacted now, he would likely have to fight his way out of this warehouse.

Instead, he put on his headset and whispered into his two-way radio and said, "Code D, repeat Code D, over."

"Code D acknowledged, repeat Code D acknowledged, over," Tom's voice replied.

Brett slid his pistol out of its holster and waited.

CHAPTER TWENTY-TWO

T his was no longer a game.

The realization hit Tom hard. The call for a diversion came in, and the next step, potentially a perilous step, was all on him. Tom had to move quickly.

"Okay—suck it up; let's go," he said to himself.

Still, his first concern was his horse; he didn't want to spook Buck. This part of the forest was dense with trees; pine needles were thick on the forest floor, and they filled the air with their refreshing scent. In a few minutes, that scent would be ruined by smoke and gunpowder. He quickly found a clearing with open skies and thinned trees, a cutback in natural acoustics, and a bit of grass for Buck. He rode Buck to the back edge of the clearing, trying to move him away from where he would fire the revolver, and then he dismounted and wound Buck's reins around a dead branch sticking out of the side of a sixty-foot-tall Ponderosa pine. Tom then hustled to the middle of the clearing, separating himself from his horse. He slid his pistol out of the holster, grasped it with both hands for a stable hold, aimed skyward thirty degrees, turned toward the camp, and fired. The sound was deafening. He wondered why he hadn't thought of ear protection. He aimed the pistol again and shot three more blasts, rapid-fire. He paused for effect, counted eight seconds, and then fired the last of his two shells. He dropped to his knees and pulled out a full box of blanks. Tom emptied the spent cylinders and quickly reloaded. The pistol was a lot easier to load when he was out of the truck and in daylight. He wanted to vary the gun's angle and its echo, so he skipped backward, closer to Buck, raised the pistol, and this time aimed almost straight up into the air. He fired three times, counted ten seconds, fired two more, and then felt one last shot would accomplish the diversion, took a couple more steps backward, again closer to Buck, and fired the final round.

The last blast was too much for Buck. As the explosions got closer, he became nervous. When Tom took one too many steps toward him and fired, he reared up, and with his sturdy neck, pulled the tied reins back hard, and then, not surprisingly, snapped the limb right off the tree. And Buck wasn't finished; he spun and galloped away into the forest with a three-foot piece of deadwood bouncing off his shoulder.

———

Mark was making good progress scouting and photographing his section of the camp when the code D transmission came in. He was on a knee, hiding behind some tall bushes and taking a photo. Mark quit the project, slid the Ricoh Camera back into its belt case, and scurried back to Rondo. Once he was back in the saddle, he adjusted his cowboy hat, dug in his heels, and urged Rondo forward. Tom couldn't be more than a mile east and shouldn't be hard to find, but it wasn't that simple with spider webbing trails leaving many alternatives. He decided to stay on the trails that were close to the camp, knowing Tom probably hadn't moved too far south since he also had been on a photo mission. Picking his way along, he kept Rondo at a canter.

Then he heard the gunfire; it was shockingly loud. If he thought that was loud, so would the bad guys. Mark needed to find Tom fast. He might need backup. The good news was that the second set of shots acted like an audio beacon, giving Mark confidence that he could narrow the source. It sounded like it came from a rocky area uphill and to his left. So they turned south and searched.

––––––––

Brett was resting on one knee, feeling trapped, listening to the two men chat away. They still sounded a little like a couple of guys who had nowhere to go and nothing to do. Then, the sound of gunfire interrupted their quiet morning. Even inside the outbuilding, the shooting sounded loud, close, and definite. One of the men hurried back inside, slapped the overhead door's control button, and promptly walked under and out of the doorway just as the door rolled down. A few seconds later, Brett heard the van driving away.

––––––––

Sage was beside herself. She felt stuck at the truck, and she didn't know what was going on except that Brett had called in a Code D, and her dad responded. She heard the gunfire clearly, even though it was a long distance away. She hoped that her dad's pistol was the only gun fired.

She thought about cutting loose the horse trailer and powering Mark's giant truck right through the crappy barricade built on the road, but she tabled that thought—for now.

She hit the transmit button on her radio and calmly said, "This is base. Status, please." Thirty seconds passed. "This is base, status, please." Thirty more seconds passed. "This is base; status needed NOW, God damn it."

"Base, everything quiet, still waiting; everything's okay," Tom sounded like he was out of breath.

"Base, I'm coming in to provide backup," Mark said purposefully.

"Base, everything's okay; will advise," Brett said.

"Thank you. Base out."

———

Jay was already standing in front of the lodge when Rick and Arnie drove up in the white van. It didn't take them more than a minute to cover the three hundred yards.

"Have you guys seen anyone sneaking around here this morning?" Jay yelled.

"We just went by both buildings, and everything was clear," Rick said.

"Somebody is doing a lot of shooting, and I don't know who or what they are shooting at. I just know I don't like it. We need to be careful, and we need to find out what the hell is going on, and we need to put a stop to it. This is total bullshit. If somebody is looking for a fight, we'll give them one. Got it?" Jay announced.

"Got it, Boss," Arnie said, while Rick nodded his head in agreement.

"Rick, you cover the front entrance east, and I'll cover it west," Jay said. "Arnie, take an ATV, go out the east side, ride south and scout the area. And before you go, strap on your guns and remember what Carlson said; if there is a confrontation, shoot first and ask questions later."

All three men ran to get their weapons when Jay paused, looked toward Arnie, and yelled, "Hey Arnie, don't wreck the fucking ATV this time!"

———

Tom walked through the trees, searching for the area where he had last seen Buck. He found the broken branch that had been swinging from Buck's reins. It was lying on the ground in an open spot between trees. Tom was glad to see it; it confirmed that he had been searching in the right direction. He was also relieved the branch had fallen away from Buck's reins; the way it was swinging, it could have hurt his horse.

Tom yelled, "Hey Buck, come back, buddy—everything is fine. Hey Buck, come back, buddy—everything is fine..."

The terrain was pretty rough. It was rocky, and the footing was uneven. It was the type of area where you could quickly turn an ankle. Tom was reminded that the cowboy boots he was wearing were made for riding, not hiking. He kept searching, working his way through the Ponderosa pines, when he ran into a small trail with moist dirt that showed hoof prints. Somewhat encouraged, he continued his chant and worked his way down the trail, checking both sides as he walked. The trail widened slightly and then intersected a much larger and definitely a higher-use trail.

Tom had a choice. Left or right, which way would a horse turn?

He guessed left and increased his pace, and then he saw it, a large fresh pile of horseshit. And it had never smelled so good.

Tom increased the speed of his pace and the volume of his chant. "Hey Buck, come back, buddy—everything is fine. Hey Buck, come back, buddy—everything is fine..."

Brett was sorting through the large garbage bin against the sidewall. There were many fitted pieces of Styrofoam and other discarded packing materials, along with the boxes they came from. If the boxes were initially on the shelves of burglarized retail stores, they might have been labeled with price tags or promotional stickers. He discovered they were, but—the tags had been carefully blacked out with a marker, leaving any useful information obliterated. Still, a black marker might not hide enough; he ripped off several box tops with the ruined tags and slipped them into his coat for further study. He also photographed several more boxes for the same reason.

He next examined the two boxes that were sitting on the shipping table. Both boxes looked ready to be shipped. They were relatively heavy and well packed. They were both addressed to the same name and address in Sparks, Nevada. However, the sender's name and return address varied on each box.

He flipped the boxes upside down and, with a box cutter, sliced opened the bottom of each one. He quickly checked out the merchandise inside. There were cameras, lenses, binoculars, and some high-end accessories. Some of them were in their original boxes with no price tags or labels affixed. Others were in plain white boxes and packed with non-standard packing materials. He estimated their value was probably at least ten grand in each box. Brett photographed a selection of merchandise from each box, and he photographed the affixed mailing labels. He then repacked the boxes, taped up the bottoms, and left them in the same spot where he had found them.

Brett slipped out the back door after he carefully made sure he left no sign of his visit. It was pretty quiet around the building and the nearby garage. He was worried about Tom and the potential confusion and conflict the diversion could bring. He hoped that after Tom had fired the blanks; he had stuck with the plan and had ridden away, met up with Mark, and then together headed back to Sage and the truck. The fence was a little harder to cross in the uphill terrain upon his return. The jump was a little more challenging, but the inner athlete in Brett made the crossing easy. Pepper had eaten most of the grass around the area he was picketed, yet he seemed content, and the horse was happy to see Brett.

———

Jay's snarky comments about Arnie's ATV wreck motivated Arnie to slow down and keep the ATV under control. He was focused on the job, driving slowly and checking the lay of the land for whoever was shooting. The east side of the camp checked out with no sign of activity, but the south side would take more time with its variety of trails. His knowledge of the trails and forest on this side of the camp was better than Jay's or Rick's, mainly because he loved to ride the ATVs during the quiet times. He had been on most of the trails a dozen times, which was probably why Jay sent him.

Arnie started his search on the trails close to the camp and then worked his way south. If anyone was still out here, they were probably within a quarter-mile of the camp's south border. The trick would be finding them without making too much noise. He drove up a narrow trail that showed signs of game, but little else. The trail petered out, so he branched off and headed back on a more significant trail when—he saw it. A riderless horse, fully saddled, trotted through the trees alone and in a bit of a hurry.

———

Tom continued hiking up the trail, repeating his chant, hoping his horse would hear. He entered a rocky area where the trees were more dispersed, allowing a little grass to grow. Buck was standing about fifty feet away. He stood there, with his head down and his ears bent back slightly, a sign of defiance. The horse appeared unharmed but didn't seem happy to see Tom. His reins were hanging free, just short of the ground. He was breathing hard and had a look of disappointment in his eyes. Tom was relieved.

"Hi, big guy—how's my buddy—you are such a good boy," Tom's soothing voice caused the horse to flick his ears. He took a few steps forward, and Buck shied away, just a little. "Come on, Buck, I am so sorry, it is my fault. You are such a good boy. Please forgive me." Buck flicked his tail and took a step forward. He really *was* a good boy.

Suddenly, a voice interrupted the exchange.

"So, you're the asshole who lost his horse, huh," Arnie shouted. He was uphill from Tom, sitting on a smooth-sided boulder with both feet dangling above the ground. The thug was wearing Levi's, a Boise State Hoodie, and a baseball cap. He wore a mocking expression and had a rifle at ready across his knees.

The guy on the rock didn't really ask a question, so Tom didn't reply. He just stared back. Tom took a good look and made an educated guess based on Mark's and Brett's description. This is the jerk named Arnie.

Arnie got a kick out of Tom's startled reaction and chuckled obnoxiously. "After I heard the gunfire, I checked out who was making all the noise, and then your horse ran by. So I stopped looking, found a seat and waited and see who'd show up, and here you are, ASSHOLE! So, why are you up here shooting that fancy pistol on your belt?"

"Why do you think it was me?" Tom asked.

"Fuck you, man!" Arnie replied. "And don't even think of grabbing that gun, or I'll blow your fucking head off. So, spill it, asshole, what are you doing up here?"

"I'm just up here riding my horse, seeing the sights, and doing a little target shooting—for the hell of it."

"So, are you with those other cowboys that were here before, you know the big guy and the doc?"

Tom was eyeing the rifle lying across Arnie's lap. Arnie was gripping it, keeping it poised to bring into action.

"I'm not sure I know who you are talking about, but yes, I'm not alone. I am here with a large group of friends," Tom expressed confidently.

"And what are you and your *large* group of friends doing here?"

"Like I said, we're just out riding our horses and doing a little target shooting."

"That's enough of your bullshit. Your buddies had been warned, and now you're back. Look at that gear you're carrying; binoculars, cameras, and of course, your fancy pistol, and you think I didn't see the rifle strapped to your horse. BULLSHIT!"

"Hey, I'm not looking for any trouble here, mister," Tom said as he held his palms up.

Arnie snapped his rifle up and aimed it at Tom. "Watch those hands, or I will shoot you. You got it?"

"No problem, no problem at all. If you want, I'll drop my pistol on the ground."

"Keep your fucking hands away from that gun! Now tell me, what in the hell are you doing snooping around our camp?"

"Like I said, we are up here riding our horses."

"Bullshit, asshole! Do you think I'm an idiot?"

Tom did.

"You are not up here joyriding. This is your last chance. What are you doing snooping around our camp?" Arnie shouted.

A spark of anger created by fear crawled up Tom's back, and by the time he could take another breath, it turned into rage. He suddenly became a creature of emotion, and then he stepped away from any form of reasonable caution.

"Now listen to me! I am up here with a large group of friends, and if you shoot that gun—there will be hell to pay. So, you better back off right now, or you'll be dead, asshole!" Tom yelled.

"I'm giving you one more chance—spill it!" Arnie said as he held his rifle steady, still aimed at Tom.

"Fuck you," Tom sneered.

"Okay, we are going to play a little game here. It's called shoot the asshole," Arnie slid the rifle's stalk against his cheek, placed his left hand under the forestock, and slid his finger near the trigger. He was careful and more precise, aiming the rifle at Tom, and was ready to shoot. But he wasn't finished talking. "First, if you move, even a little, I am going to shoot you. Second, I am going to count to three, and when I get to three, I am going to shoot you." Arnie took a breath and grinned.

Tom stiffened.

Arnie counted, "One… two…"

There was a surreal moment, where everything moved in slow motion, and the sound of gunfire seemed all-encompassing.

Mark drew his pistol, aimed, and shot Arnie.

The bullet sent him flipping backward, his head disappeared behind the boulder as his heels went vertical, and he tumbled out of sight. As he was struck by Mark's bullet, Arnie fired a wayward shot—too late.

At the same moment, Tom sprang forward in a desperate dive. He laid on the ground in a pile of dirt. The sound of gunfire came from both behind and in front of him. Tom's mind was blown. He didn't know what happened. He was alive, and his arms and legs seemed alright. He crawled into an adjacent pile of rocks as fast as he could.

Mark was still in the saddle, in a borderline catatonic state. He had shot no one before, and he had never thought or dreamed of shooting someone, ever. His pistol was still aimed at the spot where Arnie used to be. He slowly slid his gun back into its holster, stepped hard into his stirrup, and dismounted from Rondo. And then he turned away from his horse, took three small steps, bent over, and threw up.

Tom's shock level was at least on par with Mark's. He wasn't quite sure why he was alive. He pushed up from the rock pile and shook. He was alive; thank God for that. He was also all scratched from crawling around in the rocks. He stared at Mark, put two plus two together, and there was clarity instead of haze. Then he too bent over and threw up. The smell of blood, vomit, and gun smoke ruined the air.

They both just stood silently for a minute, and then Tom sucked it up and climbed up the hill to check out Arnie. He found him lying awkwardly behind his perch. There was a lot of blood, and it was coming from multiple parts on his body.

"Hey Doc, this dude is still breathing," Tom yelled.

Mark snapped out of his stupor, turned, and looked for Rondo, who hadn't wandered far. He was twenty feet away, standing nose to nose with Buck. It would be interesting to know what those horses were thinking. Mark had his outdoor med-kit tied up behind the seat of his western saddle. He quickly removed it and hustled up the fifteen-foot rise to where Arnie was lying.

Arnie laid on the ground with his legs tangled awkwardly. He looked like he was tucked in some type of impossible, unforgiving Yoga pose. He was breathing regularly, and he was out cold. Mark did a quick body check and discovered two problems. First, a gunshot wound to his arm and shoulder; it looked like the bullet followed a path cleanly through as Arnie was firmly holding the rifle's forestock while aiming. Second, as he fell backward off the boulder, he cracked his head *hard* as he took the full brunt of his failed backflip. Both his shoulder and head were bleeding heavily.

Tom had a hard time showing any sympathy for the little man who tried to kill him.

Arnie didn't look so tough now.

"What do you think, Doc?" Tom asked.

"He'll survive this. The worst of it is the head wound. He was probably knocked out from the impact. He tore up his scalp; that's why there is so much blood, and he could have a concussion."

"His head is worse than the gunshot wound?"

"Yeah, the bullet tore up his arm and shoulder, exited and kept on traveling, a half-inch to the right, and the shot probably would have missed him. It's going to be a messy cleanup, and it will probably leave an ugly scar, but with some stitches and bandages, he'll be fine."

"Are you relieved?"

"Yes," Mark choked out. "I'm not made to hurt people."

Arnie regained consciousness with no medical help from Mark. They had moved him uphill, out of the rocks, and into a smooth depression of a dirt-sand mix. It was a more comfortable position for Arnie, but a long way from being clean.

Mark quickly slipped into his doctor mode and enlisted Tom's help. Tom was nervous but happy to be Mark's go-for man, bringing blankets and water, plus it also allowed him a chance to grab his rifle from the saddle holster on Buck. His old west replica blank pistol was useless at this point. The horses were calm and happy to be together. They were untethered, watching the boys, and staying close.

Overall, their current location felt pretty safe; they were a short distance away from the trail in a wooded area, so they would be easy to miss, as long as they were quiet. Still, Tom encouraged some urgency, since the troops at the camp would come searching, and eventually, they would find them. The question now was how long Mark's medical care would take.

Tom knew he had to support Mark's medical effort, especially after Mark felt personally responsible, but it wasn't that simple. Arnie had tried to kill him, an experience he would never forget.

At first, Arnie's eyes wandered over his surroundings, neither awake nor asleep. Then, a look of awareness filled his eyes; awareness with a good deal of understandable confusion. "Doc," he said as he looked at Mark with a note of question.

"Yeah, Arnie, it's me. You have been shot, and you have hit your head hard, and I'm here to help," He held up his hand. "How many fingers am I holding up?"

"Three," Arnie said.

Tom suddenly grabbed Mark by the shoulders, turned him, pushed him away from Arnie, and took Mark's spot. "That is good enough; I've got him right now, give me a minute."

"Absolutely not!" Mark said, wide-eyed and alarmed, vehemently protesting.

"This guy just tried to kill me. Give me a couple of minutes, and you can have him back." Tom glared.

Mark glared back but didn't respond this time.

Tom moved face-to-face with Arnie. "You remember me, asshole?"

"Yes," Arnie squeaked.

"You were going to kill me, remember that?"

"I guess."

"And then what happened, do you remember?"

"There was gunfire, and—did you shoot me?"

"No asshole, I didn't shoot you. You had me covered, remember?"

"Yeah, so who did?"

"You really don't remember?"

"No, everything is—I don't know."

"So, I'll explain," Tom said.

"No, let me explain," Mark said. He felt it was his responsibility to answer.

"I'm doing the talking here! Back off for a minute, Doc," Tom said aggressively.

He moved in closer, his face inches away from Arnie's. "You were sitting up there on that boulder, and you were counting to three, and then you were going to shoot me. Remember that, asshole?"

Arnie closed his eyes as if his pain level increased, "Yeah."

"When you counted to two, I dove into the dirt, and you—you weren't set, so you lost your balance and fell backward right off the boulder and landed headfirst into a pile of rocks. But the best part is, you little piece of shit, the best part is you fired your rifle on the way down, and guess what? The ricochet hit you. You shot yourself, asshole! Now, do you remember?"

Arnie's head was hurting, and he looked somewhat stupefied. "Yeah, I remember."

Mark could hardly believe what he heard, a revision in history that got him off the hook, but all he really cared about right now was treating his patient. "That is enough, you're finished, and I need to take care of this man, right now!"

Tom blocked his access as if he were an offensive lineman protecting his quarterback. "No! I'm not finished yet; give me a couple more minutes."

Then he started back at Arnie, "You see the doc here cares, and I don't. You have some artery damage, and you could bleed out. What I care about is answers, answers from you. If you give me the answers quickly, you may not die, but if you don't… and don't you dare pass out. Got it?"

"I've got it," A terrified Arnie said.

Tom pushed the video record button on his chest-mounted camera. He deeply hoped Mark would forgive him. "First question: You're the guys who burglarized Teton Outdoors and tried to rob Valley Camera, right?"

"Yes," Arnie whined.

"Second question…"

CHAPTER TWENTY-THREE

Sage thought she heard a motorcycle's winding sound, but she couldn't see anything yet. She sat in a folding chair behind the trailer while taking in the view of the trailheads and the old logging road. Sage had a pretty good vantage point; it would be difficult to sneak up on her unnoticed. She lounged in her chair, sipping a Coke she found in the trailer's cabin. And she had a book on her lap that she wasn't reading. Sage kept her eyes peeled while playing her part.

The guys had been communicating with the radio set, talking to her and each other. The code system kept their talk down to essentials but left many unanswered questions, at least on Sage's end. Tom and Mark called in and reported that they were together and okay, and they were cleaning up after a confrontation, whatever that meant. Brett was riding fast on a trail that ran wide of the camp. Brett wanted to make sure that Tom and Mark were okay. And Sage was sitting there, wondering if she could do more to help.

———

Jay and Rick rode together on their UTV, scouting the south side of the camp. They were searching for trespassers, and for Arnie. They hadn't seen or heard from him for a long time, but it was Arnie, so he could be way out, patrolling half of Boise County. Jay called Arnie's cell and ended up in voice mail, which was typical; the reception was pretty spotty. It had been a while since they had heard any gunfire, just a couple of shots since the early barrage. So far, the two of them had seen no sign of trespassers or any trace of vehicles or horses. Hopefully, the noisemakers were a long distance away.

————

Sage heard the engine sound again; this time, it sounded closer. She scanned the area and finally spotted the UTV. It stopped behind the pile of trees blocking the logging road, but it was there. The two men aboard shut it down, stepped out, and climbed around the barricade. They were dressed like outdoorsmen, in boots and coats, and they were looking around the area. Then they spotted her. One of them had a pair of binoculars and used them to check her out. Sage felt a little uncomfortable, then thought it over for a second and reacted. She stood up from her chair and looked straight at the Peeping Toms. She beamed out her beautiful smile and waved a friendly wave at the duo.

One of the two men raised his hand and responded with a weak wave of recognition. Their body language looked uncomfortable as they climbed around the barricade, stepped back into their UTV, and drove away.

"Mission accomplished," Sage said to herself.

————

After Mark sewed up Arnie's head, he cleaned, disinfected, medicated, and bandaged his arm and shoulder. It would be sore and messy for a while, but as long as it didn't get infected, it would heal and leave a rough scar, especially in the spots where the skin looked like ground beef. Mark once again left Arnie with medicine and instructions and ordered him to rest. He advised him to see a doctor, especially if he had any concussion symptoms or infection. Arnie was appreciative and thanked Mark. He wouldn't have been so grateful if he knew who shot him.

Tom searched the area until he found Arnie's ATV about an eighth of a mile away. He made a simple decision not to trust Arnie, even in his wounded condition. He hid Arnie's rifle and ammo and explained that they would be safe until he healed up enough to return and search for them. Tom gave him a couple of hints that would help him locate it and warned that it would take some time. With Tom on one side and Mark on the other, they walked him to his ATV, where they helped him get set for the one-armed drive home. They then lied and told him they were camping a little to the south and warned him to stay away. Arnie agreed quickly. He wanted no more of these guys.

Tom was eager to get back to the truck and trailer. He wanted to get out of there before anything else crazy happened. He was eager to see Sage, and he was concerned about Mark, who seemed to be quietly steaming. They were riding side by side, closing in on the trailhead.

Tom broke the quiet and said, "Mark… thank you."

"For what?"

"You save my life back there—thank you."

"You're welcome, but I just wish you didn't have to go Dirty Harry on that guy."

"I understand, and I'm sorry. I couldn't pass up the chance to solve this whole thing. You know, we probably learned enough to bust the entire crime ring, which was our goal."

"Yeah, we did a pretty good job, but we may have crossed the line a bit there. My God, you told him he had artery damage, and he could bleed out. You scared the hell out of him."

"Yeah, I'll give you that, but we talked, and you told me he wasn't that bad. You said he only needed bandages and stitches, so I felt I wasn't putting him in any real danger. If he was at risk, I would have never done that. But honestly, I don't give a shit if I scared him. He sure as hell scared me."

"Okay, I guess that makes me feel a little better. I'll admit that this guy was a total asshole."

"Mark, look at what we may have accomplished. I think we've done it! We're going to bust these guys and were going to stop the burglaries. We may have saved my business."

"Sometimes you have to do what needs to be done, right?" Mark smiled.

"Absolutely, but you know what we did back there? We played good-cop, bad-cop," Tom jabbed.

"Yes, that's what we did, but next time, Tom—I want to be the bad cop."

"What are you talking about? You were this time."

Suddenly, they heard a noise ahead, and Brett and Pepper rode up from an intersecting trail and burst into the area in front of them. "Hey, guys. I'm glad to finally find you. I've been riding every trail around here. Are you okay?"

"We're good," Tom answered.

"Right, we're good," Mark agreed.

"Alright. We'll talk about it later."

He called in on his radio. "Base, all accounted for—Code H."

"Code H, acknowledged," Sage returned. "They're coming in hot. Get moving."

"Follow me!" Brett yelled. He turned Pepper toward home, and they took off at a gallop.

CHAPTER TWENTY-FOUR

The Riders Club was a cheerful bunch. Their confidence was soaring, their attitude upbeat, and their emotions were sky high. They were ready to celebrate. Brett couldn't help but wonder how the crooks at the camp were feeling. If they could connect the dots, it might lead them back to the joyriding cowboys. Still, they probably didn't know what happened this morning unless Arnie talked, which seemed unlikely.

It was good to be back at the barn. As usual, the rider's priority was to unload and take care of the horses. When they arrived back at the trailhead, Sage had the trailer ready for loading and a quick getaway. Usually, they unsaddled the horses, let them cool down, and cleaned them up before loading. This time, they loaded the horses, saddles on, and got out of there. Once they were back at the barn, they got busy unsaddling, brushing, watering, and feeding. After they got everything taken care of, the horses were in the pasture, happily grazing.

Mark raided the fridge and started a fire in the pit. He set out a cooler with a selection of local beer, along with hotdogs, buns, chips, ketchup, and mustard. Four chairs ringed the fire pit, seating four wannabe chefs, each holding a hotdog or two on a stick. They were roasting them to perfection.

"Hey guys, this is fun, but don't you tire of hotdogs and beer?" Sage asked.

As a unit, the three men turned and looked at her as if she was crazy.

"Sorry, stupid question," she said.

Everyone relaxed and enjoyed lunch, and then Brett brought the group back on to the point. "I wanted to let you know how good I feel about the job we did this morning. We acted as a team, and everyone contributed at a high level. Sage, that means you, too. You not only did your part, but you also provided leadership at a critical time."

All three men raised their beers as Sage smiled.

"So now," Brett continued, "Let's get everyone's perspective on what happened today. I'd also like to borrow the memory cards from your cameras. I'll pull the photos, videos, and audio files from them, and I'll try to compile them in a way to illustrate what we've learned."

Sage told everyone her story about how the two guys on the UTV checked her out and then ran off after she waved. The crooks probably would have trashed the truck and trailer if she wasn't there. Brett explained his experience and what he found, leaving the big story from Tom and Mark for last. Brett detailed how the outbuildings exhibited the look of a wholesale distribution center: well-designed, and no doubt efficient.

Tom's story started where he fired the barrage of blanks with his pistol. He was thrilled that it was so loud, everyone agreed, and Brett even asked Tom if they could go out and shoot sometime. He'd like to see it in action. Then Tom explained how he lost Buck and tracked him down. The story seemed humorous at Tom's expense until they got to the point where he told them how Arnie got the drop on him. It was horrifying.

"Mark, is it alright if I turn it over to you now?" Tom asked.

"I guess," Mark was hesitant; he wasn't proud of his actions. He gazed down when he talked. "Well, here's the story. After Brett called for the diversion, I packed up and rode east and looked for Tom. I was lucky to find his trail. A couple of patches of horse manure sent me in the right direction, and then I heard their voices; they were yelling at each other. Arnie looked ready to shoot when I rode up, and with his focus on Tom, he didn't see me. So, I stopped —just in time. And within a few seconds, Arnie started his one, two, three-thing. I shot him on two…" Mark sobbed.

Tom interrupted, "That is enough. I'll take it from here. Mark told me he isn't made to hurt people, and that's true. He is too good of a person. Still, Mark helped Arnie. He cleaned him, sewed him up, and gave him medicine. It was a good outcome, and Mark has nothing to feel guilty about, ever. And Mark *saved* my life.

"After Mark had determined that Arnie would be okay, just beaten up and sore, but not in serious condition. We did a good-cop bad-cop thing on him. I asked him questions and pressed him for answers. He completely folded and told us everything, and we recorded the entire confession."

"I can't wait to watch the video, but give us the short version. What questions did you ask?" Brett urged.

"Okay, let me think… Did you rob Teton Outdoors and Valley Camera? How many people are involved? How often and how long have you been doing this? Where did you bring the stolen merchandise? What do you do with it? What is the purpose of the camp? Why is it here? Who is your boss? There may be more, but there you go."

"Holy shit, Tom. You should be a professional interrogator. So, they start here, and then they travel to other cities like Spokane or Salt Lake?" Brett asked.

"Exactly, and then they ship it out to Nevada to be sold off," Tom replied.

"How long have they been doing it?" Sage asked.

"A few years."

"Oh, my," Sage then asked Brett, "Doesn't that solve the pattern question you have?"

"I'm not sure I see a pattern," Brett said.

"Spokes on the wheel, that's the pattern."

"How's that?"

"You see. Boise is the hub, and places like Spokane and Salt Lake are on the wheel. The crooks don't travel from Spokane to Salt Lake. They rob Spokane, come back down the spokes to Boise, get rid of the merchandise, go up another spoke to Salt Lake, and repeat the process. They control their travel, drop off the merchandise, and head out in another direction. It is very efficient and appears to be random, but it isn't."

"But their camp isn't convenient. It's out in the middle of nowhere."

"I disagree. When the thieves are on the job, they probably drive on Interstate 84 and take the Highway 21 exit. Then, they stay on the highway and drive sixty-five all the way to the camp. They don't drive through town like we have to. The camp is less than an hour from the interstate, and it's in total seclusion. It's a perfect setup."

"Spokes on the wheel, huh? It makes total sense. Why didn't I see that? Great analysis, Sage," Brett complemented.

"Thanks, I look forward to seeing all the evidence tonight. It will be *so* interesting," Sage said.

"Tom, who did he say was his boss?" Brett asked.

"He said his name is Jay. I don't think he gave us his last name," Tom replied.

"Okay, that helps. Remember the guy on the ATV who told us to stay away after the first trip? I knew I had known him from somewhere. Now I've got it. Jay—his name is Jay Peters. He used to play linebacker for Boise State. He played the last couple of years

I was at Wyoming. He was a good ballplayer, and sometimes the press compared us to each other. But he was a dirty player. They called him Jay the Pain because of his dirty hits. Everybody said he would make it in the NFL, but he didn't. He had the ability, but he didn't have the smarts. He played dirty instead of playing smart. A good football player is smart, but not this guy. It sounds like he hasn't changed."

CHAPTER TWENTY-FIVE

Roger Carlson was a man of mixed emotions, but his primary emotions were fear and greed, and for him, greed almost always won out. Today was different; he was considering calling his partner in crime, and this partner was all about the emotion of fear.

Tony Levitt didn't manage Prime Goods Brokers, but he had oversight at the highest level, as he no doubt had at multiple other businesses. His corporate title was chairperson, but he related to the unofficial moniker of fixer. He was a fixer; that is what he did, and that is who he was. So far, his involvement with Roger Carlson and the boys had been smooth and profitable, and he was happy with that. Plus, Tony expected the trend to continue forever. The truth was, Tony scared Roger. That is where the emotion of *fear* came in. Roger's feeling was more than reasonable. Tony Levitt was foremost a man to be feared; he built his career upon a hard-core system of zero tolerance. Still, if you are involved with the Devil, his help can come in handy. If you need help with a negative issue, one you can't stomach, call him, he can fix problems like no other.

And then there was the greed side of the equation. Tony had the skills to help, and his assistance could help build profits. Since the beginning of their association, Tony had offered Roger an open door. Roger remembered the conversation.

"If you have a problem that is too big for you to handle, call me. I'll take care of it. If you have an issue, you're not sure how to handle, give me a call. I'll take care of that, too. If you are involved with a question you want to deal with, but you need a little help or a second opinion, give me a call on that, too. I'll check it out for you and try to help. I've had a lot of experience with tough issues. We have a business relationship here, and we need to depend on each other. It is a two-way street. Together, we should make a pile of money."

Roger pulled his cell phone from his pocket and tapped in a number he had committed to memory, Tony's phone number. After one ring, Tony answered, "Hello, Roger. How is everything in Idaho?"

———

Earlier that day, Roger sat with the boys at the camp's main lodge. Arnie removed the bandage that ran from his left elbow and extended up to his shoulder.

"Wow, it looks like someone stuck a screwdriver in your arm and then ripped you right through your shoulder. And someone told you it was a gunshot wound?" Roger asked.

"Yeah, and they said it traveled as you said, like a screwdriver, but it was a bullet."

"I don't see any gunpowder burns," Roger commented.

"That's because it was a ricochet."

"From your gun?"

"That's what they said."

"They said. There is that comment again. Is that what you remember?"

"I guess. I was knocked out cold, so it's fuzzy."

"But your head wound wasn't from a bullet. It was from a fall, right?"

"Yeah, that is what they said—sorry."

"So, who are they?" Roger pressed.

"It's the doc. I don't know his name, but he is a doctor. He's the one who bandaged me up and stuff, both times."

"And the other guy?"

"I don't know his name, but he is a real asshole. He's a middle-aged guy, six feet, blondish, and kind of husky. The doc was okay, but the other guy is a piece of work."

Roger opened his 13-inch laptop. He connected to the Teton Outdoors home page, clicked on the about us tab, pulled up a photo of Tom, and showed it to Arnie.

"Yeah, that's him," Arnie read the listing and said, "He's the owner of Teton Outdoors. Holy shit."

"What were they doing out there?" Roger asked.

"This Tom guy was out there, riding his horse, and he was all by himself. He had this fancy, old-style revolver, and he was shooting it and making one hell of a racket," Arnie said.

"I never saw him, but I sure as hell heard him. That's why I sent Arnie out there to see what was going on while Rick and I checked out our borders," Jay added.

"And you guys saw no one?" Roger said.

"Right, we did a full sweep and didn't see anyone. We went back and checked the buildings, and they were locked and untouched. We got nothing," Jay replied.

"So, at the same time, Arnie got shot. This is so weird. Arnie, tell me what happened."

"This asshole guy Tom had lost his horse, and I found it. What a dipshit. He probably scared the horse when he was shooting his guns. He had binoculars and a camera. I figured he was snooping around. I got the drop on him and asked him what was going on, and then I ended up shot and shit. And that's when the doc showed up and fixed me up."

"What did he say he was doing up there?"

"He said that he was riding around and doing some target shooting. But I think he was full of shit. I think he was snooping around."

"If they were snooping around, it's probably not a problem unless there is a connection with the police. Has anyone seen even the slightest sign of police activity?"

The guys all shook their heads no.

"I guess the cops don't ride horses around here, so that's a good sign," Roger commented."

Everyone chuckled.

"Jay, do you have any thoughts on the whole deal?" Roger asked.

"Not really, Arnie saw these guys about a half-mile away, and Rick and I covered everything closer in, and like I said, saw nothing. I don't know if these guys are a problem or not. They may be just a bunch of jerks that lose their horses. I don't get it; it's just so weird."

"Yeah, that's the operative word: weird. I don't know if we have an issue here. I want to get back in business, but I don't know what to think of these guys. Are they a problem or not?"

"I don't want to sound like a broken record, but should we ask Mr. Levitt what he thinks?" Jay asked.

"I like to take care of our business here independently. I take pride in the fact that our team is strong enough to hold up our end with no outside help. I only call Levitt if we have a problem we can't solve. However, *weird* may qualify. We know who two of the cowboys are, and I think I can figure out who the good doctor is. Yeah, the time has come; let's see if Levitt can help," Roger said. "And Arnie, I forgot to ask you something. When the doc was sewing you up, did they ask you questions about what is going on up here?"

"No," Arnie lied.

CHAPTER TWENTY-SIX

Brett felt comfortable being in charge. He had hooked his laptop up to the big screen, a bit of overkill, but better than four people crowded around a small screen. He had downloaded all the SD cards and organized the images. The Riders Club were all there, plus Sage; it was time for serious business. Everyone felt keyed up, almost nervous.

Brett could tell they were ready to go. "I'm going to start with the recording of Arnie's confession. It is by far the most critical piece of information we have, but I have to warn you; it is rough, real rough. Arnie is injured and scared, and Tom doesn't show much sympathy."

The video started with a wide-angle shot of Arnie's mid-section. His face was out of the frame, but you could see his left arm and what was left of his shirt after the bullet had gone through. There was a large patch of bloody, ripped-up flesh, but it was nothing the group couldn't handle. As the video progressed, there were multiple camera angles as Tom changed positions, including some head and shoulder shots showing Arnie's agony and fear. Everyone watched apprehensively.

Tom questioned Arnie in a steady, almost business-like manner, probably a practiced benefit of management dealings with customers and employees every day. He was used to being the boss, and his comfortable verbal strength showed. He moved from question to question, covering the key areas, and he continually increased the pace of the interview because he was feeling time-pressure from Mark. Everyone watched in silence. It was tough to watch, but Tom's focused questions brought illuminating answers that brought gasps.

Arnie struggled when Tom asked, "What did you do with the merchandise, and where did you ship it?" Arnie was wearing out; he was very stressed and panicky. He was pale, and his eyes seemed to have sunk in as he lay in the dirt and answered questions, almost irrationally. Twice, Arnie begged for Tom to stop, and asked Mark the doc to stop his mythical bleeding. As panic set in, he slurred his words. The interview was falling apart fast.

Mark asked Brett to pause the playback, "What did he say? 'They sent the merchandise to sharks.' What the hell does that mean?"

"Play it another thirty seconds," Tom said, "I think I asked him again."

"I told you we shipped it to sharks—please—stop," Arnie pled.

"That didn't help," Brett said with a shake of his head and a small smile. "He's either talking about a name, a business, or a destination. It's hard to tell. When I was in their warehouse, I shot photos of a couple of their shipping labels. We can check them to see if there is a connection."

The outdoor photos of the camp helped show the lay of the land, but had little value otherwise. Brett thought the images of the outbuildings were more critical in defining the crook's crime ring. And he was right; everyone leaned forward and studied the photos of the garage and the warehouse. Both told the story, but the shots in the warehouse connected the dots. The crooks returned from their burglaries and dropped off the merchandise at the warehouse where they sorted, cleaned, and, if needed, re-boxed it. And then they shipped it out to a company or someone with the ability to sell stolen goods.

Brett displayed the shipping labels on the big screen. Where the return addresses varied from box to box, the shipping address remained the same. The packages were all sent to PGB, Inc. in Sparks, Nevada.

"So, Arnie was saying Sparks, not sharks; that makes sense, but I've never heard of PGB Inc. Tom, does that mean anything to you?" Brett asked.

Tom sat in a comfortable leather chair at the corner of the coffee table facing the big screen. He leaned forward with his palm on his forehead. "Yes, it does. I'm very familiar with them. I do a fair amount of business with them. Jesus, could they be involved in... all of this?"

It was hard for Tom to take—getting screwed by people he trusted.

"Dad, is that one of Roger's companies?" Sage asked.

"Yeah, he reps them, but he doesn't own PGB if that even matters."

"Can you catch us up here?" Brett asked.

"Sure. PGB stands for Prime Goods Brokers. They're a wholesale company that sells class two, used and overstock goods to retailers at a cheap price. They are the dominant player nationally in their space. And they specialize in electronics, photo, and optical products."

"What is class two?" Mark asked.

"Have you ever wondered what happens to all of those products people return to the big online retailers? Often, they don't resell them as new, even if they are perfect. Instead, they classified them as 'class two.' It's kind of like refurbished products. Companies like PGB buy them up and will sell them to other retailers," Tom quietly laughed to himself. "At least I thought they bought them. They have a limited warranty and can be an excellent value for the consumer. From time to time, we have purchased them. It makes me wonder if I have unknowingly repurchased some products that they stole from us."

"So, who is Roger?" Mark asked.

"Roger owns a company called Carlson Distributing. He represents several major brands, one of which is PGB. We are old friends—hell, we've had him over for dinner and drinks. That's why Sage knows him. He has a summer home outside of town toward Idaho City. Oh, my God, his place is about halfway to the crook's camp." Tom slapped his forehead.

"Is that the same Roger you introduced me to at your store?" Brett asked.

"Yeah, it is the same guy."

"He came off with quite the personality. He asked me about football and moved on to horsemanship, the whole deal. He certainly got me talking. I told him everything. He knows about the barn and our horses. I told him how the three of us go riding all the time."

Everyone was silent for a couple of minutes. Everyone was thinking.

"We have to assume that by now, Roger knows everything about all of us. He knows where we work, where we sleep, and what we do. And if he knows all of that, who else does?" Brett wondered.

CHAPTER TWENTY-SEVEN

Tony Levitt was sitting in his corner office on the 12th floor of an older yet still viable casino-resort in Reno, Nevada. He was thinking about Roger Carlson, his problem child in Idaho. After talking to Roger, Tony contacted two key employees he often used to deal with security issues. Both men were masters of their approach; one dealt with computer information systems, where he could quickly and effectively vet history and backgrounds. The second man was more of a soldier who dealt with challenging issues in person. Tony had confidence in both men. They had worked together for years, and he felt they were both loyal and capable. He wished he felt the same way about Roger Carlson.

Carlson's call had set the ball rolling, which pleased Tony. If there was a security issue in their line of work, it needed to be addressed immediately. Typically, Roger had been a little too distant, which may have been a sign of independence or possibly a sign of denial. Tony felt it was likely the latter. Roger was afraid of him, and he was scared to make the tough decisions needed when you worked in the shadows of legality. Tony felt Roger was a sneaky, vain man, certainly not a person who could be considered a friend. But business is business, and as long as Carlson could bring in the goods, everything was peaches. Still, Tony's gut told him Carlson might be a risk. Tony would check out the situation in Idaho, and if his gut feelings proved correct, it could be the end of Roger Carlson.

Tony's phone rang for the second time today with an incoming call from Idaho, this time from Jay Peters.

Tony checked the caller I.D. and answered, "Hello Jay, It's good to hear from you. You're my second call from Idaho today."

"Thank you, Mr. Levitt, so Roger did call you. I'm glad."

"I am too. Give me your thoughts on these problem cowboys."

Jay and Tony discussed the situation, and Jay told a very similar story to the one Roger had relayed to him earlier in the day. Jay could give a little more thorough background on Brett Wyatt, namely his history as an NFL football player who had a significant enough career to support him in style for the rest of his life. When they finished their discussion, Tony understood Jay's discomfort and confusion with the cowboy problem, and he understood the possibility that this investigation may be an exercise in futility. It might merely be a case of a few rich guys pretending to be cowboys. Why adult men would ride horses and pretend to be cowboys, he couldn't figure. The only horses Tony had ever seen were in the movies. The situation was possibly a farce, but he couldn't get by his core belief that weird coincidences don't exist.

"So, you used to play college football, and that is where you knew of this Wyatt guy?" Tony asked.

"Yeah, I played against him at the beginning of my time at BSU. I don't know the guy; I know of him. But Roger has met him."

"What? Roger knows Wyatt?" Tony was startled.

"Yeah, he met him while he was at a business meeting at Teton Outdoors."

"What do you mean?"

"Teton Outdoors was our last successful job. Roger knows our victims, so he went down there to see how quickly they recovered, and then I think he tried to sell them more stuff."

"Well, that sounds pretty smart, as long as he doesn't get too close. Roger told me he dealt with Coogan, the store owner, and if I understand it right, he knows all of his victims, and he cases their stores. But I didn't know about Wyatt." Tony's voice leaked concern.

"Roger told us Tom Coogan introduced them while they were both at the store. I think it surprised Roger too. They just had a brief conversation, and I don't think there is anything to worry about."

After a momentary pause, Tony said, "I'm sending a specialist to investigate. He will fly in tomorrow. No one knows anything about this except you, him, and me. And I want to keep it that way. Do you understand?"

"Yes, sir," said Jay. "Would you like my help with anything?"

"As of right now, if he needs any help, he will contact you. He knows about the camp and he may visit you there. If he does, I want you to give him your total support. He is an expert, and if he deems it necessary, he will take charge. Do you have questions?"

"No, sir."

"I appreciate your support, Jay. I'm concerned that Roger may not be able to handle the tough problems, so I'm counting on you."

After the conversation ended, Tony made another call.

"Joe here," a voice said.

"Did you receive my information?" Tony asked.

"Yes, I did."

"Do you have any questions?"

"No, it seems clear."

"One extra item, Roger Carlson, could be a little too close to a couple of these cowboys. He knows Coogan very well, and Coogan owns Teton Outdoors."

"I don't like that twist; having a prior burglary victim involved is concerning. That brings up the risk level."

"I just found out he knows Brett Wyatt too. Coogan introduced them."

"That is even worse," Joe commented. "So now I need to add Carlson to my list and check him out. I wonder what he's thinking. These are his victims."

"I need you to fly to Boise in the morning. Check out the situation and report back. If I find out anything else on my end, I will let you know." Tony said.

"Alright, I will have wheels up at dawn."

"This may be a fire drill. These cowboys could be clueless fools who are harmless. If that is the case, scare them off. If not, harsher measures will be needed. Either way, their presence is disrupting business, and we need that disruption stopped.

"And above all, if Carlson is talking to the wrong people, then we all could be at risk. The situation is fluid and is growing; the Carlson question is now your top priority."

"Agreed, I will follow up with you tomorrow," Joe said.

"This could be a cakewalk, or this could be a war," Tony advised.

"Either way, I don't care."

CHAPTER TWENTY-EIGHT

Brett contacted Agent Terry after the meeting at the clubhouse. His old friend was as helpful as ever, happily volunteering to meet at Brett's house. He dressed casually, wearing chinos, trails shoes, and a dark polo shirt. In the office, he usually worked in a dark suit, a starched white shirt, and a reasonably conservative tie. Of course, on the job or in the field, he wore whatever was appropriate for the investigation at hand, whether it was a t-shirt and jeans or a tux.

In his casual clothes, it was apparent he was built like a rock. Agent Terry took the time needed to keep fit. He ran early every morning, lifted weights several times a week, and consistently practiced his combat skills. He had a natural gift of observation, with cop eyes that swept every scene. He was average height with neat short black hair, large brown eyes, and a strong jawline. He was younger than Brett and had joined the FBI after one enlistment term in the Marine Corps. Agent Terry was an impressive figure and a skilled agent, and Brett felt good having such a powerful advocate on their side.

DeShawn had never visited Brett at his house off of Willow Creek Road. Being a man with acute observation skills, he was wide-eyed when he walked into the entry. Brett led him into the kitchen where his laptop was waiting. DeShawn looked across the family room with its back wall made of glass. "You have one hell of a view here," he said.

"You want to go out on the deck and check it out?" Brett asked.

"Yeah, I would."

They slid open the door on the house's back wall and walked out on the suspended deck. The deck was large for any home, especially a two-bedroom bachelor pad. A local furniture store tastefully furnished it with a matched set of furniture, including a heavy metal outdoor table, comfortable cushioned chairs, and of course, a barbecue grill and a gas fire pit. There was a motorized roof that covered over half of the deck, for the times when the sun could be a little too intense. DeShawn walked to the edge of the deck, stood, and admired the view. Then, he looked down at the fifty-foot drop onto a steep downslope covered in sagebrush and grass.

"If I lived here, I don't think I would ever go inside," DeShawn said.

"I know how you feel," Brett replied. "Sometimes, I sit out here all night."

"It's beautiful, man."

A short time later, they sat down at Brett's kitchen table with a pot of coffee and Brett's laptop. Brett had cleaned up the quantity and the order of the images, leaving out a lot of the redundant elements. His presentation began with the basics and then built from there. He started with the camp's layout, the well-designed outbuildings, the main lodge, and the individual living cabins. He explained his theory on the use of the different vehicles and the warehouse functions. He then showed his photos of the received merchandise and the outgoing shipments. After which, Brett scrolled to the warehouse photos of the mailing labels, with the addressee: PGB, in Sparks, Nevada. And then he explained the tie-in with PGB's representation from Roger Carlson.

Brett saved the video of Arnie's confession for last. The impactful confession helped connect the facts, and those facts supported the spokes on the wheel theory.

Agent DeShawn Terry intensely watched the video. His expression continually changed from deadpan to surprised to uneasy. Brett could sympathize, he reacted the same way when he first watched Arnie squirm and suffer while Tom Coogan interrogated him. Still, Brett stayed silent and let the FBI agent come to his conclusions. He didn't want to color the video with his take; he wanted Agent Terry's findings to be strictly his own. When the footage concluded, Agent Terry turned to Brett and shook his head, astonished.

"What do you think?" Brett asked.

"That was unbelievable. I can't say I've ever seen anything like it. It was like a scene out of Desert Storm."

"In your opinion, how clear is the evidence?"

"Crystal! But, will it be admissible in court?"

A few minutes later, Brett watched Agent Terry as he took control of the laptop and double-checked some details. He had asked for some time to review the entirety of Brett's presentation. He was sorting the data, checking it for logic, and he was mentally building the case. Brett could almost read the FBI agent's mind by the flashing of his eyes.

"Where do you think we are at?" Brett asked after he hoped he had given Agent Terry enough time.

"I believe it is time. We need to act now, and we should move quickly." Agent Terry replied.

"I agree."

"The case has a few problems that we need to tackle. Arnie's confession is probably a non-starter. We can use it outside the courtroom and probably scare the hell out of any defense attorney, but that is about it. I'd be shocked if it was allowed in court. Plus, we don't have a name to pursue in this PGB Company. It smells like an organized crime venture to me, which could expand the case, but we must have names. And since this Carlson character knows who you are—so could some other people, dangerous people. It is possible that right now, someone could be watching us, or you and your friends. You all could be in danger."

"And this Carlson character; what do you know about him?" Agent Terry asked.

"He is a master salesperson, the type of guy who talks to you like he is your best friend, all for show. He has an odd sense of vanity in his appearance, sort of a prissy, pretty boy, which is odd for his age. And I get the feeling he enjoys the money side of the burglaries and has no stomach for the dark side." Brett replied.

"Do you think he could fold under questioning?"

"Yeah, but he is smart and may cry for his lawyer if he maintains his balance."

"I'll need to put together a few teams to deal with this. We should have a couple of agents make Carlson's arrest and hopefully get a confession, where he gives us some names. And ideally, have an FBI team hit the camp up by Idaho City, and have another team hit PGB in Sparks. I want to shut down both operations in simultaneous raids." Agent Terry said.

"Is the confession critical?" Brett asked.

"I wouldn't say it is completely critical. We could probably take down the camp without it, but if we want to take down PGB, we need to have names, and Carlson is our best bet as a possible source."

"How long will it take to put the plan together?"

"I want to go fast; still, it will take a day, maybe two."

"I have a suggestion. We could enlist the help of Tom Coogan. I believe getting Tom involved could negate Carlson's potential attorney request, and then between the three of us, we could improve our chances of getting the confession and the names we need. Tom knows Carlson better than anyone, and he'd want to help."

"What's your plan?" Agent Terry asked.

"We will need a wire. I want to get Tom together with us, and we can get into the details."

"So, he will confess and won't even know he is doing it."

"Right," Brett replied.

"I like it. But, if we do this, first, I want to talk to your friend Tom. We need to keep him under control. We don't want any blood this time." Agent Terry smiled.

Brett shook his head and agreed.

"How about we get together early tomorrow morning and put it together?"

Agent Terry stood and extended his hand, "I look forward to working with you. We meet here?"

"I've got a better idea. Let's meet at the barn where we keep our horses. It is very private. It's just up the hill and around a corner. I'll show you."

"Meet you at your barn? Heck, I kind of like it here." DeShawn admired.

"DeShawn, when this is all done, I'm going to put you on a horse and take you riding. And if you like this place, you are going to love the barn."

Agent Terry looked at Brett with a quizzical expression. "I'll have to take your word on that. Is there anything else for me today?"

"Yeah, just in case someone's watching, I'd recommend you leave your FBI issued sedan behind and drive a pickup."

CHAPTER TWENTY-NINE

T he small Cessna Citation Jet ripped through the sky and made quick work of the flight between Reno and Boise. Landing at sunrise, it taxied past the Boise International Airport and rolled to a stop in front of the private terminal, Snake River Jet Center. Joe departed from the jet. He was wearing a dark suit, gray hat, and designer sunglasses. A duffle bag hung from his left shoulder, and a hard-sided case was secured in his right hand's firm grip. He was a short, trim man with erect posture and a purposeful stride. He entered the small terminal and walked past the only employee in the vacant waiting area, whose attention was focused on her smartphone's screen. By the time he stepped into the medium-sized gray SUV parked and waiting in the adjacent parking lot, the Cessna Jet was airborne and flying home to Reno. One minute later, the SUV disappeared into light traffic flowing north.

He drove north on Vista Avenue and parked in the McDonald's parking lot directly across the street from Teton Outdoors. After a quick reconnoiter, he drove across the street and parked in the Vista Park Shopping Center lot. As he exited the SUV, he looked like a different man, wearing blue jeans, trail shoes, a lightweight hoody, convenience store sunglasses, and a nondescript baseball cap. On his walk to and from Starbucks's corner location, he swept past Teton Outdoors and checked out Tom Coogan's store.

He threw his full paper cup full of Starbucks coffee into one of the Vista Park's trash cans, slipped back into his SUV, and continued driving north toward the Boise Front, which was illuminated by the morning light. Joe felt good. Everything was moving along as planned. It looked like it was going to be an easy day.

His plan today was to scout the territory. Tom Coogan's recently burglarized store was already behind him with his first stop. The quick walk-by gave him a good feel of the layout and location. His second stop was in west Boise, Teton Outdoors Fairview location. Both stores were closed because of the early hour, which was convenient. Today he was concerned about location, size, and the basic layout. He might swing back later to check for the owner or the store's management. He'd like to get a look at them.

He spent the next hour behind the wheel driving up Highway 21, also dubbed the Ponderosa Scenic Byway, which led him to Idaho City and further north, the camp-headquarters of Carlson's burglary gang. It was nice to drive through some scenic country which could impress if you cared about that type of thing, which Joe did not. Joe didn't care about much, except his next paycheck.

After driving through Idaho City, he circled back, parked the vehicle, and then walked through the town's two major streets. There was a small grocery store, a general store and a gas station, a couple of restaurants, and several good-looking bars, which of course, weren't any help. He pulled out his cell phone and called Jay Peters at the camp.

"Hello," Jay answered in a quiet, guarded voice.

"Jay, this is Joe. I assume you were expecting my call. I will drive in shortly; please remove any physical obstructions that may block my approach."

"Okay," Jay said, and then realized the call had ended. He

looked at his phone and quietly muttered, "Jerk." Then he yelled for Rick and Arnie to come and help him pull down their roadblock.

Joe drove through the camp's open gate, wound past the garage and warehouse, and parked behind the main lodge where only moments before, Jay, Rick, and Arnie had returned in their UTV. He stepped out of his vehicle and strode up to the awaiting group. "Good morning, gentlemen," he said. He made quick individual eye contact with the group and said, "Jay, Rick, Arnie, please to meet you. I'm Joe."

Joe was not quite what Jay, and the guys expected. The man standing before them stood about five foot eight. He was trim and slightly dark with greasy black hair combed straight back. He looked young, in his early thirties, and had a military straight and stiff posture. His voice was deep and commanding, and he emanated confidence.

Jay, as requested, gave Joe a building-by-building tour of the camp. Joe reviewed each building quickly, opening cabinets, checking shelves, and even taking a hard look at their garbage containers. His demeanor seemed reminiscent of an inspector, sizing up every area as if he cared more about its order than its function. Joe spent most of his time in the warehouse building. He asked about pending shipments and in-process inventory, and he reviewed the contents of their hold shelf, asking specific questions about each piece of merchandise set aside. He appeared to be impressed with the area, and he treated Jay with a level of professional respect.

Next, the two men jumped on the UTV. As Jay drove, Joe reviewed the grounds with a critical eye, looking for security weaknesses. Several times, Jay stopped the UTV, where Joe stepped out and physically tested the strength of the fence posts and checked the tightness of the barbed wire. He also pulled out his binoculars and, from the perimeter, looked back into the camp, checking to see what if any critical knowledge could be gleaned from viewing outside of the property's border.

Joe and Jay were standing at the front gate when the sound of a loud pickup truck interrupted the tour. It roared up the dirt road, slowed down, and then crawled through the turn that led to the front gate. The pickup was a dirty brown Chevy, about fifteen years old. Taped to the right front passenger door was a poorly made hand-printed sign that read, "Official Volunteer Forest Ranger." The driver who was the lone occupant of the truck, stared at Jay and Joe. He was an older man, probably in his late seventies or early eighties. His long white hair was unkempt, and his ragged beard disheveled. His beady eyes peaked through an uncontrolled patch of eyebrows, and he wore an angry sneer. And behind the driver, a 22-caliber rifle hung in a rack.

"Oh shit, not now," Jay said.

"Who the hell is that?" Joe asked.

"That is Crazy Larry."

Arnie and Rick must have seen him coming. They drove down the hill in a UTV and parked next to Jay's. Arnie, who was riding shotgun, carefully exited the vehicle, walked up, unlocked the gate, and then turned back toward Jay and Joe. "I've got this," he said.

Arnie walked up to the driver's side door, stood at attention, and with his right arm, saluted the old man. "Good Afternoon, sir," Arnie bellowed. "I was ordered to give you a report. The head ranger completed his inspection of our property yesterday. He rated the property to be in excellent condition, and he said, thanks to you, all is well here. Thank you for your service, sir."

The old man stared at Arnie, and Arnie stared back. And then, the old man ground his truck's transmission into reverse, backed up, and drove away.

"What the hell was that?" Joe asked as Arnie locked up the gate and rejoined them.

"I don't know his real name, but folks around here call him Crazy Larry. He's a common topic of conversation in the bars. He drives around and inspects the forest. He can hardly speak; I've only heard him say one word, inspection. He comes by here and silently stares at the camp. It's creepy." Arnie said.

"The first time he showed up, we kicked him out, and it got kind of ugly. Now we've learned to play along with him, as you saw. It works a lot better." Jay added.

"How long has he been doing this?" Joe asked.

"For a few years. Crazy Larry shows up irregularly; sometimes we don't see him for months, sometimes he shows up a couple of times in a row. The poor guy is senile. He doesn't have a clue." Jay said.

"Does he have anything to do with the cowboys we've talked about?"

"No," Jay said.

"Crazy Larry isn't a problem; he is just crazy," Arnie said.

"Yeah, I get that. There is no way that old man is a risk."

Joe was quite satisfied when they rolled back up to the main lodge. He was impressed with the operation, and more so, he liked it. In his inspection of the perimeter, he could not find any real risk issues.

He felt the setup and location helped ensure the burglary organization's privacy, and from his initial assessment, he doubted any security risk existed here. His next step would be to finish tracking down and assessing the likelihood of a threat from these trail riders. His boss had ordered background reports on each of them, information that would help define how long he would be in Idaho. Their source was pretty fast, so he hoped to see the reports soon. If the trail riders were ordinary guys, he might go home tomorrow. This investigation was probably a case of unneeded nervousness. Time would tell.

"Alright guys, I will probably be in the area for a few days or less while I finish my risk assessment. When I finish my work, I will report back to our office in Reno. My next step will be to investigate the trail riders who have been bothering you. Is there any information about them, you think I should know?" Joe asked.

All three men replied negatively, except for Arnie. "These guys are just a bunch of want-to-be cowboys who are riding their horses around and getting lost and shit." Arnie lied.

"Anything else?"

Everyone stood surprisingly silent.

Since their last encounter with the Riders, Jay and Rick had distanced themselves from the event. Arnie was the only one who saw the cowboys, and rather than speaking second hand or speculating—they kept their mouths shut. They felt they shouldn't have missed the last incident, and they were embarrassed.

"Okay, we'll go from there; everything looks good to me. I'll follow up with you." Joe said.

Roger Carlson's vacation home was a half-mile west of Highway 21, about two-thirds of the way to Idaho City. It was perched on a tree-lined lot in the middle of a hillside with a mountain view. It was a large cabin style home with a varnished log exterior, an expansive wood deck, and a steep green metal roof. The house's layout took advantage of the view, with massive panes of glass separating the great room from the deck. The wooden deck was an exterior extension of the living area. It was well-designed.

Joe drove up the dirt road that led to the property until he found a non-encumbering spot to pull off. He hiked from there, trying to blend in, hoping to escape notice by Carlson or his neighbors. It wasn't too hard; it appeared neither Carlson nor any of his neighbors were home. He navigated a route that circled the cabin, and he envisioned angles providing the best line-of-sight toward it. On the view side, he found a hidden knoll where he could see all the deck and, depending on the light, see through the glass front. It was the perfect spot for surveillance. It was still early enough in the day that the cabin's glass was reflection-free, and with his binoculars, he could see the interior's detail. Satisfied, Joe hiked back to his SUV and drove back to Boise.

He exited the highway on the east side of town, turned north toward the foothills, and drove up to Willow Creek Road. His first stop was Brett's house, where he found a situation that was the opposite of his last stop at Carlson's. Brett's place was built on a cliff, and there was no way to get near it except to knock on the front door. Binoculars were useless, and as far as finding a line-of-sight angle, forget it. Joe was frustrated with the lack of a stealthy approach. The only way to deal with a problem here would be with head-on force. He couldn't see any opportunity for an advantage.

Tom's house, a short distance up the road, was more manageable, the entire back yard bordered open country. Hell, there was hiking and mountain biking paths that were within fifty yards of the back patio. Joe felt better about this location. It was easy in and easy out, with ideal angles of view, perfect.

A little further up the road, he found Mark's place. Joe spent a couple of hours walking down trails and bike paths to get close to the small ranch. It had a variety of structures, including barns, corrals, and the residence. He was able to go unnoticed by playing the role of a passing hiker. Joe found the entire setup ripe with potential. Here, if he needed to, he could make a point. There were a lot of horses too. Not that Joe would ever ride a horse, but he didn't dislike them, and he wasn't afraid of them. Access was good. Joe could enter Mark's place the easy way, turning off of Willow Creek Road, or he could walk in cross-country. Stealth versus speed. At least he had options.

He had a relatively long hike back to the SUV. His cross-country route sent him through a set of public trails that led to a small parking lot at a popular trailhead. The day was getting long, and the sun was low in the sky. He had covered a lot of ground, and he felt good about it. Now all that was left was to learn more about the men involved. Were they outdoor enthusiasts, or were they trouble makers?

He carried a cell phone that was known to only a select few. When it rang, he looked down at the screen and saw his boss's ID. After one ring, he touched the incoming button, lifted the phone to his ear, and answered, "Good evening, Mr. Levitt."

____

CHAPTER THIRTY

"This is not a barn!"

"Yes, it is," Brett replied.

"A barn does not have a wet bar."

"If you walk past the bar and through the kitchen, you'll see horses, hay, and oats—the whole deal." Brett gestured toward the stall area.

"Do the horses hang out and watch football on the big screen?"

"It depends on who's playing," Brett smiled.

There was a bit of a racket out front, along with the sound of familiar voices. A couple minutes later, Mark and Tom walked in.

Brett stood and smiled at his buddies, "Hey, come over here. I have someone you need to meet." He stood with the pair and introduced them to their guest. "These are my friends Mark Taggart and Tom Coogan. And this is FBI Special Agent DeShawn Terry."

It was one of those introductions where everyone was familiar with each other, but they had never met. They were all excited to see each other, all-knowing they had been working on a common problem.

Brett was happy this day had finally come. A lot had happened in the last couple of weeks, certainly not all good. But now they were all in the clubhouse, sitting and waiting to finalize their effort to shut down the burglar's crime ring.

With the introductions complete, Brett stood and addressed the group. "As you guys know, Agent Terry and I have met and discussed our case. He feels we have strong enough evidence to arrest these crooks and shut them down. Agent Terry would also like to shut down the Nevada side of their operation simultaneously, but we need to do a little more work to go there.

"Tom, our plan would involve you. You and I would visit Roger Carlson and question him. Our goal would be to convince Roger to give us the name of his contacts at PGB. We think your presence would be vital in this meeting. He may speak to you in a way that he would never speak to the FBI. We're asking, not telling, are you in?"

Tom flashed his famous smile, "You couldn't keep me out."

"I figured you would say that," Brett smiled knowingly. "Agent Terry, you are up."

Agent Terry stood before the three men. His posture was erect, his stomach tight, his shoulders back, and his piercing gaze forward.

"Gentlemen, first, thank you for your effort and support. When we finish this operation, the credit will belong to you. I know it hasn't been easy, and I know all of you have stepped up and made an enormous difference. We plan on shutting down the criminal enterprise you have uncovered here in Idaho, plus we intend on shutting down its counterpart, an organization with deep criminal ties that operates out of Reno and Sparks, Nevada.

"Our initial plan was to deploy a small group of agents, including myself, to Roger Carlson's residence. Once there, we would interrogate and arrest him. We have enough evidence today to completely shut down his operation here in Idaho. However, we hope to get a confession that will implicate his partners in Nevada through Carlson's interrogation. We need Carlson to give us the names of his primary criminal contacts at PGB. If we move into

PGB and start making arrests without knowing who is in charge, we may end up arresting only low-level managers. Or worse, we could very well prosecute innocent individuals that unknowingly shipped stolen goods. We need names.

"When we arrest Carlson, our biggest concern is that he might shut down and play the attorney card. He is a slick individual who may not fold and instead turn us over to his attorney and then cease all communication. If that happens, his attorney may recommend that Carlson comes clean and cooperates, or he may not. We want to avoid the entire scenario.

"Our plan involves sending in Brett and Tom. Because of Tom's relationship with Carlson, we believe he may get Carlson talking, and I'll be outside listening. Tom, are you ready to wear a wire?"

"Yes, sir. Wow! I find the concept exciting. I've never thought I would do something like that. And I relish the opportunity to bring these bastards down."

"Thank you. I had no doubt. I knew you are a strong man."

"Agent Terry, is there anything I can do to help?" Mark asked.

"This is planned as a three-person operation. Tom and Brett will be inside with Carlson, and I'll be outside listening until I come in and make the arrest." Agent Terry replied.

"If I may make a recommendation," Brett said, "If we have a conflict and someone gets hurt, Mark is a hell of a good man to have around."

Agent Terry gave Mark an appraising glance, "Alright, Doc, you're with me."

CHAPTER THIRTY-ONE

With his shoulder and upper arm ripped apart by a bullet and his head rhythmically aching with his pounding pulse, Arnie was a mess. He slept little. He tossed and turned, scared he'd roll onto his left side and screw up his stitches. Arnie wished the doc would have given him more pain pills, and lamented taking his three-day supply, yesterday. Why couldn't he follow simple directions?

He finally got out of bed and sat down on his old leather sofa. Arnie felt he was getting the short end of the stick with the job, and he was tiring of it. This new boss, who showed up out of nowhere, had no sympathy or even acknowledged the existence of his injuries. What an asshole.

Finally, there was a glow of sunlight behind the hill to the east, so he gave up on the hope of any relaxation, changed his clothes, and left. He was getting some dexterity back into his left arm, but it still hurt to get dressed, especially when he struggled with a fresh shirt. Limping along, he trudged up to the main lodge. Something to eat might help, and a cup of coffee, or three, sounded good. Maybe it would help take the edge off.

Arnie was the earliest riser of the crew living at the camp. Being the low man in the group set him up for an unnecessary life of supervision from everyone, all of whom figured they were his boss. Sometimes in the morning, he would bring coffee back to his cabin, sit on his porch, drink and relax, while the other guys slept. He was the only one who seemed to appreciate the mountains, and he enjoyed spending time outside, especially in the crisp, clean morning air.

The path to the main lodge was a sandy trail, strewn with pine needles, and shadowed by the tall trees. The smell of pine, along with streaks of warm morning light, all helped walk off some of the pain. He hoped to loosen up his legs and stiff back. Scrambled eggs, toast, and coffee sounded good. He would whip it up and bring it all back to his porch. Rick and Jay had been up drinking late last night. Hopefully, they would stay down for a while.

A trio of paths came together in a clearing in front of the lodge. Arnie strode up the half-cut log staircase, and with his right arm, shoved open the front door. Joe was sitting at the main table; he had a coffee cup in his hand and a frown on his face. Arnie knew trouble when he saw it.

"Where are your buddies?" Joe demanded, sounding clipped and irritated.

"Up in their cabins, I guess."

"Go get them—now!"

———

Joe wasn't surprised very often, but he was last night when Tony Levitt called. Everything had been going so well. Too easy, Joe found out. He should have known better. What looked like a simple rubber stamp job, after a quick check, quickly turned south.

Mr. Levitt had received the background reports on the trail

riders. Two out of three of the checks were what they expected. The doctor and the retail merchant were just fine, clean as a whistle. However, the retired football player's report was a surprise, a negative one. After retiring from football, Mr. Brett Wyatt worked in two separate law enforcement careers, the last one as an FBI agent.

Now they had a problem. This situation was not a case of a few rich guys playing cowboy. Weird coincidences don't exist.

With the recent information came an alternative plan. Joe and Levitt agreed on performing a *Clean-Up*. A *Clean-Up* was a method designed to erase the existence of the involved problem-spot. If a criminal enterprise disappears, police cannot take action against it. If the players involved disappear, communication with them becomes eliminated. It just depends on how far you want to go.

Joe thought back to the conversation with Mr. Levitt.

"How far should I go?" Joe asked.

"You implied the camp was impressive. Is it worth saving?" Levitt returned.

"I believe it is. If this blows over, we could come back to a great setup."

"Then, sanitize it and go."

"Where do we stand with Carlson?"

"I will call him next."

"After we sanitize the camp, what about the men?"

"I will leave that to your discretion."

————

Arnie beat on Rick's door, and finally, Rick ripped it open and angrily stood nose to nose with Arnie. "What the hell is wrong with you?" He spat.

"Get up and get your ass down to the lodge—now!"

"What are you talking about? Leave me alone. I'll come down there when I damned well feel like it."

"The boss says to come down now."

"No way, Jay's as wasted as I am." Rick turned away and closed the door.

"Not Jay, I'm talking about the new boss, that asshole Joe."

Jay was also slow on the uptake when Arnie woke him. "Why are you in such a hurry?" He asked.

"Because that asshole Joe is down at the lodge, and he sent me up here. He's down there drinking coffee, and he's acting like he is King Shit."

"What did you say?"

"I said that asshole—" Jay interrupted Arnie and grabbed him by his shirt.

"Shit! Watch it, Jay, you are hurting my bad shoulder," Arnie whined.

"Listen, Arnie; you need to watch your mouth. If I hear you call him an asshole again, I'm going to kick your ass, and I don't care if you are already injured. You have no idea who he is, and you have no idea what he is capable of. You need to be very, very careful around him, understand?"

———

Joe and Arnie waited on opposite sides of the main room, sitting silently, ignoring each other, and both power-drinking coffee. It took a little longer than it should for the other two to show up, and when they did, Joe wasn't stupid; he could see what slowed them down. The idiots drank too much. They were hungover.

Joe decided not to push it. He needed them to be in better shape so that they could get to work, and there was plenty of work to be done. He let them all have the time to eat breakfast and ingest enough caffeine to get their systems going. But he was disgusted;

they were adults and should have known better. Their jobs, their time here, everything was in flux. And now they were hungover, except for the weasel Arnie.

When the men felt good enough to function, he sat them down and explained the situation. "Okay, guys, we need to be on top of our game for the rest of this week. Set the bottle aside for a while; we'll have plenty of time for that later. We have a big problem, and you've drunk too much. It's time to clean up your act. You look like a bunch of losers with Arnie all banged up and you other guys barely sober. It is unacceptable."

Joe's eyes flared; he wasn't looking for a response.

"Now, these trail riders we've checked out, one of them is a problem. The big guy, you know who I'm talking about?"

All three nodded affirmatively.

"As it turns out, he is an ex-cop and an ex-FBI agent."

"Oh shit," Jay said.

"Yeah, oh shit is right. I don't know who is behind these trail riders, if anyone, but we could get raided. It could be these cowboys as a group of self-appointed vigilantes, or it could be the local cops, state cops, or even the Feds. Take your pick.

"Everyone needs to get ready for a fight, so from this moment forward, it is time to pack a gun. All three of you, get your firearms cleaned up and ready. We are going to clean out this camp and leave absolutely nothing behind. And that means anything that could tie us to it, even fingerprints."

"We're ready to ship out everything left in the warehouse, but what about the extra vehicles, tools, and stuff like that?" Jay asked.

"We've rented a warehouse in Boise. We can store it there for the time being."

"What about us?" Rick asked.

"Get your personal effects together. We're heading south to Reno. We've got rooms reserved at a downtown hotel casino."

"That sounds great, but are we finished here, for good?" Arnie asked.

"Hopefully not, after the dust clears, and if it is safe, you'll come back. This place is an ideal setup. We want to keep it going."

"What about Carlson?" Jay asked.

"That's my next stop. I'm going to visit Mr. Carlson right after I leave here."

CHAPTER THIRTY-TWO

gent Terry was driving one of the FBI's older pickups, this one an eight-year-old Chevy, most likely forfeited by a criminal who was no longer in a position to use it. Brett was sitting shotgun, and the pair were unusually quiet as they drove past Lucky Peak Reservoir. They were on a scouting mission, hopefully just a quick drive-by Roger Carlson's house.

Carlson's vacation home was in a small development of good-sized, high-end cabins, built on large wooded parcels that were spread well apart from each other, giving privacy, views, and an escape from urban living. It was less than a half-hour drive from Boise's east side and about halfway to Idaho City on Idaho 21. The private road to the development quickly turned to dirt after they turned off the highway. Carlson's place was simple to find, standing on a hill, set for a view. There was a driveway at the base of the slope below his cabin. A paver walkway led to a wooden set of stairs that climbed up to the cabin's main entry. A black Mercedes and an older Jeep were both parked at the bottom, both vehicles belonging to Carlson. The driveway sat below and to the cabin's side, completely hidden from the main living area's view. If Carlson didn't hear them coming, he wouldn't know they were on his property until they knocked on his door.

Driving past Carlson's place, Agent Terry picked out a flat outlet cut into the road, kind of a general turnaround, probably designed to service lost drivers. It was ideal for his listening station, being nearby, private, quiet, and away from any other homeowner's property. Brett and Agent Terry felt good about the setup. Mission accomplished; not much could go wrong here.

———

Sage and Tonto ventured out together. Tonto was ready to run, and Sage was excited to learn the ins and outs of the local trails that wound through the foothills. This morning she followed her primary route, involving a couple of connected trails that had enough incline to scare away the mountain bikers. She was getting spoiled with the ride's privacy, and she selfishly didn't want to share the area with anyone.

As she rode back into the pasture, she noticed her dad's truck parked outside the barn. She rode into the stall area, unsaddled Tonto, gave him a treat, and readied him for the pasture. Activity had increased next door after an older truck drove in and parked. She'd been curious about what was going on with her dad and the guys. What was their next step, now that the criminal's status was evident? She didn't want to be left out, so she marched through the tack room and into the clubhouse. It seemed like a good time to check things out.

Her dad, Mark, Brett, and a man she guessed was probably the FBI agent were all there. She smiled and said, "Hi guys."

She looked to her dad, "Do you have a second?" She asked.

They slipped into the music room. "So, I'm no longer needed here." She said.

"That's not it. The case is now an official FBI investigation, and I am not calling the shots. I didn't plan on leaving you out."

Tom told Sage how much they appreciated her, and he explained in detail the status of the case. She understood. Her dad and Brett were undercover. Mark was on standby in case of a medical emergency which was sensible, but she was out—again.

They had a good plan that didn't include her. Sage felt like the girl who sat on the end of the bench on a basketball team, knowing she would only play if her team had a big lead.

––––––––

Roger Carlson sat on his deck, reading the *Wall Street Journal* while drinking a morning beer. He, of course, knew Joe was around, probably working with his men up at the camp. If Roger was a team player, he would be up at the camp, helping his crew or at least offering leadership. But Roger didn't care to get his hands dirty and had developed a bad attitude. If Tony Levitt wants his man in charge, he can be in charge. Plus, what did Tony mean when he called this guy Joe a security specialist? The answer, like everything else, would likely scare him.

Roger's primary residence was in Seattle; his wife lived there, and when they were young, so did his children. Now, even when he was home, he never saw the kids. They were a pretty worthless bunch; none of them had the grades to attend the University of Washington in Seattle. What a disappointment; his wife raised a bunch of losers, which means they took after her. No wonder he spent less and less time back home. He'd rather sit by himself on this deck and drink alone. It was time for another beer.

––––––––

Tom was a detail man and usually the boss, at least in most factions of his life. To him, the whole idea of wearing a wire was both exciting and worrisome. But he had questions like, how should he dress? Should he wear a baggy shirt to hide the wires, transmitters, and battery pack? He felt he needed to take charge, and he needed to do something before he *lost it.*

The entire group had huddled a little earlier and would meet again shortly, so it was decision time. Tom had Agent Terry's number; it was time to call him.

"Hello Tom, what's up?" Agent Terry answered.

"I don't mean to bug you, but I have a few questions."

"Great, happy to answer them. Fire away," he responded.

"Since I'm wearing a wire, how should I dress?"

"On a normal day, when you meet with Carlson, how do you dress?"

"Kind of business casual; I wear khaki pants and a button-down shirt."

"That sounds fine; I'd stick with an outfit like that or something similar."

"Do I need to shave my chest or wear a t-shirt with the wires and the tape?"

"No, just come dressed as normal, and relax. We are ready."

Thirty minutes later, Agent Terry walked into the barn. He had a holstered pistol on his belt and was carrying a small box. Brett, Mark, and Tom were sitting around the coffee table. Agent Terry sat down and engaged the group.

"First, thank you—for everything. I've come directly from our office, where we have a backup team ready if we need help. Hopefully, this will go smoothly, and we will not need any help. I checked the latest satellite feed, and both of Carlson's cars are still parked next to his house. So, we are going to keep it simple. Mark and I will drive up first, and Tom and Brett will follow fifteen minutes later. Fifteen minutes will give us ample time to set up, and if we see any reason to abort, I will call Brett and Tom while they are in-route. Once we are all in place, we will do a quick communication check. Tom, please remove your watch and leave it here. I have a new one for you."

Tom pulled off his watch and set it on the table.

Agent Terry opened the box he had brought with him, removed a watch, and handed it to Tom.

"This looks like a fitness watch. We sell one at the store that looks a lot like it." Tom said.

"This is not a normal watch, even though it tells time. It is a state-of-the-art digital audio surveillance transmitter-receiver. With this system, I can listen to your meeting with crystal clear sound and record it from more than a mile away."

"Wow, and I thought you were going to tape a two-pound battery pack to my chest."

"We've left that technology behind." Agent Terry pulled out a second watch, one with a more traditional design, and gave it to Brett. "Brett, this is a personal record-only unit that we will use as a backup. Both devices are voice-activated, have automatic sound sensitivity control, and they do an outstanding job."

There wasn't much involved in operating the watches. Agent Terry taught them how to go through the test procedure and run the incoming and outgoing alarm system. All the other functions were automatic, and with the time already set, they were good to go.

"Any questions?"

Everyone looked confident and said nothing.

"Okay, Mark, let's go."

Joe sat on an outdoor patio at a pretty cool burger joint in Idaho City. It had an indoor counter where you ordered, which was right next to the beer taps. Beer sounded good, but Joe never drank while he was on the job. Out of the side door, a large deck sprawled along the length of the building. There was even an area reserved for dog owners, and one table had a sleeping Golden Retriever resting at its owner's feet. Joe picked a small table underneath a shade in the corner. He was eating the special house burger with fries. The burger was excellent. Joe, as a hamburger fan, gave it a personal rating of five stars. And he discovered something, a condiment called fry sauce. French fries would never be as good without it. It made sense that something as great as this was popular in Idaho. He just wished they had it at home.

It took him longer than he planned to escape the camp. He'd still be there, working with the team, if Carlson would have shown up. It was Carlson's outfit, after all, and Carlson knew the *cleanup* was in motion. A little leadership would have helped a lot today. Rick and Jay were hungover, and as a result, they were moving in slow motion. Arnie, of course, was working with one arm and whining continuously. The little punk had an attitude. All Joe could do was get the guys organized and focused. The *cleanup* was running late, but now at least he had the guys working together, all except Roger Carlson.

He made the right decision to stop in Idaho City and have lunch. His prior consumption had comprised multiple cups of coffee, and nothing else, which left him unsteady and a little edgy. This late lunch helped steady his nerves. Maybe now he could deal with Carlson and hold back the urge to kick his ass. Joe felt Carlson was an older guy who acted like a narcissistic child. He may have to teach him a life lesson.

He left ten dollars on the table for a tip, and then he stopped and pet the Golden Retriever on the way out.

———

Agent Terry was getting used to driving the pickup, and he liked it. The extra clearance helped smooth out the bumps on the private dirt road that led to Carlson's place. He drove by the cabin slowly, looking for questionable elements. He saw none, so he continued past and went to the turnout he had picked out earlier in the day. He parked the truck tightly against the trees on his right side, giving room on the left for another driver who might want to use the turnout for its original purpose.

Tom and Brett turned off of the highway fifteen minutes later. They drove to Carlson's cabin slowly, while they also checked out the area for any red flags. Seeing none, they parked next to Carlson's Mercedes, sat in the car for a moment, ran a communications test on both of the wristwatch-surveillance devices. The test was simple; they touched an icon on the watch's face, and then a confirming image blinked back. Tom and Brett glanced at each other, and after a quick nod together, they open their respective doors and stepped out.

Carlson was lying on his lounge on his cabin's back deck, and he was sound asleep. He'd been feeling sorry for himself, being alone with no one around to talk at. He'd been sucking down a beer while soaking up the sun, and after his fourth, he fell asleep. He woke feeling unsettled, knowing he needed to take a leak, but there was something more. What in the hell was that noise? It was a pounding that started and stopped and then started again. And then it hit him; someone was knocking at the door. *Oh, shit*, he thought, *too much beer*.

He stood up and stumbled away from the lounge, and he weaved toward the screen door that separated the deck from the great room. He was in a half-sleep, half alcohol-induced fog, when he walked into the screen door, bounced backward, and almost knocked it off its track. At the same time, the knocking at the front door continued as he awkwardly slid the screen door open, walked through, and didn't even bother to close it behind him. The knocking erupted again, so he yelled at the front door, "Hold it for a goddamn second, give me a break." Then, he turned left down the hall, marched into the bathroom, stepped inside, and took a leak. At least that pressure was over.

The typical prissy, GQ styled, Roger Carlson was unprepared for visitors. He was wearing a t-shirt, shorts, and flip-flops, all of which were brand new, but not his regular vanity driven attire. His t-shirt was pulled loose from his shorts, no longer hiding his gut, and since he was in such a hurry to take a leak, he forgot to zip his fly. Bleary, bloodshot eyes replaced his toastmaster posture and bearing, and his comb-over had broken free from its cemented layer of hair spray and instead jutted up and out like a loose feather on a Cockatiel's head.

He swung open the front door in an angry, aggressive move that would let whoever was behind it know his privacy meant more than whoever was knocking. He somehow expected one of his landscape service workers, probably there asking a stupid question or hoping to get paid. Instead, he found Tom Coogan, and standing behind him was his friend, the big ex-FBI guy, Brett Wyatt. And neither man was smiling. Roger was more than surprised; he was stupefied. If he hadn't had the sense to take a quick leak, he would have pissed his pants.

Roger wobbled slightly, trying to recapture his stability. He looked at Tom and partially slurred, "Tom—hi uh, I'm surprised to see you."

"I'm sure you know why we are here," Tom replied firmly, and then he said nothing.

Whoever speaks next loses.

Roger let his head fall forward. His emotions pushed the beer buzz away. His hands shook as his eyes watered, and for fifteen seconds, he lost not only his practiced oratory voice but even his real one. Finally, with tears sliding down his cheeks, he choked out, "Yes, it is all true, the burglaries, the camp up north. Me trying to ruin your life. It is all true, it was all my doing, and it's all my fault. I am so sorry."

He was confessing. It was a good start.

"It's a little more than you trying to ruin my life. We know about the burglaries. We know about your gang of thieves. We know about your center of operations up at the camp. We know all about what you and your buddies do with the goods after you have stolen them, and we know about PGB and who runs it."

Roger looked at Brett standing behind Tom and asked, "Are you still an FBI agent? Are you here to arrest me?"

"I haven't been an FBI agent for a long time. I'm here because Tom wants to find a way *not* to arrest you. He's the one who you screwed with the burglary two weeks ago, and we know it wasn't the first time. We need answers, and we need to know what you plan to do to resolve it. We need satisfaction and saying you are sorry won't cover it.

"Now I'm not Tom, so I'm convinced you are a scumbag. You have a couple of options. You can show good faith and work with Tom, or we can send him outside to wait by the car, so you and I can take care of this mess?" Brett stepped around Tom and took the position directly in front of Carlson; his six-foot five-inch frame and mountainous physique was intimidating. He said, "Why don't you invite us in."

It was decision time for Roger Carlson. Should he try to find a way out of this problem: run, deceive, lie, or beg? With his little crime empire falling apart, Tony Levitt may very well kill him.

Roger waved them into his entryway. It appeared at least for the moment; he had lost his ability to speak. Uncharacteristically, Roger Carlson stood in silence. His bloodshot eyes were moist, and he stared at the floor. He was concentrating, hoping his next words would be acceptable. He slowly looked up and turned to Tom. "I understand why you are here and why your friend is with you. We robbed you, and you are dealing with me directly. I don't know what you plan to do to me, but whatever it is, I no doubt deserve it. I will do anything you ask. You are entitled to satisfaction, so tell me what you need, and I will do it. I have lots of money, a good chunk of it yours. You can have it all back."

Roger almost looked like he was relieved it was finally over. And then, for a moment, a light lit up behind his eyes. "Oh my God," he said. "We've got a problem—you can't be here. It's not safe. You need to leave now; we could all be in danger."

"We're not going anywhere," Brett said.

"I'm serious. He told me to stay away from you. There is a guy around, and he could be watching."

"Who told you to stay away from us?" Brett asked.

"Tony told me. He said, whatever I do. I had to stay away from you. He has sent a man here to take care of this mess, and he can't see us together. We all could be in danger. I'm not kidding."

"You mean Tony from PGB?" Tom faked.

"Yeah, PGB and a lot more, he's a big-time organized crime guy. He owns casinos; he sells stolen goods internationally and has a small army of enforcement goons. If there is an organized crime business anywhere in the west, Tony Levitt probably owns or is deeply involved in it. And he is scary as shit—you guys need to leave, now."

"We're not going anywhere, Roger," Tom said. One of the reasons we are here is to find the truth and not just the big picture. We want details. We're here to get answers to all the questions: who, what, when, where, and why. We're entitled to it."

"Yes, I understand, please, believe me, I'm with you. Like I said, whatever you want, I'll do. But your truck is parked right below the house. Joe could drive by and see it. Can we meet some other place where no one would see us?" Roger was winding himself up into a panic. As usual, he was scared.

Brett's experience told him Roger was afraid. "Who is Joe?" Brett asked.

"Joe is the guy Tony Levitt sent to take over. I don't know his full name, only Joe. I think he flew down yesterday morning, so he is here, right now. Levitt called him a security specialist, whatever that is."

"What do you mean he sent him down to take over?" Brett followed up.

"They were checking you guys out because you kept bugging us, and they found out you were an FBI agent. They are taking over the operation and shutting us down, for now, at least. They mean business! They're not screwing around. They are tough guys, and I wouldn't be surprised to see Joe drive up here. That's why you need to leave. We need to get together someplace safe for all of us."

Between the beer and the confrontation, Roger looked sick. He was trying to be rational, but he was struggling. His face had turned bright red, his hands were shaking, and he was grabbing his stomach as if he could throw up at any time.

"Roger, I get it," Brett said. "Let's calm down and decide what to do. Where is your kitchen? We need to get you some water or coffee and help you settle down? Then, we will figure out how to keep us all safe."

They walked into the kitchen, and Tom opened the fridge, not finding much except for a six-pack of beer and a few bottles of Coke. "Roger, would you like a Coke on some ice," Tom suggested.

"I think I drank too much beer. Maybe a Coke will help." Tom handed Roger a Coke, and he took a long pull. "You see, I talked to Tony yesterday, and he was angry, and he told me to have no communication with either of you or your doctor friend. It sounded like a threat."

"This sounds serious. We need to decide *how* serious. Should we walk away from here and plan a secure meetup, or should we take you with us right now? If we leave together, we can make sure we are all safe," Brett said.

"Roger, I think we should sit down. We all need to get off our feet, calm down, and figure this out." Tom suggested.

The kitchen led right into the great room, where on the right, there were several brown leather chairs and an overstuffed leather sofa, all set up in a nice grouping and positioned to enjoy the view. On the left side of the room was the doorway to the deck. The screen door was still open, and a few leaves and debris had blown in onto the wood floor, leaving a small mess. Roger noticed the screen door, and he walked over to close it.

The bullet hit Roger before anyone heard a sound.

CHAPTER THIRTY-THREE

"**G**ET DOWN!" Brett shouted as he dove to the floor.

Tom was shocked, and for a second, he hesitated. To his left, the bullet's impact twisted Carlson around until he lost his footing and crashed to the floor. Hard. Tom turned toward Brett and saw him skidding face-first across the wood floor, after completing a successful belly flop. Quickly coming out of his confusion and disbelief, he collapsed to the floor in a yard-sale maneuver. He was fortunate he didn't crack his head on the coffee table. Carlson was the only one shot so far.

The second bullet struck and punched through one of the big view windows. A third and fourth pursued a tight pattern. The three rounds impacted and buried themselves into the kitchen's back wall. The cracking of the glass and the pounding boom against the wall were simultaneous horrific sounds. Spider web cracks spread across the glass. The window looked fragile, ready to collapse; one touch and it could go.

The first four shots had come in quick succession. After ten seconds, it felt like the shooting was over, but it wasn't. After another pause, a fifth bullet traveled through the glass and pounded the back wall. The situation was still in flux.

"Crawl into the kitchen, stay low and call for help," Brett yelled to Tom.

Tom quickly belly crawled to the far end of the kitchen, then scooted to his right and hid behind the counter that separated the kitchen from the great room. He rolled onto his butt, leaned back into the cupboard, and started shouting at his watch. "Mark, get down here with your kit. We've got a man down." He was still yelling when the back door sprung open, and Agent Terry slid into the room.

Agent Terry pulled his pistol, gripped it with both hands, and breathed deeply.

Brett crawled to the right side of the great room, then stood up and wedged himself into the corner, past the edge of the window. He took a defensive position, with his pistol out of its holster and ready. Carlson was lying on the floor right where he fell. His breathing was ragged, and he was convulsing. Mark, trailing behind Agent Terry, arrived at the back door. Agent Terry held up his palm, ordering Mark back and away from the line of fire.

Mark stood right outside the back door. He hugged his med-kit and breathed with pursed lips. Brett also wanted to get the doc inside, but Carlson laid on the floor, potentially in full view of a shooter who might still be out there. Brett, desperate for a solution, crawled behind the overstuffed sofa and, with his stout legs, shoved it across the room. He positioned it in front of Carlson, hopefully blinding the shooter.

Agent Terry signaled Brett toward the back door. Brett scampered over, and after a ten-second conversation, they exited the cabin and split apart, both men working on an agreed-upon search pattern. They moved in quadrants, starting in the backyard, then searched both sides, and finally approached the exposed front. The shots originated from a position level with or above Carlson's front deck. However, if the shooter was still on the hunt, he could have moved to a new position and kept the element of surprise on his side. Carlson's cabin was perched on a hill, with the deck and front of the house optimized for a splendid view. Unfortunately, that left several hills and ridges with an opposite view—a shooter's dream.

Both men looked for the shooter. They had to move through the terrain slowly and carefully. They worked from tree to tree, avoiding open areas, keeping their eyes searching for any sign of movement. After they completed their initial sweep, they believed the shooter had escaped.

The search then quickly changed. Now that Agent Terry and Brett were in front of Carlson's cabin, they could project the shooter's shooting angle. With that, they started looking for exactly where the shooter had set up and taken the shots. They checked the line-of-sight terrain until on a small brush-covered ridge; Agent Terry found the spot. There was a hidden knoll that offered both camouflage and a clear sightline toward Carlson's deck. And it looked like someone had recently been there. The ground was disturbed, the grass flattened, and a dirt patch was left with a pair of small holes gouged into the dirt. Brett guessed Joe was likely the shooter. He must have been in such a rush to exit that he didn't have time to adequately cover his tracks. A bipod had created those holes, a shooter's bipod. Interesting, but more important at the moment was that the evidence now showed the shooter had left the scene. It was all-clear.

———

When Brett and Agent Terry returned to the cabin, they found a worried doctor treating his seriously wounded patient. Carlson laid flat on the floor, at the spot where he fell, with Mark kneeling on one side of him and the big leather sofa set on the other. The sofa was no longer an asset; instead, it was blocking Mark's light and crowding his patient. Brett and DeShawn noticed the problem and quickly resolved it when they each grabbed an end of the sofa and carried it away. They crammed it next to the wall on the other side of the room.

"Thank you," Mark said. Carlson was unconscious; still, Mark gave him a shot to ease the pain and help him rest. Unfortunately, rest wasn't the answer to this problem. The bullet had missed his heart, but it still created major critical havoc. Mark's goal was to stabilize Carlson's condition enough to transport him to the hospital.

"Brett, come here," Mark asked. "Grab a pair of gloves out of my kit, put them on, and kneel next to me."

Brett put on the gloves and knelt next to Mark, ready to help. Mark calmly pointed out a heavily bleeding area on Carlson's chest and told Brett to apply pressure to slow down the blood flow. Brett was a cool customer, and Mark knew he could handle the situation. Once the medical handoff was complete, Mark turned to Tom.

He ripped off his gloves, pulled out a cardholder from his kit, reviewed it for a second, and handed it to Tom. "Tom, call Les Bois Hospital at this number and ask for Wendy. Let her know we have a major medical crisis. First, she needs to call and use my authorization with Life Flight, get them air bound, and let them know we are scouting out a landing zone. Second, she needs to notify Doctor Taylor that we have a gunshot victim on the way. Third, have her call Doctor Gates; she is the best trauma surgeon around. Let her know we are coming and ask her to get to the hospital fast. And tell her I'll be there soon."

"I'm on it," Tom replied. He walked back into the kitchen and called. Wendy answered immediately.

When he got off the phone, he drifted back into the great room where Mark was working hard. He could tell by his body language that Mark was dealing with a life and death struggle. Carlson couldn't have a better man at his side.

The room's air seemed thick with tension, and it drew in both Brett and Agent Terry. They were watching Mark. Tom walked between the men, touched both of their shoulders, and whispered, "Let's go scout out the landing zone."

The guys rushed out of the cabin and surveyed the area. The turn off to Carlson's cabin was wide, flat, and treeless. It was a perfect landing area as long as there weren't any vehicles driving up or down the road. They solved that problem by using their trucks to block both sides of the intersection.

They also set out some orange cones that Agent Terry kept in his truck. The helicopter landing site was ready and would be easy to spot from the sky.

Tom, Brett, and DeShawn Terry stood admiring the site. And then they heard the rhythmic sound of an incoming helicopter.

The drive to Les Bois Hospital from Carlson's cabin usually took at least forty-five minutes; Life Flight's helicopter did it in ten. Their reputation was well earned. Mark was stooped over, kneeling next to his patient when the Life Flight team arrived. He stepped aside and let the experts transfer Carlson onto a medical cot and load him into the helicopter. Mark joined them, and they flew off to the hospital together. Brett and Tom tried to stay out of their way and then jumped into Tom's truck and followed them to Boise.

It would be awhile before they saw Agent Terry. He stayed behind at Carlson's, now that it was a crime scene. He was organizing and protecting the area until he turned it over to the crime lab, which the FBI had dispatched. The specialists would work through the scene, documenting every drop of blood, every piece of broken glass, every bullet hole, and of course, beyond Carlson's property, they would perform an in-depth study of the shooter's perch.

When the guys arrived at the hospital, they were surprised to see Sage, Tess, and Cindy. They were sitting downstairs next to the

Starbucks kiosk. Coffee sounded good to Brett, so he ordered both Tom and himself a sixteen-ounce medium roast.

Tom gave Tess a quick hug and said, "I'm surprised to see all of you here. What's going on with Carlson?"

"He's in surgery with Dr. Gates. She was here ready and waiting when they landed, and they went straight to the operating room." Tess replied.

"Mark said she is the best trauma surgeon around. Carlson should be pleased with the high level of care and pleased to see you all here in support." Brett commented.

"I'm not that good of a person," Cindy said. "I'm not here for Carlson; I'm here for my husband. I know you guys are his best friends, and you've known him for a long, long time, but you may not know how he feels about his job. He didn't become a doctor because he wanted to make a lot of money. Mark understands and embraces modern medical technology, but he envisions himself as a cowboy doctor saving lives with what he carries in his little black bag. He thrives on working alone and relying on his skills, smarts, and guts. He wants to make a tremendous difference."

"But he made a difference. You would have been proud of how hard he worked today, and you better believe Roger Carlson would have never made it to the hospital alive if it wasn't for Mark." Brett said.

"You guys are a lot like Mark with the horses and the riding and your fondness of the old west. You're idealists and dreamers, so I'm sure you can relate."

"That's probably true, and I think we all can relate to that era, and sometimes dream we belong there; still, we are all firmly planted into the present, even Mark," Brett replied.

"That wasn't true today, at least not for Mark. He was up there with you, treating a gunshot victim with what he had in his kit. He was an independent doctor, working against the odds, at least to my understanding. It was the type of challenge he embraces. I know Mark, and if his patient doesn't make it, he will be devastated."

"I'm sure that is true, Cindy. He would be crushed, and that is okay. If he didn't feel that way, he wouldn't be Doctor Mark Taggart. We all know he can handle it. Mark is a tough man, and he lives each day with courage."

A couple of hours passed without any sign of Mark or any update on the status of the surgery. It was going slowly, which could be either good or bad. Brett's phone buzzed with an incoming text from Agent Terry.

"Meet at the barn in ten for an update?"

Brett and Tom were getting a bit stir crazy, so the invite was more than a welcome distraction. They disappeared out of Le Bois Hospital in a flash.

They parked in front of the barn, and Agent Terry followed after just a couple of minutes. As soon as they entered the clubhouse, Agent Terry excitedly collapsed into one of the oversized chairs.

"Hey guys, we have quite the force of forensic experts crawling all over the scene up at Carlson's cabin, and they are putting a lot of hard evidence together. I left to meet my boss downtown, so while I had the chance, I thought I'd quickly bring you up to date. But first of all, how is Carlson doing?"

"As of right now, we don't know, he went into surgery shortly after Life Flight landed, and he is still there," Brett said.

"Well, I sure hope he makes it. I hate to sound cold-hearted because I do hope he makes it in general, but it will probably help the case if he survives. Even if Carlson doesn't give us any more information, the case is strong. The reason I'm getting together with my boss is to help jump-start the entire process. In a tactical move, our team in Reno is taking the lead. They are preparing all the warrants needed to search several Reno and Spark's locations, plus the offices of PGB and their distribution center. We are also going to arrest Tony Levitt and his core employees. We believe Levitt's empire extends well beyond Carlson's, and we want to take him down. You guys did an outstanding job getting Carlson talking. His confession is compelling. If he survives, his testimony will help, but either way, we have an excellent case. Our Washington Office is already processing warrants to search his business in Seattle, plus his office at home.

"We have been monitoring the camp off of Highway 21. We are concerned there is a flight danger; they could bolt, but we believe they are days away from shutting down the camp. The three men living there, plus their large staff of part-time burglars, will spend time in jail; they just don't know it yet. We don't want to tip off Tony Levitt's bunch in Nevada. We plan to raid Reno and Sparks first, and as soon as we are clear there, we will hit the camp in Idaho. We expect to surprise them while they are still cleaning up. We want them all, and we want this mystery-man Joe."

Brett appreciated Agent Terry keeping them informed. He knew Terry didn't have much extra time; he would probably be hustling back up to Carlson's cabin, wrapping up that part of the investigation after meeting with his boss.

On his way out, Agent DeShawn Terry dramatically shook both Tom's and Brett's hands. He said, "Here is the bottom line. Whether Carlson makes it or not, it's over. You all have done a great job and it would never have happened without you. We did it."

———

When they got back to the hospital, the ladies were still waiting for Mark. He had walked down and visited with them for a few minutes while Tom and Brett were out. Carlson had made it through the surgery, but he was still in critical condition. They transferred him to the ICU.

"How was Mark doing?" Brett asked.

"Tired, but he'll be alright," Cindy replied. "He assisted Doctor

Gates throughout the surgery, so he's had a long day. But like you said, he can handle it."

A few minutes later, Mark stepped out of the elevator and walked out to see his wife and friends. Cindy hugged him and asked, "It's getting late, hon. Are you coming home with me?"

"No, I have a report to write." And then he turned to the group and said, "All of you should go home; there is no reason to wait here. Dr. Gates did a masterful job repairing the gunshot wound, but the damage was too much. He couldn't recover. Roger Carlson died."

CHAPTER THIRTY-FIVE

ack at the camp's main lodge, Joe called a special meeting. He sat around the main table with Jay, Rick, and Arnie.

"Roger Carlson is dead," Joe said.

It was rough to start a meeting with those words.

"What happened?" Jay asked.

"He took a bullet to the middle of his chest. There was no way he could have survived it."

That answer stopped the questions. Joe paused for a moment and then continued in an emotionless business-like manner, while Jay stared at the table, and Arnie and Rick both wore dumbstruck expressions.

"I spoke with Mr. Levitt and updated him on where we stand. He is taking direct ownership of this organization. Because of some tactical errors in planning, you have missed a couple of weeks of business. None of the mistakes are your fault, but you're the ones who have missed paydays. Mr. Levitt is going to cover those paydays and more; he will issue extra bonuses. You can expect them both right away.

"In the short run, we will set up a new headquarters. You will work out of that location until it is clear to return here. Carlson lost his nerve and, unfortunately, was turning on all of us. This afternoon, he was meeting with Tom Coogan and the big guy, Brett Wyatt. Our concern is law enforcement involvement, and as of right now, we believe there is none. That, of course, could change.

"We have made progress here at the camp, but we need to increase our effort and quickly finish the job. We have shipped out all the merchandise in our warehouse. We need to move the tools, supplies, and company vehicles to the backup warehouse in Boise. Every cupboard, refrigerator, and closet in the lodge needs to be cleaned out. If anyone comes here, we want them to find a perfect, uninhabited, campsite ready to rent out to visitors. Your cabins need to look clean, empty, and available. You can store whatever you want at the Boise warehouse. Beyond that, stow all of your stuff in your vehicles. I want to get out of here tomorrow night or the next morning at the latest.

"We still need to deal with these cowboys or trail riders, whatever you want to call them. Later tonight, Jay and I are going on a mission. We will let them know it is time to back off, shut up, leave us alone, and stay away from the cops. They are out of their depth. We will make that *very clear*. All we need is a little time and space, and they will never have to deal with us again.

"Let's get the job done and get the hell out of here. Any questions?"

"What happens if they won't back down? They don't seem the type." Arnie asked.

Joe looked at Arnie as if he were an idiot. "We will take them out, just like their friend Carlson."

———

It was three in the morning when Joe and Jay drove out of the camp. Arnie was still working, cleaning up his cabin, but decided the rest of the work could wait, and instead, he walked over to Rick's for a visit, if he was still up. Arnie had a lot on his mind and wanted to talk.

Rick was up but ready to crash when Arnie arrived.

"Hey Rick," Arnie called as he knocked on his door.

"What's up," Rick asked as he stood in the doorway.

"Did you see that Joe and Jay just took off?"

"Yeah, so?"

"Ever since these cowboys showed up around here, things have been going to shit, and now Carlson is dead."

"Yeah, Arnie, that's a tough one, but remember, we knew we were going into a risky business when we signed up."

"I know, but I've been thinking about our meeting and about how Joe said we might have to kill those guys."

"Yeah, I hear you. That is kind of tough to swallow."

"This might sound stupid because I know I'm a criminal."

"What's your point, Arnie?"

"I'm a thief, but I don't think I'm a murderer. Are you?"

"I'm going to have to sleep on that one. Goodnight, Arnie."

CHAPTER THIRTY-SIX

Tom Coogan was in bed with his wife, enjoying a deep, restful sleep, and all was well, except he was about to be hassled, big time.

The telephone rang. Tom rolled over and squinted at his alarm clock's red LED display. It was five-thirty, another early morning phone call, and no doubt trouble of one kind or another.

"You have got to be kidding me," he groaned.

"Just stay there, and I'll get it," Tess said, as she slipped out of bed and padded over to the small table and chair sitting against the wall on the other side of the bedroom. Even though it was pitch dark, she quickly found her way to the phone.

"Hello," Tess spoke into the telephone, then frowned as she listened. "Yes. Who is this?" Tess asked intensely. "He is right here. I can get him to you."

"Is it the alarm company?" Tom shouted.

"What did you say?" Tess choked.

Tom turned on the lights, and the first thing he saw was tears sliding down his wife's cheeks. He jumped out of bed, leaped across the room, and snagged the phone from her hands.

"Who is this?" He boomed.

Tess sat on the edge of the bed, wilted.

The phone was silent for a few seconds, and then, "Mr. Coogan, Shut up and listen. You need to back off, and you need to behave yourself."

"You are not telling me what to do." Tom retorted.

"It is your choice, but if you don't comply, we will kill Tess, Nick, and your daughter Sage. And then we will kill you. Do you understand?"

"Why are you saying this to me?" Tom asked, deadly serious.

"We want you to stay completely away from us, and we want you to stay completely away from the police. No contact—period. We will disappear in three days, and then you will never see us again. Three days, that's all. And Tom, we left a parting gift to show our sincerity. Enjoy and—back off."

The connection ended.

Tom frowned as he slowly released his grip.

Tess was shaken. She looked at Tom with tears in her eyes. Tom sat next to her, wrapped his arms around her, and buried his face in her shoulder.

"I'm so sorry," he said.

"You have nothing to be sorry about."

"Maybe I've screwed up and have gotten us in too deep."

"No, I don't believe that." Tess was calming down.

"It seems like I may have gone below my depth. These guys are professional criminals. Instead of taking them head-on, I should have left it alone and let the police handle it."

"And what would the police have done? Would they have handled it differently than they did with the last burglary or the one before?"

"I don't know—but probably not. It just seemed like nothing would change."

"Exactly, remember when the three of you discussed the burglaries, and you guys did some real investigating and solved the case. You are a problem solver, and you are someone who won't give up once you start. You are a strong man, sometimes to a fault, sometimes you're too strong."

"Yeah, and I'm still hurting from getting the shit beat out of me. So, when does it all end?"

"Honey, I don't want you to get hurt again. It was almost too much for me to deal with, but I can't tell you when it all ends; only you can answer that question."

"The guy on the phone said I had to back off and stay away for a few days. That's what he said to you too, isn't it?" Tom's hands were shaking from anger or from fear. Who knows which, it didn't matter.

"Yes. And that they would kill us if we didn't comply," the tears reappeared on her face.

"It may be different this time. The guy threatened me, you, and the kids—with violence. For Christ's sake, I'm not talking about stolen store merchandise. I'm talking about taking care of my family. Maybe I should take the safe stance and back off."

Tess wiped the tears from her eyes, and a sense of calm seemed to embrace her. She pulled away from Tom, still sitting next to him, just reclaiming a small amount of her personal space.

"So, help me with this. A criminal calls on the phone, and I answered. It's a man you and your friends have been trying to incarcerate. Instead of talking to you, he tries to scare me. And now, you might follow his directions. I figured I might have to stop my husband from doing something stupid, like acting first and thinking later. But you're going to back off. Are you seriously considering putting up with this shit?"

Tom looked down at Tess's hands, which were rock steady. He grasped both of them softly and looked into her eyes. "When I get too wound up, you calm me down. When I get down, you help me up. How did I ever find such a powerful wife? Sometimes, I forget how strong you are. You are right, I can't overreact to that phone call, and I can't under-react either. What I need to do is simple. I need to do the right thing. Whatever that is. I'm going to get the group together, and we will work through the alternatives, and then, we'll make a plan. You are right. We can't put up with this shit. We need to nail these punks. They will be sorry they ever threatened us."

"Just be smart about it." Tess reminded.

"You got it, honey."

About fifteen minutes later, the sun was rising, and this time Tom's cell phone rang. Tom looked at the display and saw it was Mark.

"Did you receive a threatening phone call?"

"Yes, one hell of a call."

"I think we need to get together and decide how to deal with this."

"Okay, but that isn't why I'm calling. Go out onto your back porch and look our way. We'll talk later."

Tom grabbed Tess by the hand, and together they walked outside and looked east toward Mark and Cindy's.

"Oh, shit…"

CHAPTER THIRTY-SEVEN

Thick smoke gave way to flames as the roof collapsed. The fire was eating the structure from the inside out. Just a few minutes ago, there was still hope. Now it was abundantly clear. The barn was a total loss. Flames were extending vertically at least thirty feet above what used to be the roofline. What had been a thick smoke bomb, probably related to hay storage and confined interior air space, was now an oxygen-fed fireball. Even Brett's horse trailer, parked in the gravel next to the barn, was ruined. Its tires had melted, and its body was smoking—too hot to move. It was untouchable. Mark's trailer was parked further away but still in an overheated zone. Mark, ignoring all reasonable safety precautions, successfully hitched the big trailer to his truck, then towed it to his house. They heard the wail of sirens coming from the city below. It was too little, too late.

Fortunately, the early summer season had its blessings with cool nights, light rains, and a healthy growing season. When the black smoke cloud filled the sky, the first question on everyone's mind was if the horses were safe? They were not kept in the barn that evening. Mark had let them out in the pasture, where they were grazing. While their human counterparts were full of frustration, the horses happily munched on the remaining sweet spring grass.

Mark and Cindy were the first to see the fire, right after being rousted by their threatening early morning phone call. Brett arrived on the scene quickly. He paced the perimeter continually and stopped to encourage anyone who would listen. Tom, Tess, and Sage huddled together, a safe distance from the flames. Sage kept breaking away to comfort a couple of curious horses who were watching from the fence line. Two fire engines arrived, and as hard as they tried, the firefighters fought a losing battle with a limited amount of water. An older pickup drove in and parked, and a scruffy-looking Agent Terry stepped out and marched over to the perimeter.

The fire department had to pump water out of Willow Creek. The closest city fire hydrants couldn't be accessed because they were too far away. Flames had broken through the roof by the time they had adequate water pressure. Still, the firefighters attacked the fire and slowed its growth until the clubhouse's front wall fell in, and then the fresh air made the flames explode again. Now, the firefighter's only option was to soak the area and keep the fire contained while it consumed the barn.

Everyone who watched had to move back from the wet spray zone on the backside of the barn. They regrouped together at a safe distance. The sight was mind-numbing. Brett stood next to Mark and gently distracted him enough to talk.

"Are you okay, Doc?" Brett asked.

"Not really, are you?" Mark shrugged.

"I'm fine. We need to keep this fire in perspective. The horses are pastured and safe. I can't even imagine how I'd feel right now if Pepper or Trixie were in danger. This barn was beautiful, and it will be again. We have the blueprints, so we will rebuild. What is important is family, friends, and our horses; everything else is just —a thing."

"You got the phone call, right?" Mark asked.

"Yeah, I did, although he wasn't on the line very long."

"He was on too long with me. The guy was confident and cocky. Why don't you do me a favor and kick his ass?" Mark chided.

Brett smirked in agreement.

"Okay, but I'll have to find him first. But we need to be calm, and we need to think before we react. So, keep it cool. I'll be back. I'm going to check on Tom."

Tom was with Sage and Tess. Brett artfully explained what everyone already knew and needed to hear. They would rebuild. They just needed to stay calm and work their way there. With a smile, Brett wrapped his arm around Tom and pulled him away.

"Sorry to break you away from your family, but I wanted to talk to you about the phone call. What did he say to you?" Brett asked.

"The guy was arrogant and demeaning, and he was cocksure of himself. He told me to stay away from them, and I'm sure he met the crook's camp. He also told me to stay away from the cops, and if I didn't, he would kill my family and me. It was kind of creepy, scary, the way he threatened my family."

"How much time did he give you until they'd disappear?"

"Three days, and I believe that is what he said to Mark. I'm assuming he called you too."

"Yeah, but he didn't elaborate. He just said he would kill me, and he demanded three days. That number seems a little high. If I needed time to get out of town before I got arrested, I wouldn't take three days to do it."

"That's an interesting point, although I'm not sure if it makes a difference. Tess thinks we should stand up to these guys, but I'm not sure. Do you think we should give them their three days, or do you think they are blowing smoke?"

"Tess is a strong, strong lady, and I lean toward agreeing with her, but this is not my decision, Tom. It's our decision."

"I like that. Honestly, I'm struggling with this one. So, should we grab Mark and talk?" Tom asked.

"First, we all need to calm down, and then you need to take care of your family, and I mean, you need to make sure they are safe."

Mark had been watching and marched over to the pair. "What's going on guys, you look like you are plotting and scheming over here."

"We were discussing what our next step should be and how we should deal with the threats. I recommend that you both take the time to take care of your family and make sure they are safe. And let me know if I can do anything to help. It's time to circle the wagons. If we are all comfortable after dinner tonight, let's get together and try to make some good decisions." Brett replied.

Agent Terry had been roving the area around the burning barn, playing the part of the curious citizen. He made eye contact with Brett, who sent a silent signal. *Stay away*.

CHAPTER THIRTY-EIGHT

M ark had his son's number saved on his cell phone. He hadn't called him for a long time, and he didn't need to since Cindy talked to him at least three times a week. That didn't mean he wasn't close to his son; their relationship was more person to person. They enjoyed their time together, but sometimes… If Mark was concerned about anything, it was the way his son might react. Mark knew his son might, or more likely would, overreact.

He took a deep breath and touched the "Steve Mobile" icon on his phone.

Steve quickly answered.

"Hi Dad, you're calling early. What's going on?"

"I was hoping to get hold of you before you went to work. I have a favor to ask."

"Sure, what do you need?"

"First, how are Jenni and my granddaughter?"

"They're both good, and they miss you and Mom. So, what is the favor, Dad?"

"We had a fire here this morning, the barn burned, and I need to go to a meeting after dinner, so I was wondering if you could stay with your mother while I was gone?"

"The barn—what started it?"

"The fire department said it was arson."

Steve lived in the west end of the valley. Middleton was a great place to raise a family; the only problem was that it was at least an hour's drive from his parent's house.

Steve was quiet for a few seconds, then said, "Okay, I'll be there in an hour and a half."

"Hold it. You don't need to come right now, what about your job?"

"I'm taking the day off, tell Mom not to worry—and Dad."

"Yes, son."

"I know you would never have called me if this wasn't huge. I'm bringing my guns."

———

Brett didn't have anyone to call for support, and he didn't need it. He was more concerned about the threat to his friends and their families if there was an *actual* threat, which was questionable. The smart move was to play it safe and follow the caller's rules until the unified group decided not to. For his protection, he policed his house, checked it for any security weaknesses, and strapped on a compact Glock 26 concealed carry pistol.

He contacted Agent Terry and filled him in with the details of the phone threats that all three men had received. That alone explained why Brett avoided contact during the fire this morning. Agent Terry used his pull with the Boise Police Department to increase the number of patrols driving by Tom's and Mark's houses. The extra patrols should make both families feel better.

———

Sage was incensed, and her big brother wasn't too far behind. Tom's concern was that they might wind each other up; it had happened many times before. He called Nick early before he went to work and asked him to take the day off. He told him the short version about the fire and who was behind it, and it was enough to bring the big guy home. Sage had taken it upon herself to explain the extended version to her brother. As Nick learned more, it pissed him off. He felt that he'd been left out of crucial family matters.

"Sage, I completely get it. Dad left me in the dark because I work for him. That wasn't fair, because he left me on the outside, which stinks. I should be treated as a family member first. But you, I don't work for you, and you kept the whole deal a secret. That completely sucks, Sage. You should have told me!" Nick challenged.

"And I'm sure you've picked up the phone and called me every time I've needed to know something. I live in California, so you blow me off. But I don't care about that right now. They burned down the damn barn, and they threatened Mom and Dad. These jerks think they can scare us—bullshit. If I have the chance, I'll *shoot* them!" Sage not so calmly responded.

"That's the only smart thing you've said yet—maybe we should get the guns out."

"I already did; most of them are in my room."

"Let's go look!" Nick boomed.

"Okay!" Sage boomed back.

CHAPTER THIRTY-NINE

Tom was surprised to see that Mark had beaten him to Brett's. Mark and Tom had something new in common. They were both motivated to get the hell out of their house and away from their crazed children. Sometimes, good intentions can be a little hard to take.

The back half of Brett's house was built for the view; it jutted out into the sky, and with a wall of glass, it felt open and inviting. Neither Mark nor Tom had ever seen its drapes closed; today was the exception. The wide-open bachelor pad had become a dark, private place. There was no line-of-sight angles here. Brett had policed the house for security, and a severe new environment came with it.

After Tom entered the house, Brett locked the deadbolt on the front door, stepped into the kitchen, and set up his bar. He offered ice water and coffee. And then, from the adjoining hall, Agent Terry walked into the room.

Mark stood by the counter; he seemed surprised and amused. "So much for not contacting the cops," he said.

Brett grimaced and shook his head. "Sorry for the surprise,

guys, but I guarantee you no one saw Agent Terry arrive here, and no one will see him leave. The man can be invisible."

"Hey, don't mind me, I'm just a smartass. Agent Terry belongs, and I'm glad to see him. Agent Terry, welcome," Mark said.

"Thanks, that means a lot. You guys are something else, and I feel like we are friends. So, do me a favor, if we are in a courtroom, call me Agent Terry, but if not, call me DeShawn or just Terry, okay?"

They all smiled and shook their heads, affirmatively.

"DeShawn, what is your take on the situation," Mark asked.

They all found seats around the coffee table in the living room.

"We have a plan, and we're prepared to execute it, but the arson and threats this morning may lead us to make changes. I'll explain the FBI's plans, and I'd like to understand your perspective. Brett contacted me and filled me in on the basics of what happened this morning. Now I need to hear from you and make sure we have missed nothing important. Hopefully, we will all be comfortable when we leave here tonight."

Brett interrupted, "Before we get started, I have a question. How is everybody doing, and I mean all of us? We've had a hell of a day. So, Tom, are you okay?"

"I'm okay, but to be honest, the threat on the phone, it got to me. It was frightening. The chicken-shit even called out my family by name. I had a moment where I was ready to back off, but Tess was there to settle me down. She told me to man up, and she was right. What kind of coward calls on the phone anonymously and pulls this kind of shit? The more I think about it, the more certain I am; if we need to finish this, I'm in."

"Do you feel your family needs protection?" DeShawn asked.

"Hell no, if I get any more protection, it could be dangerous. As of now, my two adult kids have every gun in the house loaded and ready. I hope they don't get confused and shoot the paperboy in the morning. I'm kidding, but just barely." Tom joked.

"That is exactly my situation," Mark said. "My son lives in Middleton, and he has walked off his job, left his family, and moved back into his old room. And he drove down with his truck loaded with a small arsenal. He's walking a patrol around the property as if we lived on a military base. I showed up early so I could get the hell out of the house."

"Sounds like my motivation." Tom agreed.

"I'm okay," Mark said, "but I am pissed off big time. The more I think about the fire and the phone call, the angrier I get, but don't worry about me. I can handle it. And as Tom said, if it comes down to it, I'm in."

"I'm in too," Brett said, "and I'm pissed off too. My blood is boiling, but that's okay, I think it may be good for me. We all received similar calls, telling us to back off for a few days or he would kill us. My call was short and sweet, almost business-like, Mark's was similar, but Tom's was more extensive. The guy spoke with both Tom and Tess. Do you think there is a reason for that?"

"I think he knew more about my background because I was a victim of their burglaries. So, I think he looked at me as an authority figure. As such, he became specific and repetitive in his message." Tom explained.

"How was it repetitive?" DeShawn asked.

"In two ways, first, he repeated the statement that I should stay completely away from them, meaning the camp, plus he said to stay away from the police. Between his conversation with my wife and me, he said that three or four times. Second, the jerk said they would disappear in a few days, and then it would be over. He then changed his terminology to a more precise, three days. He attempted to make sure the time limit was clear."

"It's kind of odd that he would be so anal about the message, but I don't know if it makes any difference to us," DeShawn said. "We plan to raid their operation in Reno tomorrow. We are still working on the logistics. Since Reno is the organized crime side of the burglary ring, we wanted to hit them first. And then we planned to follow up with the Idaho end of the operation."

Tom jumped in, "When he asked for three days, I felt like he was trying to lead me or sell me. I may have been in the business world too long, but I have learned to know when someone is trying to sell bullshit. The three-day limit seems like bullshit to me."

"I agree," Brett said. "It may be bogus. If they have an inkling that a raid could come, it will work to their advantage to slow us down and keep us quiet. Hell, we know they are cleaning up and getting out. They could abandon the camp tomorrow."

"Shit, you guys are turning our plan upside down. We may have to change our timeline, but if we hit the camp first, the word could leak to Reno—shit." DeShawn frowned.

"I have an idea," Mark said.

"God, help us." Tom grinned.

"Seriously, hear me out. So, if the FBI or the police raid the camp, I can see how the crooks up there would tip off their bosses in Reno. But remember, the police haven't bothered them at all. We have. They probably look at us as a bunch of want-to-be cowboys who have been a colossal pain in their ass, but not much of a threat."

"We are a bunch of want-to-be cowboys," Tom added.

"Exactly," Mark agreed. "Why don't we ride out one more time, and this time, take them down?"

"There it is," Brett said, "another bad idea. Remember what happened last time. It was a disaster." He shook his head and frowned.

"It wasn't a complete disaster. We stopped the burglary, remember."

"I remember you were about as upset as a man can be."

"I know, we just need a better plan, and we need to do a better job, which we can."

"The last trip up to the camp, you shot a man, and you were upset. You felt you had violated your medical ideals, remember."

"Yeah, and I've surprised myself by how fast I recovered. I think I'm getting used to our risky ways."

"Their security efforts will be high. This situation could be dangerous. This bust has to be a police action." DeShawn advised.

"Humor me for a minute. We can ride in on horseback and approach through the woods. They won't see us coming, and then we can sneak up and make a citizen's arrest."

"I'm sorry, but you aren't trained for an operation like this. Once again, this has to be a police action," DeShawn said firmly.

"Well, you aren't completely right. We have Brett, and—can you ride? I've got a spare cowboy hat." Mark was getting excited.

"I hate to encourage him, but Mark's argument has some merit. If they saw us coming, they would probably be angry as hell, but they wouldn't react as if we were the cops." Brett said.

"Guys, I haven't ridden a horse since I was a kid, and then just a few times. I am not a cowboy." DeShawn confessed.

"That's alright; we can help you with that. I've got a big mountain horse you can ride, a fast stallion who will lead the way. All you will need to do is hang on." Mark said.

"A stallion—what do you call him?" DeShawn was worried.

"He's a good-looking guy. We call him Dynamite."

"Dynamite, you're kidding?"

"Yeah, I'm kidding. I have a gentle horse who won't give you any problems. Trixie is her name, and she is a sweetheart."

"When the FBI performs a raid like this, we come in hard and fast with tactical squads in tactical armor, not cowboy hats on a horse named Trixie," DeShawn stressed. "That is the FBI's method and for a good reason."

"Could you get us some of those Kevlar bulletproof vests?" Mark asked.

"That's a good idea," Tom added.

"Okay, guys, let's calm down just a little," Brett said. "Here are my thoughts. If we trailered up and parked a half-mile past the camp's turnoff, we could ride back from the north and then picket the horses out of sight on the high ground above the camp. From there, we would hike in. We could work in pairs, with DeShawn leading one pair, and I would lead the other. Tom and Mark, you would have to back us up, and you would have to promise to take orders from us, no matter what. I'd recommend that we ride in before dawn and work toward an element of surprise. And if things get rough, DeShawn and I will take the point, and you guys will be our wingmen. I prefer to take them without a fight, and by hitting them early, we should be able to.

"So that would be my recommendation in broad strokes. DeShawn and I would have to take some time and work out the details. We know they are cleaning up to abandon the camp. It would be good to know how far along they are with that project. It is even possible that they have already left. Before we make a final decision, I need to make another midnight reconnaissance mission. That will give us the information we need to define the situation. And then, if we are not confident, we will call it off."

"I think that sounds like a solid plan," Tom said.

"Where you lead, I will follow." Mark smiled.

DeShawn was looking down as if he was examining the floor. "All my training tells me this should be a police action."

"I understand, but I think we need you on this one," Mark said.

"If we do this, and it blows up, my career will probably be over. And somehow, it still feels right. I'm in," DeShawn agreed.

They all reached toward the mid-point of the coffee table and did a fist bump.

"Hold it," Tom said. "Brett, can you give us one?"

"One what?" DeShawn asked.

"Brett lives by a code, and sometimes he'll quote one, and it always seems to help."

"You have a personal code?" DeShawn asked.

"No, I don't, but the State of Wyoming has a code of ethics, and I believe they are the only state in the United States that does. I admire the code, and I sometimes quote parts of it. I think I have a short one that fits."

"So, one more time, let's put our fists together," Mark said.

The men all reached out again and touched fists.

"Gentlemen, let's… Ride for the brand."

"Oh, I like that." DeShawn smiled.

CHAPTER FORTY

It was almost nine in the evening when Jay, Rick, and Arnie drove back into the camp in the cargo van. The sun was low in the sky and was casting warm, dramatic shadows. With daylight savings time in effect, they had another half-hour left before dark. They had been up working since early morning and, to a man, were tired. They stopped in Idaho City for takeout at a small drive-in that made better burgers than any of the national chains.

Arnie carried two dinners into the lodge where Joe was waiting. They all sat down together at the main table. Arnie set a bag in front of Joe. "Here you go, boss. You've got a double cheeseburger, large fry, chocolate milkshake, and per your request, a cup of coffee."

Joe stared at Arnie suspiciously. "What's wrong with it?"

"Not a thing. That outfit makes the best food around, and in my opinion, the world's best milkshakes. You are going to love it."

Joe pulled the large milkshake from the bag and tasted it. "That's a pretty good milkshake, thanks."

"You are welcome, boss."

Those were the first civil words between the men in the last couple of days. Arnie had an epiphany. Don't rock the boat; it isn't worth it. He just needed to make it another day, and he would get away from this *asshole*.

While they were eating, Joe fell back into his role as supervisor. "We are getting close to finishing this operation. While you were in Boise, I've been on guard duty patrolling the perimeter. It's been quiet all day, and by tomorrow, we should be in the clear. I'm feeling pretty good; we should have seen something by now if the cops were involved. We have little daylight left, so our primary goal for this evening should be to load up the repair shop, and in the morning, we need to clean the garage out and leave no trace. All that's left is the main lodge and your cabins. So, this evening pack and clean your cabins. All of your stuff will need to go into your vehicles, including the sheets and towels you use tonight and tomorrow. Your cabins need to look like a maid went through and cleaned it. Any questions?"

The three men looked bored.

Joe stood up and started pacing and scanning the room. "I'm going to crash here on the couch tonight. While I'm here, I'll clean out the fridge, check out all the cupboards and closets and get the building in order. If you need anything else to eat, grab it now, and remember no garbage anywhere. Leave no trace."

"This milkshake will take care of me," Jay said.

"No shit," Rick offered.

"Jay, you'll work in the garage tonight, and we'll put a team together to help you finish it up in the morning. Rick, I need you out on guard duty as soon as you finish here. Arnie, you'll take over for Rick at midnight and patrol the perimeter until we send out a replacement tomorrow morning. I'm giving you a simple job. We wouldn't want you to hurt your delicate shoulder."

Joe smirked. He enjoyed the moment at Arnie's expense.

"Shit," Arnie muttered quietly, almost only to himself.

"Do you have a problem?" Joe barked.

"No problem," Arnie muttered.

"You're sure?" Joe circled behind the table.

"I'm sure, boss."

Joe slipped behind Arnie, and with a full-body twist behind the blow, hit Arnie in the back of the head with an open palm punch. Arnie's head snapped forward, his face impacted the table, and they could hear his nose crack.

"That wasn't necessary," Rick said as he stood up.

Joe pulled his pistol and pointed it at Rick. "I decide what is necessary around here."

"No problem," Rick said as he kept his hands up in a non-threatening position.

"What about you?" He said as he swung the pistol toward Arnie.

Arnie, holding two napkins to his bleeding nose, replied with an unintelligible response that sounded agreeable.

Rick walked toward the front door. "I'm on guard duty."

Dinner was over. The puddle of blood was enough to ruin any appetite.

At midnight, Arnie found Rick leaning against a fence post near the main gate. Silently, Rick pulled the binoculars off his neck and handed them to Arnie.

"So, Rick, do you think we will make it out of here alive?" Arnie spoke with a rough, broken nosed, nasal tone.

"What the hell do you mean by that?"

"Well, Joe calls this procedure we are working through a 'cleanup.' The idea occurred to me that the term may apply to more than the buildings and their contents. Maybe, the term refers to us."

"I don't think so."

"I've got to question if we have any real value to these guys. They may not need us when we finish the job tomorrow."

"He said we are driving to Reno, and we'll get a bonus."

"And then what, if they needed us in Reno, we would have been there all along. It's not like they have open jobs waiting for us."

"I think you are reaching this time, Arnie."

"Oh, I don't know. Joe almost killed you tonight because I said *shit.*"

"I remember. But it was your fault, not mine."

"Thanks for sticking up for me tonight. I wouldn't do it again if I were you; it may cost you your life."

"God damn it, Arnie, what do you want from me, anyway?"

"I guess I just wanted to know how you felt about something."

"What's that?"

"If things get dicey tomorrow, even a little, I'm going to run and never look back. If I do, are you going to try to stop me, ignore the whole thing, or what?"

"I'll give it some thought." Rick turned and walked away.

CHAPTER FORTY-ONE

he Riders needed to get prepared now. Right after their meeting broke up, Tom and Mark left Brett's house and went to work, finding backup saddles and tack for all four horses. Unfortunately, this morning's fire took more than the barn itself. It consumed seven saddles, eight bridles, and a lot of matching tack, some of which were collectible. Between the Riders, they should be able to put together enough older tack to get them through. Old saddles are one of those things a lot of folks have a hard time parting with, like musical instruments, firearms, and even automobiles. A fire wouldn't keep them out of the saddle.

Brett pulled out the satellite and the topographical maps of the region around the camp. DeShawn had stayed behind, so the two men could study them together. With Brett's multiple trips, he had a good understanding of the camp's location and the spiderweb of trails that were near. Riding in from the north would be challenging due to the mountainous territory, but doable. The terrain offered a backside approach that should allow them the element of surprise. After a couple of hours of planning, they felt confident. Their plan was straightforward.

———

After DeShawn's departure, Brett moved on to his last job of the night. It was time to pull out his Honda and take another ride. It seemed like a long time ago when Brett made that late-night recon trip to the camp. Actually, it was just last week. Looking back, he questioned his judgment. He wondered if he should have torched their truck that night. Could the barn fire be payback for the truck fire? Probably not; everything changed when Joe took over. There was no way Brett could answer that question for sure, not now anyway. Maybe tomorrow he could learn the truth, and if the two fires were related, he knew there could be plenty of paybacks to go around. His primary focus was to define the situation that they would ride into tomorrow morning, and his secondary focus was Joe. He'd like to identify the man.

He was going to have to pass on his pregame ritual tonight. That was okay; he had made this trip before. He knew where to go, knew where to hide the bike, knew where to cross the fence, knew the camp's layout, and knew what needed to get done. He quickly assembled what he considered his stealth pack. It included his helmet, riding jacket, heavy leather gloves, lightweight backpack, black ski mask, water bottle, standard binoculars, night vision binoculars, red beam flashlight, snap gun, tension rod, compact pistol with laser sights, holster, and ammo pouch. He changed into his black running clothes and double-checked to make sure he had forgotten nothing. He was satisfied, felt good, and was ready to go.

At midnight, he rolled out of his garage on his Honda road bike, hit the accelerator, and started his low flight to the crook's camp.

Once he turned on to the dirt road, he turned off his headlights and carefully picked his way forward. Visibility was low, the night sky was partly cloudy, and there was no moon. There was positive and negative in that. It was hard for Brett to see, and it would be hard to see him. It made finding his way difficult, but beyond that, the lack of light helped him.

The trail he took last week was easy to find, even in the dark. He rode into the same wide spot where he previously hid his bike and parked it behind the same cover. One advantage of the cycle was that he didn't have to worry about Pepper's food and water. He stripped off a layer of clothing, which left him in the comfort of his running clothes. He remembered the trail, started running, found a good pace, and quietly covered the camp's distance. After he sprung off of the fence's lower rung and vaulted over the top into the camp itself, he followed the fence line toward the front gate. He reactively slid behind cover when he spotted a figure resting near the entrance. Using his binoculars, he magnified the image. The man was leaning comfortably against a fence post. He was wearing a baseball cap, and in his left hand, he was holding a cell phone. Brett's angle was offset so he couldn't see the man's face, but the phone's screen flickered, and Brett could tell that he was wearing headphones. Brett had to smile. The guy was watching a movie, or maybe a sporting event; it was hard to know. The man extended his arms, stretched, and opened a little better viewing angle. Of course, it was Arnie.

Knowing that the quality of security was lacking, Brett moved about the camp carefully but a little more comfortably. The cabins looked quiet, two were dark, and the third partially lit. The status of the outbuildings would answer some of his questions. A familiar trail led up to the building that functioned as a warehouse and shipping center. All of its lights were off. Brett pulled out his snap gun, then tried the door, and to his surprise, found it was unlocked. He entered the building, and using his red flashlight, searched the interior section by section. It was empty.

The garage's door was locked; Brett couldn't win them all. It allowed him to use the snap gun again, which worked quickly but created an unnatural clicking sound. Arnie sure as hell didn't hear it with his headphones on. Hopefully, no one else was listening. There was a large van in the garage, heavily loaded with tools and parts. Beyond that, it looked as if a little cleanup would put the building on par with the warehouse.

There was no doubt. The crooks were abandoning the camp. They had removed a lot of vehicles, tools, merchandise, and supplies. Where? Brett did not know. The Riders Club had made the right decision to take the camp now.

Seeing enough to define the situation, Brett slipped by the main lodge. A single light was on, and it was illuminating a man sitting alone inside. Brett used his binoculars to view through a window and inspect the camp.

Brett saw the fresh face and figured it was Joe. He didn't look like much.

CHAPTER FORTY-TWO

Most families have a resident night owl; in the Coogan household, it had always been Sage. Even in her high school and college days, she couldn't or wouldn't go to bed at a reasonable hour. It concerned her folks, who suggested several sleep strategies, none of which ever made a difference. Worst of all, it was hard on Sage in the morning.

It had been a long day with the fire, the phone call, her brother, and all the other family dynamics. There had been too much stress, way too much to sleep. Sage sat in the kitchen, alone in the calming quiet of her family home. She was reading a novel and letting her angry mind take a break when she heard her dad tip-toe in from his bedroom.

He was surprised to see her. "Hi honey, why are you up so late?" he asked.

"You know, Dad. Sometimes I just don't feel like crashing. Anyway, I'm used to Pacific Time, so it's not as late for me. What about you? You are never up this late."

"I've got a lot on my mind, so I thought I'd gather up and work on some of the riding gear that I've been keeping at home. Since the tack room and everything in it burned up with the barn, I've been going through my extra tack, trying to put together some saddles and other gear, and move it to the hay barn, for now."

"Yeah, I saw the old saddles in the garage. They're still in good shape; it looks like you'll be alright. How did your meeting go last night?"

"It was fine. Well, I'm going to go out to the garage. Goodnight." Tom curtly said and then turned to walk out of the room.

Sage wasn't in the mood to have any of her dad's exclusionary ways. "Hold it for a second," she barked. "What do you mean, the meeting went fine? You were there for quite a while. You guys are up to something. What is it?"

"Oh," he grimaced, "we're bouncing ideas off of each other, that's where we're at, but that's about it, for now anyway," he awkwardly lied. "So, go to bed, honey, I'm going to run this stuff down there."

"At three in the morning, Dad?"

"Yeah, I can't sleep. I might as well keep myself busy."

"Wait a second, and I'll grab my coat and go with you. I'm not tired either."

"No, stay here and get some rest. We can't all leave the house with all this crap going on, right?"

"You're hiding something. I think something's going on. Come on, what is it?"

"I said nothing is going on! Go to bed and get some sleep, for God's sake. Why can't you do what you're told, for a change?" Tom marched out to the garage, loaded his truck, backed out, and drove away. He felt terrible about lying to Sage, but he thought he had to.

Sage sat on a stool in the kitchen, snapped her book closed, and steamed. That wasn't like her dad, he was hiding something, and she wasn't happy.

———

By the time Tom arrived at the hay barn, Brett, DeShawn, and Mark were already there. He looked at his watch; it was 3:30 in the morning, and he was the last one to arrive. Tom wanted to be here first, not last. So much for everyone meeting up at four; he sure as hell was riding with an eager bunch this morning.

They planned to load up all four horses into Mark's trailer and drive to an alternative pull-off north of the dirt road they had used in the past. The new pull-off was further up the highway but offered a stealthier approach. The drive should take them around an hour, leaving them with plenty of time to saddle up by 5:30, at least a half-hour before sunrise.

Mark's pickup and trailer were parked next to the hay barn. The property's dirt road passed by the barn's charred remains and then continued to the hay barn, which up to now they'd used for hay storage only. But there was enough room for it to do double-duty for a while. The Riders had already agreed to build a make-due-corral with a feeding and watering area for the horses. They would get a load of wood, dig some post holes, and get the whole thing built in an afternoon. They also planned to clear out space inside and create an area to organize, store, and keep their gear. But right now, they missed the barn they had designed and built. They were hanging out in front of the tall hay barn, and everything felt upside down. They didn't even have a decent place to prep the horses. And they sure missed their comfort zone.

Mark walked out to Trixie, who was lazily grazing in the pasture. He attached a rope to her halter, walked her back, and spent a few minutes with her to make sure she was calm and ready to be loaded. He led her over to DeShawn, who had been intently watching. "Trixie, I'd like you to meet your new friend, DeShawn," Mark said while stroking her nose. "Rub and scratch her nose a little. She always likes that."

DeShawn gently rubbed her nose. He did an awkward layperson's job, but Trixie still liked it. She mildly threw her head toward him when he stopped. It surprised him a bit, but he got it. Trixie didn't want him to stop—she loved the attention.

"She's trying to tell you she likes you," Mark said. Now, take the rope and walk her around a bit. Don't stare at her; just look forward, keep her close, and walk together. Talk to her in a calm voice and tell her about yourself. And let her know you think she is a sweet girl. Try to bond a little before we load up."

DeShawn looked at Mark, he wore a quizzical look, and then he turned and walked away with the Palomino. "Hi Trixie, I'm DeShawn. I can tell we're going to be great friends. I've always loved horses and…"

Brett liked the match, smiled, walked over next to Mark, and watched. The pair looked good. Trixie was relaxed while DeShawn talked to her, and he too was smiling.

"So, you are pairing DeShawn up with Trixie, good choice," Brett said.

"Yeah, they'll be fine together," Mark replied.

"They look good together already, and you're taking your mountain horse?"

"Yeah, Rondo, it is. A trip like this is what he loves."

"Absolutely."

And then it was time.

"Hey everybody, let's circle up," Brett yelled.

Everyone came together and looked toward their leader.

"We have made this trip before, so we know what we are doing. Double-check your gear; you all know what to take. We want to be more concealed on this trip, so leave the light-colored cowboy hats behind. We don't want to stand out. I'd say everyone's clothes look dark enough; we should blend in fine. After we ride and find a suitable spot, we will picket the horses and hike in the rest of the way. As far as firearms, Tom and Mark, as we mentioned before, you could be in a cover position — rifles will give you the best accuracy and range."

"Got that covered," Tom said.

Mark nodded in agreement.

"Questions or comments?"

The group stood silent and committed.

"Great guys. One more thing, DeShawn brought in a piece of extra gear. DeShawn, show them what you've got."

"Thanks, this one is originally Mark's idea, and if I remember right, it was his request." DeShawn reached into a duffle bag and pulled out a vest. "These are Kevlar bulletproof vests. They are the latest models in the FBI's arsenal. They are lightweight, and can prevent a bullet from entering your upper body. The vest leaves a lot of your body unprotected, so we still need to be careful. When I say it prevents a bullet from entering your body, that doesn't make you bulletproof. If you get shot, it will hurt like hell, and you will probably be knocked down and could be out cold for a while. Potential injuries could be broken ribs, internal damage, or worse, but it's a hell of a lot better than getting pierced. So, have respect for every gun you see and be careful." He passed out the vests, and everyone nervously looked them over.

"I checked out your mobile radio system. The radios are state-of-the art; we should be able to go hands-free with open communication. Tom, are we set up with headsets?"

"Yes. We have four radios and four headsets."

"Good. We have the right equipment, and we have a solid plan; the rest is up to us. So please, do not forget the basics this morning. We plan to take down the crooks at the camp, and we want to take them without a fight. We will surprise them and keep them from communicating with their accomplices, and then, we will arrest them. We want to avoid any gunplay. Do not fire your rifles unless we are fired upon or under direct orders from Brett or myself. We have already learned that we are dealing with dangerous men. We have to be extremely disciplined and careful. We are a team, and we need to act like one. We do not want any individual heroics. Remember our agreement. You will follow orders at all times. We are going to make a difference today. Thanks for stepping up."

"Alright, gentlemen, let's load up and hit the road," Brett said.

They rolled out, all in Mark's F250, pulling his four-place horse trailer loaded with Trixie, Rondo, Buck, and Pepper. The horses loaded up quietly and seemed settled. It was early in the morning for them, too. They slowly drove up and out of the pasture and turned downhill onto Willow Creek Road. All four men were keyed up, nervous, and eager to get out of town. They weren't paying attention as they drove down the hill.

Sitting behind a parked car, an observer was waiting and watching.

———

Arnie awoke in a fog, groggy. He shifted his weight forward, accidentally clipped his left shoulder on a wooden post, winced in pain, collapsed, and rolled face-first into a pile of dirt. He had fallen asleep while watching a movie on his phone, anything to avoid boredom. He laid on the ground and hoped no one saw him sleeping on the job.

He had been leaning against the main gate's anchoring post, sitting in a reasonably level spot, almost pleasant, or at least comfortable enough to fall asleep. But he wasn't even close to feeling comfortable. He was so cold. The temperature had dropped at least twenty-five degrees, which wasn't unusual at night in the mountains. He shivered uncontrollably and struggled to breathe through his newly smashed and probably broken nose. He gave up and just breathed through his mouth, rolled to his hands and knees, and pushed himself up and onto his feet. His shoulder burned, and his back that he screwed up during the ATV accident was almost cramping. He was a miserable human being.

He looked at his watch, growled to himself, and started a slow walk back to his cabin. He would like nothing more than to wrap up in a blanket and collapse into bed. But that wasn't going to happen tonight. He was on guard duty all night long.

His cabin was warm and inviting. He needed to change into warmer clothing; a thick hoodie under his coat would work. Everything was packed, all ready for the exit. He unpacked a box and found his coffee maker; hot coffee was severely needed. And he found his hoodie and his gloves in his main duffle. Arnie stared at the coffeemaker as it brewed some dark roast; it didn't matter what it tasted like as long as it was hot. He sat, watched the coffee drip, warmed up, and stewed.

Arnie was getting pissed. He had never made so much money and had never been so abused at any endeavor, ever. It was one hell of an inconsistency. He was the inferior man in the group, a collection of thieves with little mutual respect. It had been horrible, and now with Joe in charge, civility had hit an all-time low. Arnie was a skillful thief. That was why they hired him, and he had done a hell of a good job, for what? Nothing except the money. And then he was injured twice in the last couple of weeks, once in the ATV accident, and then, of course, the gunshot wound. It was hard roughing it out while his inconsiderate co-workers treated his injuries as if they were a joke. They needed to be careful. Especially Joe, that punk was a real chicken shit. Joe sucker-punched him in the back of his head, smashed his face into the table, and screwed up his nose. What an asshole.

Arnie could repack his bag, drop it into his Jeep, drive away, and never look back. It was very tempting. He didn't feel secure. Joe couldn't be trusted, and yet, no one else seemed to recognize that fact. Joe promised to pay them a bonus which was the only reason to stick around, but it was a shaky rationale. His coffee was ready; he filled his thermos and then a separate cup. If Arnie hung in here, and all went as planned, he would drive to Reno in the afternoon, and they would pay him a fat bonus. He convinced himself to hang in a little while longer, but if anything went sideways, he would split. And screw the bonus.

———

The Riders reached the pull-out, unloaded, and readied themselves for the ride. The pull-out wasn't a parking area made to support a trailhead. It was a wide spot on the road where drivers could chain-up in the winter. There was a gap through the trees that led away from the highway, possibly a faint trail. Hopefully, it would connect to a better trail heading south toward the ridge behind the camp. They could park out of the way, on the edge of the hillside. It didn't look like parking there would cause any problems.

Mark and DeShawn saddled up Trixie. Mark demonstrated a breakaway cinch, which allows the rider to release the saddle with a single pull on the leather strap. DeShawn gave him a concerned glance, wondering why he might need to know such a technique. Mark chuckled to himself and explained that they all used this method, every time they saddled a horse. Mark wasn't concerned about teaching saddling techniques, he wanted Trixie and DeShawn to continue bonding, and saddling helped.

Mark kept his promise and gave DeShawn a quick riding lesson. Mark stuck to the basics, and DeShawn seemed to soak it all in quickly. DeShawn knew a lot more about riding a horse than he had claimed, and DeShawn wouldn't admit it, but he was a natural rider.

"You will be fine today; your technique is solid. Remember, give Trixie a lot of love and praise. She deserves it, but you are the boss, and you will need to let her know if she gets wild or headstrong. If you find yourself in an out-of-control situation in rough terrain, depend on her. She is a smart horse, and two heads are better than one. That's the lesson. I think you are good to go," Mark smiled.

They rode up through the gap. It looked like someone, or something, had been there before, maybe some hikers or possibly wild game. Brett and Pepper took the lead, followed by Tom and Buck, then DeShawn and Trixie, and Mark and Rondo brought up the rear. They were in the saddle before sunrise, but a glow was building behind them to the east. The light helped with visibility. They were riding slow and careful, picking their way west. It was more of a path than a trail, and it narrowed to where pine branches slapped them from both sides. Twice it disappeared completely. Both times, it reappeared after they rode around a patch of dense bushes and young trees. Maybe this was a game trail, after all. Their progress was discouraging until finally, they intersected a defined trail leading south toward the camp.

———

Arnie was too cold to leave the cabin, at least until he had to. With a full thermos, he sat and enjoyed the cabin's warmth and sipped the cup and a half that was leftover in the coffeemaker. When he finished, he dropped the appliance back in its box and went back to work. It was more like pretending to work. The sky was showing a prelude to dawn, and he figured he'd walk by the main lodge, and if anyone was watching, he could show off his dedicated guard duty skills.

Joe was up early after a restless night's sleep on the sofa. The sofa was comfortable to sit on, but it sucked as a bed. Through the window, he spotted Arnie, wearing binoculars around his neck, and looking engaged in the job. He walked past as he was making a northern sweep across the property. Joe stepped out onto the front deck and yelled, "Hey, Arnie, after you finish checking the northern perimeter, go back to the front gate. If we are going to have any visitors, they will come through there."

Actually, that was probably the last place they'd come through. But Arnie didn't want to talk to that asshole, so he continued playing the good soldier and didn't even slow his pace; he gave Joe a thumbs-up and kept walking.

———

The new trail was clearly defined, which helped the Riders speed up. It led uphill through a forest of Lodge Pole Pines and then merged with another branch that traversed a steep, rocky face. The trail crossed a slide area, littered with slippery shale slabs, a dangerous path. Trixie broke into a quick trot, using her momentum to find solid ground uphill from the slide. Her acceleration caught DeShawn by surprise, and he overreacted by pulling her head downhill. Accidentally, he pushed her into the rock slide. Trixie kept to her feet, and DeShawn almost fell out of the saddle on the uphill side while the shale gave way and slid down the steep grade, bringing DeShawn and Trixie with it. When they came to a stop, they were both stable but shook. Maybe Trixie was the real mountain horse. It was a miracle she didn't fall into the steep hillside. On solid footing for the moment, but they were in trouble. They stood on the edge of a small cliff. There was a drop off below, and above them, the terrain was impossible to climb.

"DeShawn, don't panic. You're going to be alright. Grab that horn and hold on, and let the reins go slack. You need to trust your horse, so stroke her neck, and she'll calm down," Mark yelled. "Now, lock both hands on the horn, balance yourself, and get ready for a rough ride. Give her a slight kick and say, 'Let's go.'"

DeShawn looked up toward Mark with wide eyes.

"Do it!" Mark yelled.

Trixie jumped off the cliff and landed six feet below. Her

momentum carried them into a steep downhill run for another thirty feet. Then she turned and traversed a lower section of the hill in a reckless gallop. After twenty yards, she turned and powered up the mountain until she climbed onto the trail around thirty feet in front of Brett. DeShawn was shell-shocked, but he held on and stayed in the saddle. Trixie stopped. She was winded.

"Wahoo!" Brett exclaimed. "Hell, we have a genuine cowboy on our hands!"

They all took a break and checked to make sure that both rider and horse were uninjured. They were fine. DeShawn had been on a horse for less than an hour and had a life experience. Before he stepped back into the saddle, he stroked Trixie's neck and then gave her nose a good rubbing and whispered, "Thank you."

The trail continued toward a ridge top that overlooked the camp, and they climbed a series of switchbacks to get there. At the summit, Brett stopped the group and dismounted. He walked up the final incline until he could see the lay of the land. He looked around, carefully assessed the situation, and turned and hiked back to the rest of the Riders. They huddled before crossing over the top.

"Okay, guys, we have a bit of a problem. The trail crosses the top of the ridge, and then it drops back down into the trees on the other side. On the top, the trail is wide open for about five yards, and if someone is looking, they are bound to see us. So, let's go over the top one at a time, and let's do it quickly. Follow my lead," Brett said.

They lined up nose to tail on a mild incline just short of the ridge top. The forest thinned out on both sides, giving them excellent visibility. Brett held Pepper still until he felt the group was ready to move. He nudged Pepper with his heels, and the horse eagerly and quickly trotted across the open ground and dropped into the cover of the pines below. Tom and Buck efficiently and rapidly followed. Then DeShawn rode Trixie smoothly across the top, emulating Brett and Pepper's trip as if he and Trixie were a seasoned team. Mark and Rondo followed, but Mark looked concerned when they gathered together in the trees on the ridge's south side.

"Hey, we may have been spotted. I saw a reflection. Someone might have been watching, someone with binoculars." Mark frowned.

CHAPTER FORTY-THREE

rnie gestured a thumbs-up. Joe felt that was an improvement for Arnie. It wasn't a snarky remark, or an obscenity muttered under his breath. The gesture was efficient and business-like; maybe Arnie was getting it—no, that was doubtful.

At least Arnie was awake and on patrol. Joe hadn't seen either Jay or Rick yet. With the sun rising, they should emerge soon, and then they all could get back on the job. There wasn't much work left in the lodge, just some minor cleaning after breakfast. All Joe could do right now was to relax and wait. Warm directional light was bathing the mountain peaks and the tree line. It was a beautiful sight. It showed why so many people loved being outdoors, and some people loved it so much they fled the cities and built their homes out here. Joe wasn't one of those people. He'd rather be somewhere else.

Last night, he carried his duffle and gun case in from the SUV. He felt they weren't safe in the vehicle, even out here in the middle of nowhere. Taking advantage of this morning's quiet, he began his treasured daily routine. After eating a lite breakfast and drinking his morning coffee, he always found a large flat table situated away from any contaminants. This morning, he chose the coffee table in front of the sofa. He cleaned the table thoroughly, removed all the objects on it, and removed everything sitting on the couch and the side table. Then, he opened his gun case, checked each weapon individually, and selected his primary firearm of the day. He defined his options depending on each day's potential needs. His central question always was; what risks could he face today? He loved his gun case, and he loved his guns. Today's travel pack was a treasured collection, where every single firearm was unique, memorable, and probably illegal. Should he stick with his compact pistol, a beautiful, versatile weapon, his mainstay because of its size? It was easy to carry, easy to conceal, and it was great to shoot. It was a formidable weapon, especially for its size. Or, should he move up to his custom-made, semi-automatic pistol with its quick-change twenty-four shot magazine. With its modified trigger system, it could dispense an abundance of bullets in seconds. It was larger, heavier, and harder to hold than the compact, but he could handle it, and he could still carry it with its well-designed holster. His semi-automatic assault rifle was his most potent option. It could create hell on earth, what a thing of beauty. And of course, there was his sniper rifle, which performed well the other day. He loved them all, and he was glad to have them. You never know which gun you might need.

———

Arnie walked up the hill, circled the garage, pretended to check the doors, and then continued to the warehouse where he followed the same routine. He hiked up to the northern fence line, where he took a break, opened his thermos, and poured half a cup into its lid. The morning was warming up, making it easy to relax, so Arnie sipped some coffee and enjoyed the view. He was waking up, his mind was clearing, and he felt better; even the sting in his shoulder had faded. The rising sun lit up the ridge top—the morning was breaking.

What the hell was that? Arnie wondered.

It seemed like there was a flash of movement up on the ridge. Maybe it was wildlife; it could be a deer or an elk. He hated to act like a security guard, but he was curious and couldn't help himself. He pulled up his binoculars and glassed the ridge. He then saw what looked like a cowboy on a horse ride over the ridgeline and disappear. He looked familiar.

Was that the doc? Oh, shit, it was.

He raised his binoculars and glassed the ridge again—nothing. There was a break in the tree line where he had seen the rider. He searched a broader pattern across the gap and then checked along and through the trees. This ridge side was thick with trees and bushes, thick enough to hide a horse and rider. However, he saw some dust, just a little.

The dust shouldn't be there.

So, the doc was up there on his horse. And Arnie had never seen the doc ride alone. There were probably three of them, maybe more. They were riding over the north ridge, toward the camp, and taking a challenging route. Arnie had covered this entire area on his ATV, and the north ridge trails ran out quickly. Everything about this was wrong. It was not another joy ride. This approach was tactical.

They were riding here again. It looked like Joe was right to be worried. He had explained it clearly; these guys are a problem, *the* problem. They had literally put them out of business, and that was why Mr. Levitt sent Joe here. To Arnie, they had never seemed dangerous, especially the doc who had taken care of him, *twice*. But Arnie's feelings didn't matter. The trail riders were coming, and Joe was ready to go to war. He was probably in the lodge cleaning his guns right now.

The situation was extremely volatile. If Arnie warned Joe, they would drop everything and get armed and ready for a gunfight.

They would go to war. The want-to-be-cowboys seemed docile enough, but from what Joe had learned, they were much more potent than they appeared. As Arnie thought about it, he realized, every time he had come face-to-face with them, there had been trouble, and every time there was trouble, he came up short.

However, they weren't all bad guys. It was good that doc was always there. Did that make sense? Not really. Every time Arnie had seen Doc, there had been blood, and it was always his. That perspective scared him. That did it. Arnie decided not to put up with any more of this shit. Enough was enough. He was out of here.

Arnie poured his coffee into the dirt, screwed the lid back onto the thermos, stood up straight, turned, and hiked down the hill. Like a good soldier, he marched toward the gate, his next assignment. Arnie kept a distanced line away from the main lodge; this way, even if Joe was watching him, Arnie could walk by without conversation. Once he hiked up into the trees, he turned toward his cabin. He noticed that Rick's lights were on. Arnie wondered if he should stop, give Rick a warning, give him a chance to get out.

Screw him.

———

Brett kneeled in a patch of thick bushes. He was concerned about being seen, possibly by someone sporting binoculars, as Mark had observed. It was a revolting revelation. He trudged through the trees and bushes until he found a well-covered viewing spot, and then he pulled out his glass. And sure enough, at the fence line, a man with binoculars was looking toward them. "Oh shit," he muttered. And then he asked Mark, "Take a look at this guy, and tell me who you think he is."

Mark dismounted and joined Brett, and both men stared through their binoculars. The man they were looking at was wearing a hoodie. It obscured his features and made him difficult to recognize.

"I can't see his face while he is looking through those binoculars. Come on, Mister, let us see your face," Mark said more to himself than anyone else. As if he was trying to comply, Arnie pulled down his binoculars, leaned against a fence pole, and stood there. "That is our old friend Arnie!" Mark grinned sarcastically.

"That's what I guessed, either him or Joe. But I'm glad it's Arnie. Joe is a much bigger problem."

Tom looped a rope around Pepper's neck, led him away, and took over as the lead on the ride downhill. Brett opted out of riding; instead, he hiked down the hill, moved from one viewpoint to another, and always monitored Arnie.

The trail widened, and the footing improved, making the ride smoother. Pepper, riderless, seemed to know the plan; he fell in place behind Tom and Buck. He kept looking for Brett, who ran back and forth between the trail and the hillside. The Riders continued down the path until they came upon a small creek, the type that would likely dry up as summer moved into July. In June, its flow was rapid; they dismounted and let the horses drink. With the horses watered, they rode on until they found a wide, flat, open area. It sat in a gap wedged between two groups of pine trees. Enough sun broke through the trees to develop a mini-pasture, grassy enough to keep the horses munching. Tom asked everyone to hold up and dismount; they would picket their horses here. The Riders were less than a half-mile away from the camp.

Brett jogged from viewpoint to viewpoint as the rest of the group rode downhill. By the time they found the quiet protected area to picket the horses, he had watched Arnie march across the camp, past the lodge, and eventually enter a cabin. Viewing from above had its advantage; Brett had an elevated, unobstructed view. He lost Arnie for a few seconds a couple of times, but that was all. Arnie's stride was purposeful, his body language calm, and he didn't act like a man that was alarmed. Maybe Arnie didn't see them. Perhaps the element of surprise was still theirs. Brett hoped so. But he would need to keep watching Arnie; he needed to learn what step Arnie would take next.

It was still very early, and the camp was quiet. A few lights were on, and Brett hadn't seen a movement from anyone else.

The Riders set up the picket line, and the horses were calm and accepting. DeShawn talked with each of the men, helped them with their gear, and calmly offered some coaching. They changed cowboy boots out for hiking footwear. They needed to be stable, quiet, and agile. They wore the new Kevlar vests underneath their jackets, and they were light enough that no one seemed bothered with the extra weight. They performed a successful soundcheck with all four of the radios and headsets. Everyone was wired and ready.

For the last time, the Riders checked their ammunition and firearms. Tom and Mark were both carrying open site rifles designed for accuracy and speed. DeShawn holstered a compact FBI issued pistol with a twelve-bullet clip. Brett had his six-shot revolver and his shotgun.

It was time to march quietly and carefully downhill to the camp.

———

Arnie entered his cabin for what he felt would be the last time. It had been unique and fun to live here in his personal cabin in this crazy camp in the woods. He would kind of miss this place. The camp was kind of serene and private, and it was built in the middle of nowhere, which was okay with him. Of everyone who lived here, he was the closest to being a true outdoorsman. He had ridden his ATV into the woods for miles in every direction. Deer and elk, coyotes and beavers, eagles and owls, and more, he had seen them all. His little cabin had been cozy, private, and rustic. After packing up what was left, he carried out his last two loads and stuffed them into the back of his Jeep.

The Jeep started right up, and Arnie wondered how that sound would reverberate through the quiet camp. He unlocked the padlock at the gate and removed the thick chains that securely held the gate closed. Arnie grabbed the chains and spun them around above his head as if they were a sling. With his body weight behind them, he let them loose, and the chains flew thirty feet across the other side of the road and landed into deep grass.

They would need luck to find that.

He grabbed the padlock and tossed it forty feet to his left, and it disappeared into a large group of bushes. He stepped back into his Jeep, drove it forward twenty-five feet, and parked on a high spot in front of the open gate. Then, he jumped out of the vehicle, climbed up on its back bumper, turned and faced the camp, and waved both hands over his head. It was a goodbye wave to the cowboys.

He hoped they saw it.

———

"Hey Brett, come look. Arnie is on the move again," Tom said.

Brett heard Tom clearly over the radio, "Where is he heading now?" He replied as he sprinted down the trail, searching for Tom's position. He quickly spotted him, covered the distance, and then to keep low, crawled over to where Tom was hiding behind a massive, fallen Ponderosa Pine.

Brett struggled to keep up with the Riders as he ran from viewpoint to viewpoint. Finally, when Arnie entered his cabin, Brett decided he couldn't risk missing Arnie's next move. He found himself stuck while everyone else rode on.

Tom helped out when he hiked along the ridge and found a spot where he could watch Arnie's cabin and take over surveillance. That left Brett free to run down the trail and catch up. They needed to keep glassing the cabin in case Arnie reemerged. Watching Arnie's movement was important, but it took up valuable time, which they didn't have. They were losing the dawn and the potential to catch the crooks unprepared. But they needed to know if Arnie saw them. It was a wild card element that could defeat their plan.

Brett perched himself into an obscured location with a satisfactory viewing angle. When he pulled his binoculars up, he was having difficulty holding them still due to his heavy breathing.

"Arnie just got into his Jeep and—oh, there he goes, he is driving away from the cabin," Tom observed.

"Okay, I see him," Brett said as he settled enough to get a stabilized view.

Arnie parked his Jeep, unlocked the gate's padlock, and then tossed both the lock and the chain into the rough around the road. Tom and Brett watched with confused interest.

"I'm not sure what he is doing right now," Tom commented, "Do you have any idea?"

"Not really," Brett answered, "we need to keep watching."

Arnie parked the Jeep, stood up on its bumper, eagerly waved his arms, and made a quick gesture. Then he stepped back into his Jeep and drove away.

"Did you catch that?" Brett asked.

"Yeah, he waved."

"I think it was more than just a wave," Brett said. "I would bet Arnie just waved goodbye to *us.*"

"So, do you think Arnie bailed on the rest of them?"

"Exactly, Joe just lost a man—they are down to three."

———

Rick heard Arnie start up and drive away in his Jeep. He figured Joe had sent him out to check the trailhead, or possibly some other errand. Either way, Rick thought he might be one of the last ones to get up, so he hustled and got dressed. Rick was hungry anyway; maybe he would make himself a batch of pancakes this morning.

He walked into the lodge just in time to see Joe snap the lid closed on his gun case. Rick thought Joe was rather anal about his guns, and the more he learned about him, he found him to be pretty odd. Maybe he was some kind of evil genius.

"Good morning," he said as he walked in.

Joe returned the greeting with a curt nod of his head.

"I feel like pancakes this morning," Rick said as he walked into the kitchen. Once in the kitchen, he searched for the pancake mix while he raised his voice and asked, "Where did Arnie drive off to?"

Now Joe responded, "What are you talking about?"

"Arnie drove away in his Jeep, just before I got here. I figured you sent him somewhere. Didn't you hear him?"

"No! I did not hear him. What kind of stupid question is that? Call Jay and tell him to get his ass up here, now!"

Arnie carefully drove down the rough section of the logging road that led to the trailhead area and was close to the improved dirt road when a good-sized dusty brown pickup truck roared up and met him nose to nose. The sizable dust cloud was evidence that whoever was driving the pickup appeared in a hell of a hurry. And then the pickup's horn blared. It was enough to irritate anyone. What did they expect him to do—take off and fly? Arnie stepped out of his Jeep, and in anger, pulled the Velcro strap loose on his holster. It had already been a tough day, and he didn't need this.

He figured if this asshole wanted trouble, he'd be ready with his gun.

When he walked up to the pickup's driver-side window, Arnie found out the driver had a gun too. A rifle barrel pointed out of the open window, straight at him.

Arnie couldn't believe he was this stupid—he froze and then

raised his hands high. His only chance was to talk his way out of this predicament.

"Oh, it's you," Arnie said. "I am *so sorry*. I should have never opened my holster. I was frustrated and made a stupid decision. I would have never pulled my gun on you, honest. I'll keep my hands up where you can see them, and if it's okay with you, I'll close up my holster."

The rifle stayed where it was, pointed straight at Arnie. The driver was silent.

"Okay, I'll keep my hands up, no problem. Now, don't get me wrong here, I mean no disrespect, but if you drive down this road and drive into that camp, you will probably find yourself in the middle of a terrible fight. If I were you, I would back up and get the hell out of here!"

He paused and hoped, but the rifle stayed steady, aimed at him, and the driver silently stared.

"I'm not just saying this," Arnie continued. "I'm a thief, but I'm not a fighter, certainly not a gunfighter. I don't care what you think, but I did not sign up for this shit. I am not going to get myself killed for this job. I quit, and I'm getting the hell out of here."

Arnie paused again, frustrated. Still, the driver stared, and the rifle didn't move. It was pointed straight at him.

"If you are so goddamned determined, I'll give you a little advice. I'm the man who knows the lay of the land around here better than anyone. I know every inch of the camp, and I know every trail leading in or out of it. If you drive down the road, we are on right now, it will be rough for a while, and then it will smooth out when you get close to the camp. I've been on guard duty all night and was stationed at the gate today. When I drove out of there, I left the front gate unlocked and wide open. With me gone, they only have three men left. I'd bet the front gate is clear. Drive right through it and then pull over and park your rig. Off to your left, you'll see the cabins, hike behind them until you pass the third cabin, and then circle back through the trees. You will come to a rise that gives a wide-open view of the lodge, the area below it, and the hill above. You should see everything from there, and if you stick to the trees, you should be able to hide."

God, he had hoped that would have done it, but the rifle still did not move.

"The problem is this; there is no way I can back up and let you through. The only way this will work is if *you* backup around fifty feet to where the regular road starts and then let me drive by. I'll drive out of here, and you will never see me again, and you can go and do whatever you want."

The rifle swung gently toward Arnie's vehicle. Arnie took that as a yes, and he scampered back to his Jeep and jumped in. The truck moved backward. After an awkward fifty feet, it entered the relatively smooth surface of the dirt road. As he drove by, Arnie flipped the bird and kept going toward the highway. At the intersection of Highway 21, if he turned right, he could drive to Boise and within an hour jump on Interstate 84, and from there, he could go almost anywhere. Or he could turn left, and drive through Lowman, and then Stanley. He could get lost in the Sawtooths, or he could keep going right into the heart of Montana.

Arnie had always wanted to see Montana. He turned left.

CHAPTER FORTY-FOUR

____

"You see the guy who just walked out on the deck, that is Joe," Brett said.

"So, he's the boss," DeShawn replied. "Did you notice he's carrying?"

"Yeah, it doesn't surprise me at all. I'd bet he is our sniper."

"He's a dangerous man; we are going to have to be very, very careful."

DeShawn and Brett were glassing the camp one last time. They had been making substantial progress hiking down the trail. It had been a quiet trek, with whispered communication and a steady pace. The trail continued to improve; it had sound footing, and a thick wall of trees and bushes effectively kept the Riders hidden from view. Their new viewpoint was perfect. They scanned the camp from one side to the other, and with Arnie gone, only two men appeared to be up and about.

"Okay, the other big guy who just walked inside. Who is he?" DeShawn asked.

"That would be Rick. I would bet he is a tough one, and another we shouldn't take lightly. The third man, who hasn't shown up yet, is Jay, who was in charge until Joe took over. Arnie explained that in the video, remember?"

"I'll never forget it," DeShawn replied. "Hold it, the two of them are in some sort of argument. Rick is calling someone on his phone. That's interesting; I bet they just figured it out."

DeShawn pulled down his binoculars and turned toward Tom and Mark; they were crouched down low, right behind them. He had seen enough. "Listen up," he said to the group in a quiet voice. "My guess is the two men at the lodge just realized Arnie has bailed on them. Joe looked pissed. We're getting close. I don't see us stopping again until we need to cross the fence. Be careful and stay in cover. When we get a little closer, Brett will show us the spot where we should cross over. Once across, we will encounter a lot of open ground we need to avoid. I don't want us exposed. We will try to move around the perimeter from one point of cover to another, and we'll need to hurry. Plus, we need to keep quiet, possibly only communicating through our headsets. We will work in pairs; Tom will follow me, and Mark will follow Brett. So far, so good guys, we are doing well. Don't let your guard down and be careful."

They were within 150 yards of the camp.

———

"What the hell is going on?" Jay asked as he walked into the lodge.

"We are down a man. Arnie drove away in his car." Joe snarled.

"That doesn't sound like Arnie. He is not one to miss a bonus."

"If you have a better explanation, I'd like to hear it."

"He was on guard duty, right?"

"Right, so what?"

"He may have driven down to the end of our road, just to see if anyone was looking around. He used to ride his ATV and check beyond the entrance, but with it parked at the warehouse, he probably took his Jeep."

"Seems unlikely," Joe responded. "And that is not what I told him to do."

"Yeah, but Arnie is an unusual guy. I've seen him disappear for hours. He drives around on the old roads, and sometimes he parks and hikes and looks at animals or trees. I've seen him drive out of here in the middle of the night, just to find the perfect spot to view the Milky Way. He is an outdoorsman, or at least he thinks he is."

"He can be a real lazy-ass," Rick volunteered, "I wouldn't be surprised if he found a good place to take a nap."

"If he did that, I'm going to kill him," Joe shouted.

"Now hold on, there isn't going to be any killing. Maybe Arnie would be here right now if you didn't sucker punch him," Jay countered.

"So now it's my fault?"

"I don't know. Did he respond when you called?"

Joe looked at Rick, and Rick looked back at Joe. Nobody had thought to call Arnie.

"Good God," Jay said. "You guys didn't even call him." Jay walked out onto the deck, pulled out his cell phone, and called. After about a minute, he walked back inside. "I couldn't get through," Jay said, "Cell service is pretty spotty up here. Anyway, my bet is he will be back."

Jay looked toward the kitchen, "I smell pancakes, I'm going to eat a couple, and then I'm going to walk up to the garage and go back to work."

Jay walked into the kitchen and left Rick behind, alone with Joe.

"Rick, we need to figure out what the hell is going on. Walk over to Arnie's cabin and check it out. See if it looks like he moved out." Joe said. And then he looked disapprovingly at Rick. "And you're not armed; grab your rifle while you are down there."

———

Tom kept his eyes on DeShawn and waited for the signal. Finally, DeShawn waved him forward. Tom, rifle in hand, sprinted diagonally down the hill until he arrived at a small clump of trees. He hid and waited. They were taking turns running from one point of cover to another in an attempt to cross the open hillside, unnoticed. Ten seconds later, DeShawn waved him forward again. Tom ran the final leg to a spot behind the warehouse. Mark and DeShawn were already there, waiting. It had been years since Tom had sprinted like that. He placed his hands on his thighs and breathed hard.

"How is your back feeling?" Mark asked, very quietly.

"It's sore, but I'm okay."

"What about your legs?"

"About the same, but I'll make it, Doc."

"You are limping."

"Well, there is nothing I can do about that."

"Yes, there is. Get your head up, stand up straight, take deep breaths, and walk it off. That should help you loosen up. You need to suck it up now."

Tom walked back and forth behind the building, and Mark was right; it did help him loosen up. As irritating as Mark's remarks were, he certainly was on his game. His eyes seemed bright; they showed a sense of awareness and focus beyond normal, even for Mark. He looked comfortable and confident, which could be difficult. Tom envied him and appreciated his example.

Tom stood tall, threw his shoulders back, took three deep Yoga breaths, turn toward Mark and said, "Thanks, I'm good to go."

Five seconds later, Brett sprinted smoothly to the group. Of course, even carrying his weapons and gear, he was hardly winded. He unconsciously performed six quick shoulder rolls just to keep loose. He made eye contact with each man, silently confirming he was pleased with their work so far. Strong, silent leadership. If Brett felt good, they all should.

Brett knew they had the moral high ground. He believed when you were in the right; you had an advantage. He also knew the crooks were willing to play by a different set of rules, especially if they were looking at jail time. And every one of the rider's understood what that meant. The crooks living at the camp could not be trusted. Brett had emphasized they needed to be ready for the unexpected, and he felt they were.

The four men stood together in a tight group. On his smartphone, DeShawn pulled up a satellite photo of the area around the lodge. Pointing at a wooded area uphill, he spoke to the group. "Brett and I are going to move to the west side of the lodge. You two need to position yourself here, and here. He pointed to an area displayed on the phone. Find cover with good visibility and be ready."

The lodge was in the middle of the camp. It sat in a bowl surrounded by trees on its west, south, and east. After originating at the main gate, the camp's road intersected a small two-track that led to the cabins. Then the road curved up toward the north ridge and ran past the warehouse and the garage. It then turned downhill and ended at a parking area behind the lodge. From there, a well-defined trail led to the front deck.

The points DeShawn showed on his phone were in the trees on the hill facing the lodge. They provided excellent visibility of the deck and the lodge's west side.

Brett and DeShawn planned to confront the crooks from the trail that led toward the parking area. If they had a conflict, they wanted it in the open, with Tom and Mark backing them up from the hillside behind, giving them a high-ground advantage. If the confrontation moved from the west side toward the deck's front, Tom and Mark could quickly shift their position on the hillside to match. The setup made sense. They kept the high ground in both directions.

"Do you have any last questions?" DeShawn asked quietly.

They all stood silent.

"We've got it," Mark replied.

"Let's get this done," DeShawn directed.

"Hold up a second," Brett said. "I've saved one for today."

"Let's hear it," Mark whispered back."

"Always finish what you start."

––––––––

"Try him again," Joe yelled.

Jay was in the kitchen, eating a couple of syrup-drenched pancakes and was getting sick of Joe. He had been trying to be a good company man and take orders, but it was running a little thin. Joe was a real punk. Jay had never seen a more cowardly attack than the sucker punch Joe threw last night. Even with the prospect of a massive bonus, he thought Arnie might have quit. But if Arnie had, it was all on Joe, no matter what the little punk thought. If Joe came at him like that, Jay would break the guy in half, and it would take about a second. Jay also learned he couldn't trust the man, and it was dangerous to turn his back toward him.

"Try him again," Joe yelled again.

"You mean Arnie?"

"Who in the hell do you think?"

Jay walked back out onto the front deck and tried to call Arnie. Just as before, the call did not go through.

"No answer," Jay said as he walked back into the lodge. "Where's Rick?"

"I sent him down to the cabins. He's going to check to see if Arnie packed up and left."

"Okay, I'm going to walk up to the garage and get to work." Jay wanted to get away from Joe, and he wanted to finish up.

"No, wait here. When Rick gets back, either he or you are going to post guard."

"You know Joe, this work will not get done by itself, and you sure as hell aren't helping, so I'm going up to the garage." Jay walked back out onto the front deck, walked across it, and then stepped out on to the trail that led to the garage.

"I told you to stop, you son of a bitch," Joe barked as he ran out after him.

Jay, remembering he couldn't turn his back on Joe, spun around and met him face-to-face. "Listen," he said. "We need to get to work. Our goal is to finish cleaning out the garage and then get the hell out of here. When Rick gets back, why don't you send him up to help me, and then you can patrol the area? That is probably the best use of your time."

"No, you are going to stay *here* until I say you can leave. Got it?"

"FREEZE—BOTH OF YOU—NOW," Brett yelled.

Joe turned toward Brett in shock. What the hell? He said.

"PUT YOUR HANDS UP WHERE I CAN SEE THEM!" Brett roared.

Both men slowly raised their hands to shoulder height. Jay was obedient, and Joe was skeptical.

"I don't think you have the balls to go through with this," Joe said as he slowly dropped his hands a couple of inches.

"Don't do anything stupid," Jay said quietly, "This guy is the real deal."

"Get those hands up," Brett ordered. He snapped his shotgun into the firing position. Everyone knew he couldn't miss.

Joe brought his hands up a little higher. He half-smiled, and his eyes shifted left and right, up the hill and back. His mind was flying, looking for a way out or an angle to kill.

DeShawn heard Tom's voice on his headset.

"DeShawn, I just saw some movement up the hill. It may be our missing man."

DeShawn and Brett were approximately twenty feet away from

Jay and Joe, who had been arguing face-to-face and were now standing side by side. They were close enough together that Brett could take them both out with one pull of his shotgun's trigger. But Jay and Joe were both armed and dangerous. Brett was fully aware of the problem; he needed to disarm them both.

"I just spotted him again. He is carrying a rifle and coming this way."

Brett was shouting instructions, trying to disarm Joe and Jay, entirely in charge, while DeShawn focused on Tom's voice.

"He is—he's trying to blindside you. He's pulling up his rifle—PERMISSION TO SHOOT?"

"PERMISSION GRANTED!"

Only a fraction of a second past, Tom pulled the trigger. His aim was perfect, and the rifle's repeat was loud and unnerving.

The bullet hit Rick in the chest. He didn't get a chance to fire. He collapsed face-first, impacted the rocky hillside, rolled once, and then curled into a motionless heap.

The world seemed to stop for a moment—at most a second in time—as Rick fell and rolled down the hillside.

Joe had repositioned himself behind Jay. In his right hand, he had his custom made, semi-automatic pistol. With his left arm hooked around Jay, Joe swung the high-volume gun and sprayed bullets arcing from DeShawn to Brett. He emptied half of the magazine in seconds and hit both Brett and DeShawn multiple times, and both men went down. He then fired the rest of the magazine uphill toward Mark and Tom. They were too far away to target with a swinging one-armed volley. They weren't hit, but Joe sent them both diving for cover.

Hiding behind a shocked Jay, Joe snapped out the spent magazine and replaced it with a new one.

The bullet impacted Joe from his right. He dropped his pistol into the dirt and fell to his left.

After being used as a human shield, Jay watched Joe fall. With his hands in the air, Jay was ready to quit. He kept his eyes forward and walked away.

Joe was down, but not out. He struggled to his knees and reached for his pistol.

Brett, struggling himself, pulled up to one knee. He pointed his shotgun and fired.

He hit Joe on his left side. The shotgun blast created a vicious chest wound, and it blew Joe's left arm off at the shoulder.

Rifles in hand, Mark and Tom ran down the hill. Mark was moving from one man to another, trying to define medical priority.

Brett was on his feet, just barely. He hobbled badly while he looked for Tom. When he saw him, he grabbed him and looked him in the eye. "I don't know how you did it, but you saved us all with that last shot. Thank you."

"Don't thank me, it wasn't my shot. I was face down in the dirt."

Brett turned toward Mark. "Mark?"

"It wasn't me."

Out of the trees, a shaky voice rang out.

"I'm coming down. Please don't shoot." Sage walked out of the trees; her long dark hair was blowing in the breeze, her rifle hung from her right arm. And she was crying.

Tom ran up the hill, grasped his daughter, and hugged her.

Sage was sobbing. "What have I done, Dad?"

"You saved us all."

Sage and her dad stood together. They hugged each other and cried.

EPILOGUE

"**A**ttention!" Mark boomed. "Welcome to the official reopening of our barn. It has been a long time coming, and we are happy to have you here with us for this celebration. We have a lunch buffet set up right outside the clubhouse, along with a cooler of beverages and beer. We have hotdogs and marshmallows ready to roast for you gourmets, and the fire pit is burning. Please, have at it. Thank you all for coming!"

The early October sun was high in the sky, and it was slightly chilly. A light sweater was the chosen attire for the picnic. The new barn looked a lot like the old barn, as it should because the guys used the same building plans. Every detail was identical; why change what you like? Of course, the Riders needed to replace the tack they lost in the fire and all the clubhouse furnishings. The only irreplaceable items were some instruments in the music room, especially Tom's vintage Gibson acoustic guitar. Even that wasn't an issue. Tom felt he wasn't a good enough player to be worthy of the instrument anyway; he just liked it, that's all.

Sage, who couldn't miss the barn's reopening, flew home from California. As the crowd thinned after lunch, she and Nick, plus Steve and his family, all roasted marshmallows and made s'mores.

DeShawn was excited to bring his family to the event. He introduced them to Trixie and then gave them the full tour. He felt like he belonged, and DeShawn once again commented that someday, he wanted to own a horse.

In the last three months, there hadn't been any smash-and-grab burglaries in the Intermountain Northwest. The burglary ring was out of business, and the Rider's primary objective had been achieved.

The hospital had discharged both Brett and DeShawn without an overnight stay. The new Kevlar vests had saved both of their lives. Most of their share of the high-speed pistol's bullets hit them chest high, which hurt like hell, affected their mobility for a couple of weeks, but had no long-term adverse effects. The bulletproof vests didn't catch all the bullets. A shot nailed DeShawn in the shoulder, and two grazed Brett in his thigh. Thankfully, the wounds were manageable. Mark treated the injuries and ordered bed rest, a very unpopular order. They all compromised by lounging at home, watching television, and medicating with bourbon as needed.

Jay had cooperated with the prosecutors, helping him avoid maximum jail time. Life Flight had evacuated Rick, and after a couple of operations, he survived. When they released him from the hospital, he was transferred directly to jail. The shotgun blast was too much for Joe, and even with Mark's help, he lost too much blood and died. A team of six part-time burglars were shocked when the FBI raided their homes in Boise. Six people, including three otherwise unemployed professional thieves, a stay-at-home mom, a Yoga instructor, and a country band's lead singer, found out that their part-time jobs weren't so lucrative after all.

Arnie, rumored to be in Montana, was never seen again.

The FBI's raid on Tony Levitt's businesses was widespread and conclusive. PGB was shut down and their assets seized. Several of Tony's other companies were also under investigation, the FBI arrested twelve of his key managers, and their case was still growing. Unfortunately, many innocent employees immediately lost their jobs.

Tony Levitt was calm and cooperative when he was arrested. His legal team sought bail, citing his cooperation, along with his long-standing history as a model citizen. The courtroom stood in shocked silence when a *friendly* Judge agreed and granted him bail.

Back at the barn, with the buffet area cleaned up and the remaining beverages restocked into the kitchen, Tom, Mark, and Brett prepared for a long-awaited ride. The Riders Club was getting ready to take the inaugural ride in honor of the new barn. Everyone was invited, and both DeShawn and Sage eagerly accepted.

Brett and Tom saddled up five horses and led them out into the corral. Sage stroked Tonto's neck and rubbed his favorite spot behind his ears; she hadn't seen him in months. The horse reacted and nosed her back; he was happy to see her too. DeShawn proudly wore the cowboy hat Mark had given him when they raided the camp.

The Riders stepped into their saddles and rode across the pasture toward the foothills.

"Where are we going?" Sage asked her dad.

"We are riding up to the Ridge. You are going to love it."

ACKNOWLEDGMENTS

Thank you to my editor-book coach, Stacey Smekofske, for both her excitement and polish.

Thank you to my first readers for all of their valuable feedback.

Thank you to all of you who answered my crazy questions without knowing why I was asking.

Thank you to the late Mike Canavan, who made me feel good about the book and myself. We will all miss you.

ABOUT DENNIS NAGEL

Dennis Nagel was born and raised in Boise, Idaho. He is an alumnus of the University of Wyoming and has spent most of his business career managing his family's business.

One of his business's darker times was when his retail stores suffered four consecutive destructive burglaries. The criminals that committed these crimes were never apprehended, and the stolen merchandise was never recovered. These irritating events are the inspiration for Dennis's debut novel, *The Riders Club*.

Dennis has now retired from his business career and is excited to have more time to write. The second *Riders Club Book* will be coming soon, with more to follow.

Dennis and his wife, Chris, live in Boise.

For updates, please check DennisNagelBooks.com.